Going Backwards

Max Barrington

For the love of my life,
my darling wife and my inspiration,
Lynette

First published in Australia in 2025 by Etteleah Books - Cairns Australia

Contents

London to Brisbane

Marcus Diarmuid, nearly eighteen, stood at the railing of the RMS Otranto, his hands gripping the cold iron as the ship sliced through the restless waters of the English Channel. His heart thudded in his chest with a blend of excitement and deep, unsettling trepidation. Before him, the vast ocean stretched endlessly, its dark waves lapping at the ship's hull, while behind him, the receding shores of England slowly disappeared into a hazy mist, leaving him with a growing sense of finality.

He was a fair-skinned youth, untouched by the fierce heat of distant lands. His tall frame, still thin and somewhat awkward, betrayed a life of privilege, a life that had not yet known the toil of hard labor or the rigorous discipline of physical exertion. The sun had not yet marked his skin with the bronzed hue of a man accustomed to the outdoors. He felt like a boy on the cusp of manhood, unsure of whether he was ready for the journey that lay ahead.

The steady rumble of the ship's engines reverberated through the steel beneath his feet, the sound of machinery cutting through the cold, dark waters. The vibration was a strange comfort, a constant reminder that the vessel was carrying him toward an uncertain future. His throat tightened. This was the only home he had ever known. England, the damp air, the grey skies, the cobbled streets of his youth, was slipping further away with each passing moment. The thought gnawed at him. Would he miss it? The familiarity of it all? Or would this land, Australia, with its promise of sun-drenched horizons and untold opportunity, become the place where he built his new life, leaving England to exist only as a fading memory?

He stared into the vastness ahead, feeling the weight of the unknown pressing against his chest. There was no turning back now. The ship was moving forward, as was he.

The Otranto plowed relentlessly through the turbulent seas, its bow cutting through the water as it bore Marcus away from everything he had ever known. As the ship sailed toward a new and distant world, Marcus felt the weight of his past, the remnants of his old life, slipping further and further into the shadowy depths behind him. His father,

Oliver Diarmuid, had been taken from him in the bloody fields of France, falling in the final, desperate months of the war. Though peace had been declared soon after, it had come too late for Oliver, and too late for Marcus's family.

The telegram had arrived with the certainty of death itself, its cold, unfeeling words sealing a fate that had already been written in the annals of war. Marcus remembered the day it came all too clearly. His mother, Doreen, had crumpled beneath the weight of grief, her heart breaking as the news struck her like a physical blow. She had suffered a stroke soon after, and the woman who had once been strong, vibrant, and full of life, was now frail, withered by sorrow.

She fought for her life, her resolve a testament to the strength she had once embodied, but it was a battle she could not win. The decline was swift. And Marcus, helpless and broken, had stood at her bedside as the life drained from her, watching her take her final breath. Now, mere months later, he was leaving behind the land that held the grave of his mother in a quiet corner of their hometown. The whereabouts of his father's grave was unknown.

It had been his mother's suggestion, though, in truth, it was more of an instruction wrapped in gentle concern, that he go to Australia to live with his father's brother, Miles Diarmuid. Marcus barely remembered his uncle from his infant years, but the idea of finding family in such a distant land seemed a refuge from the sorrow that clung to him in England.

The letter from Uncle Miles had arrived a few weeks after the funeral, its tone distant and functional, as though the ink on the paper could not be bothered with niceties. It was not unkind, but neither was it warm. There would be a place for him at Stratheden, the family's sprawling property in Queensland, but beyond that, nothing more was offered. No promises of affection, no reassurance of comfort, just the blunt, pragmatic statement that Marcus was expected to adapt and fall into line.

With the letter had come a set of instructions, detailed steps for how to make his way from Brisbane to Quilpie, where his uncle would meet him and escort him to the homestead. The map that accompanied the letter seemed to mock Marcus as he traced the miles, his finger running across the vast, unforgiving distances. Over ten thousand miles. A journey that would carry him halfway across the world, to a land so unfamiliar it felt like a land of myth.

He folded the letter slowly, the words imprinted on his mind like a sentence handed down by an unfeeling judge. In that moment, standing on the ship, the vastness of the journey ahead seemed both exhilarating and terrifying. Would the land of sun and dust offer the solace he sought, or was it merely the next chapter in a life already marked by loss?

Marcus was the youngest of the four men who shared the cramped cabin aboard the Otranto. The air was thick with the scent of saltwater, sweat, and the lingering traces of dampness that seemed to cling to everything aboard the ship. Two of his cabin mates were Australian soldiers, broad-shouldered men who were returning home after serving in Scotland on exchange duties. They were men of few words, hardened by the war but with an easy camaraderie between them that Marcus couldn't quite tap into. But it was the third man, a nineteen-year-old Scot named Andrew Connolly, who became Marcus's closest companion during the long days at sea.

Andrew, or Scotty as he came to be known, was a man of boldness and a free spirit, everything Marcus wasn't. It was Scotty who introduced Marcus to the pleasures of drinking, smoking, and gambling, pulling him into a world Marcus had never thought to enter. Each stop at port was an opportunity to stock up on fine duty-free bottles of whisky and cigarettes, luxuries Marcus could barely comprehend before. He had never imagined life could be so indulgent, and the allure of the open sea seemed to carry with it a sense of freedom he'd never felt back home.

Scotty was on a transfer from the Edinburgh Bank of Scotland, in Glasgow, to the English, Scottish & Australian Bank in Sydney. Born in Glasgow and never been out of the city, his first venture being a huge one to Australia. He hadn't applied for the transfer, his boss had just said to him one morning, "Connolly, you are going to Australia!"

His tales of his life in banking, of cities full of money and movement, fascinated Marcus. They were worlds apart, Marcus had never known a life defined by business or wealth, but listening to Scotty, he began to picture what such a life might be like in Sydney.

In their shared cabin, the days blurred into nights filled with laughter, smuggled drinks, and card games that went on long into the hours when the rest of the ship was asleep. But as much as Marcus revelled in the newfound distractions, he knew, deep down, that they were merely distractions. A way to escape the growing weight of what lay ahead, the unknown land waiting for him, and the family he had left behind.

As the Otranto pressed steadily onward into the vast, unyielding Atlantic, Marcus felt a quiet shift within himself. England, his past, his losses, the war that had swallowed so much, seemed to recede into the horizon, vanishing with the familiar shores. Ahead, the unknown expanse of Australia stretched out, beckoning him forward. It was a future as vast and wild as the continent itself, and for the first time in a long while, Marcus squared his shoulders and stood just a little taller. There was no turning back now.

The ship rolled through the choppy waters of the Bay of Biscay, and many of the passengers succumbed to the relentless motion, their stomachs pitching in time with the waves. But Marcus, with his stomach of iron, fared better than most. When the Otranto finally passed the jagged coastline of Spain and sailed into the calmer embrace of the Mediterranean, the mood aboard the ship lifted. The oppressive chill of the North Atlantic was replaced by a warm breeze, and the sun seemed to smile more brightly on the decks. The passengers grew lighter, more relaxed, and the days stretched out lazily ahead.

Marcus found himself spending hours walking the decks with Scotty, the young Scotsman who had quickly become his closest companion. The two of them watched the brilliant Mediterranean sea shimmer in the sunlight, the rhythmic pulse of the ship's engines beneath their feet, and the endless parade of sun-soaked bodies on the decks. They drank beers in the three saloon bars and exchanged stories of their homes, their lives, their distant pasts. The world felt a little smaller, a little more bearable with each passing day.

The ship's first major stop had been Gibraltar, where the colossal rock stood like a sentinel, its massive shadow cast over the ship as it anchored in the harbour. For Marcus, it felt like a final vestige of Britain, a parting gift from the land he would soon be leaving behind. As they sailed away, the ship moved south, toward Malta and then Naples. There, the Otranto refuelled and took on fresh provisions, and Marcus caught fleeting glimpses of bustling harbours and sun-drenched streets filled with traders, fishermen, and the vibrant energy of a world that seemed almost untouched by the scars of war. The sights, the sounds, the scents were so alien, so foreign to the England he had known, that he found it hard to believe they had ever belonged to the same world.

The journey continued, and soon they arrived in Port Said, Egypt, the gateway to the legendary Suez Canal. The ship docked briefly, and Marcus, ever the curious wanderer, found himself exploring the bars and cafes in the port. There, he discovered the allure of shisha, the fragrant smoke curling in the air as passengers gathered to relax and chat. It was a strange, intoxicating atmosphere, one that felt both ancient and modern, a world away from the staleness of the English countryside.

Then came the most thrilling part of the voyage: the Suez Canal itself. As the Otranto glided through the narrow waterway, Marcus stood at the railing, the heat of the desert rising in shimmering waves from the golden sands on either side. The stark, endless desert stretched out in all directions, and in the distance, he could make out the slow-moving silhouettes of camel caravans making their way across the horizon. The scent of foreign spices drifted in on the dry air, mingling with the salt of the sea. It felt like stepping into another world entirely, a world far removed from the damp and grey of England.

As the ship moved through the canal, vendors in small boats paddled alongside, calling out in halting English, trying to sell everything from trinkets to fresh fruit. Marcus watched, fascinated, as passengers lowered baskets on ropes, exchanging coins for oranges and dates, their laughter and bartering adding to the surreal atmosphere of the journey. This was no longer just a voyage. This was an adventure. A passage to something new, something unknown, and for the first time since he had left England, Marcus allowed himself to feel a spark of excitement. The future was waiting for him, and it was just beyond the horizon.

Beyond the Suez Canal, the Red Sea unleashed its blistering heat, and the oppressive, stifling air clung to the ship like a heavy blanket. Below decks, it was unbearable; the air thick and rank with sweat and the salty smell of the sea. To escape, Marcus, like many others, began sleeping out on the open deck, where the cool night air, though still warm, was a welcome relief. The nights, though hot, held a peculiar beauty as he lay back, gazing up at a sky so vast and full of stars it was as though he could reach out and touch them. He had never seen the heavens so alive, so brilliant.

The Otranto made a port of call in Aden, a rugged, sunbaked outpost where the air seemed to shimmer with heat. The ship stopped briefly to refuel, and Marcus stepped off the vessel to stretch his legs. Aden was a place of harsh contrasts, its dry, barren hills stood stark against the deep blue of the sea. It was the gateway to the Indian Ocean, and from there, the ship would sail on into the vast emptiness of the ocean, a journey that stretched endlessly before them.

Days passed, one indistinguishable from the next, as the ship ploughed onward toward Ceylon. During the long, monotonous stretch of water, Marcus and Scotty found themselves growing closer, forming bonds with other young men aboard, the sort who had left behind familiar lives in search of something new, something better. Some of the lads were travelling with families, while others, like Marcus, were alone, adrift in the currents of fate. The camaraderie among them provided a strange comfort as the ocean stretched out, offering nothing but its endless expanse.

When the Otranto finally arrived in Colombo, Marcus and Scotty were introduced to something they hadn't expected, opium. It was offered freely, the pleasures it promised whispered eagerly between men who had become too accustomed to the confines of the ship. Scotty, ever adventurous, had tried to smuggle some onboard, but it had been confiscated before he had a chance to enjoy it. Despite the setback, Colombo left an impression on Marcus. It was the first time he had truly seen the tropics, a land of lush, vibrant jungles, palm-fringed shores, and a riot of colours and scents unlike anything he had ever known in the dreary greys of England. The stop was brief, but it marked the first taste of a new world, one that felt as foreign and wild as the journey itself.

The days at sea seemed to blur into one another, but eventually, the Otranto reached Fremantle, the first Australian port. Some passengers disembarked here, their eyes wide with anticipation, their feet stepping onto the land they had longed to see. But for Marcus, the journey wasn't over. The ship rounded the Great Australian Bight, skirting the southern coastline, passing Adelaide and Melbourne, each stop taking him further toward his final destination. Every port they passed added a new layer of expectation, but still, Brisbane was out of reach.

By the time the Otranto reached Sydney, the atmosphere aboard the ship had shifted. There was a palpable excitement among the passengers, an electric hum that seemed to fill the air. This was the final stop for many, including Marcus's good friend, Andrew, Scotty. As they stood on the deck, preparing to say their goodbyes, Marcus felt a lump form in his throat. Scotty had become more than just a companion on the journey. He had been a friend, a brother-in-arms through the trials of the voyage, and now he was leaving. They promised to keep in touch, to write letters through the Sydney branch of the bank where Scotty worked. But the departure was bittersweet, and as Scotty disappeared down the gangplank, Marcus felt the weight of the distance between them grow.

Standing at the rail, Marcus took in the sight of Sydney Harbour, its waters bustling with ferries and fishing boats, a far cry from the quiet, uncertain sea that had carried him here. The city was alive, vibrant, a stark contrast to the quiet, sun-drenched port towns they had visited. Yet, as the ship began to move on again, Marcus knew that Brisbane, his true destination, was still days away.

At last, the Otranto entered the Brisbane River, its murky waters twisting and turning like a serpent towards Hamilton Wharf. The moment Marcus stepped onto the dock, after clearing customs, the heavy, oppressive humidity slammed into him like a wall. The air was thick with the pungent scent of mangroves, saltwater, and something wild, an earthiness that clung to his skin and made his lungs feel heavy. Around him, passengers were reuniting with family or being ushered toward the immigration office, their faces a mix of excitement and exhaustion, each with their own story to tell.

Marcus stood still for a moment, taking it all in. His fingers tightened around the letter from Uncle Miles, the only lifeline he had in this foreign land. The paper was worn, the creases deep from being unfolded and read over and over. The instructions inside were clear, outlining the long road ahead. Australia was now his home, but the journey was far from over.

At his feet lay everything he owned in the world, two large, heavy suitcases, bulging with the few remnants of his old life. On his person, tucked securely in his coat pocket, was his letter of identity and introduction from the Institutional Bank of England. His bank book, with a balance of £12,000, was the inheritance left to him by his mother. The money had been transferred to the Brisbane branch of the Bank of New South Wales, but it was still just a number to Marcus, a sum that would eventually be the foundation of a new life.

He adjusted his grip on the suitcases, the weight of them pulling at his shoulders, and began the walk toward Doomben railway station. The midday sun was a merciless force overhead, beating down on him with a ferocity unlike anything he had ever known in England. By the time he reached the station, a ten-minute walk that felt like an eternity under the relentless heat, his shirt was soaked with sweat, and his breath came in short, laboured gasps.

From Doomben, Marcus boarded the train to Roma Street Station, the heart of Brisbane's railway system. Inside the carriage, the air was thick, stifling, despite the open windows that offered no real relief from the weight of the humidity. As the train clattered along the tracks, Marcus's eyes swept over the city unfolding before him. Streets bustled with movement, wide verandas shaded the fronts of houses and shops, and trams rumbled along, clattering through intersections with a rhythm all their own. Everything felt different, so much less formal than London, the architecture low and sprawling, the people casually dressed, moving with an ease and comfort that seemed foreign to Marcus.

When Marcus arrived at Roma Street, his eyes immediately sought out the departure board for the next train to Toowoomba. His heart sank as he saw that he had missed the last service of the day. Frustration surged within him, gnawing at his patience, but the realisation quickly set in: there was nothing he could do. The next train to Quilpie was at one 'clock tomorrow afternoon.

With no clear idea where to go, he approached a railway porter for advice. The man, a seasoned figure with a permanent frown etched into his face, offered a simple direction: Wickham Terrace, an area known for its hotels and boarding houses. Reluctantly, Marcus hefted his suitcases once more and began the uphill climb, the weight of his belongings pulling at his shoulders and the humidity clinging to his skin. The incline left him breathless, but he pressed on, driven by the need to find shelter.

It wasn't long before he found a modest hotel, The Terrace Hotel, its weathered exterior and dimly lit entrance giving off the faintest impression of faded respectability. He pushed open the creaking door, and the scent of aged wood and lingering tobacco smoke hit him immediately, carrying with it a sense of quiet history.

Inside, the reception area was small and worn, and the desk was unoccupied, save for a handwritten sign that instructed guests to ring the bell for service. Marcus's hand hovered over the bell, and when he finally pressed it, the chime echoed faintly through the room, seeming almost too polite for the somewhat rough atmosphere.

Moments later, a barmaid emerged from the adjoining bar, her apron slightly askew and a cloth in her hand as she wiped it absently. Her eyes swept over Marcus, her gaze lingering for a fraction longer than necessary, perhaps sizing him up, wondering if he was really old enough to be travelling on his own. She took her time, reaching for the registration ledger, but a sudden burst of raucous laughter from the bar broke her concentration.

"Hold on," she muttered, disappearing for a moment into the noisy refuge of the bar.

The sound of shouting orders, the clink of glasses, and the brief exchange with a customer demanding another round followed. Marcus stood in the quiet reception, feeling out of place in the chaos, while she served in the bar, her movements hurried and distracted.

When she finally returned, pen in hand and completed her entry into the register, she then handed him the key to room number seven, Marcus caught the slight misstep, she had written "Mark Dawson" instead of "Marcus Diarmuid." His immediate instinct was to correct her, but the words stalled in his throat as she turned to return to the bar, her attention already claimed by the noise and bustle.

He stood there for a moment, caught in a brief, bemused silence. How had she gotten it wrong? Was it his accent, the noise, or simply her distracted manner? The thought lingered in his mind as he pocketed the key.

Mark Dawson, was it? he thought, a smirk tugging at his lips. For one night, at least, he could be anyone.

Once inside his room, Marcus let out a long sigh of exhaustion, dropping his bags onto the worn floorboards with a thud that seemed to echo in the stillness. The room was bare, its simplicity almost a comfort, a narrow bed against one wall, a heavy chest of drawers, a small desk cluttered with little more than a flickering lamp, and a window that framed a view of the city spread below, its buildings shrouded in the fading light of evening. The heat of the day still clung to him, but the room offered a small reprieve.

He loosened his collar and peeled off his jacket, damp with sweat from the stifling walk up the hill. As he sat down on the bed, the mattress groaned under his weight, offering no promises of comfort but at least some rest. Tomorrow, the train to Toowoomba would carry him further on his journey, toward Quilpie, toward an uncertain future, but for now, the world seemed distant. He had a bed, a roof over his head, and a few quiet hours before the next leg of his journey demanded his attention once more.

The evening settled in, and with it, the distant hum of the city grew louder, drawing Marcus downstairs to the bar. The scent of grilled meat, tobacco smoke, and the low murmur of conversation beckoned him. The bar was alive with the clink of glass, the occasional burst of laughter, and the easy camaraderie of locals who seemed to belong in the chaos. He scanned the room, searching for a quiet corner, weaving his way between tables and patrons, the chatter thick with the kind of familiarity he hadn't yet found.

At the bar, the sight of cold beers being poured caught his attention, the condensation sliding down the glass, the promise of a brief escape. It was tempting. No, more than tempting. After the weight of the day, the heat, the uncertainty, it was exactly what he needed. Without thinking, he ordered one, his voice steady even as uncertainty fluttered beneath the surface.

The barmaid, the same one who had checked him in earlier, barely looked at him as she pulled the drink, her movements practiced and quick. She placed the glass in front of him with a swift efficiency, took his money without question, and turned away, her focus already shifting to the next patron.

Had she assumed he was of age, or was she simply too busy to care? It didn't matter. Marcus wasn't about to ask.

His fingers wrapped around the cool glass, and he lifted it to his lips. The beer was bitter, the sharpness of it cutting through the fatigue that had settled deep in his bones. As the liquid slid down his throat, a momentary sense of relief bloomed in his chest.

The bar was a whirlwind of noise, crowded with laughter, chatter, and the clinking of glasses. The air was thick with the scents of tobacco, sweat, and the faint, lingering aroma of grilled meat. Finding a quiet spot to escape the chaos was no easy feat, but as fortune would have it, two men vacated a small table near a window. Their chairs scraped against the floor as they made their departure, and Marcus seized the opportunity before anyone else could claim it.

With the table secured, Marcus settled in, his fingers absently tracing the rim of his glass, his eyes wandering over the crowd. He could feel the heat of the room, the weight of the conversations, the life of the place pressing in on him. As he took a long pull from his drink, he caught sight of a man approaching.

The gentleman was strikingly different from the other patrons, well-dressed, with a glass of dark amber liquid in hand. His polished boots clicked confidently against the wooden floor, and his suit, though meticulously pressed, seemed a little too large for his broad shoulders, giving him the appearance of a man who had stepped out of a different world. His presence was commanding, yet smooth, and he was headed directly for Marcus's table.

With a polite nod, the man gestured to the empty chair across from him.

"Mind if I join you?" His voice was smooth, confident, with a cultured tone that spoke of someone who was accustomed to the finer things in life, someone at ease in any company.

Marcus, still uncomfortable in his skin, fumbled for the right words. He had expected to drink in solitude, but the invitation, in some strange way, eased the tension he had been carrying ever since stepping off the ship. His nerves betrayed him, and he stumbled over his words in an attempt to sound casual.

"Yes, please... I mean, no! I don't mind... of course," he stammered, the words rushing out in a blur of nervous energy.

The man chuckled, the sound rich and knowing, as though he had encountered young men in bars who fumbled just like Marcus before. There was no mockery in his laughter, just a friendly, almost paternal patience. He studied Marcus for a moment, as if measuring him, before setting his drink down and easing into the chair with an easy grace.

"First time drinking alone?" the man asked, his tone laced with curiosity as he took a deliberate sip from his glass. "I'm surprised they served you. Eighteen, or... over?"

Marcus stiffened at the question, his initial sense of relief now tinged with a flash of suspicion. The man's appearance seemed to match the comfort of his demeanour, too smooth, too assured. His business suit was slightly loose, his frame larger than most, and yet there was an air about him that didn't quite sit right.

Marcus studied him carefully, weighing his words, and wondering how much this stranger could see of his own nerves. He had been wary of strangers before, and something in the man's posture, almost too casual, too knowing, set off a small alarm in his mind.

The man across from Marcus was a study in contrasts, broad-shouldered, heavyset, with a round face that suggested a life of comfort, but his silver-white hair, a touch disheveled, gave him a somewhat untamed, almost rogue-like appearance. Deep-set eyes and a prominent nose dominated his features, while full cheeks added to his unmistakable look, one that might belong to a politician or a businessman of some influence. He wore the mark of a man who had seen many years and many worlds.

Noticing Marcus's wary gaze, the man let out a short, amused chuckle, raising his free hand in a gesture of reassurance.

"Oh, don't worry," he said smoothly, his voice carrying a subtle thread of amusement. "I'm not the police. It's of no consequence to me whether you're of age to drink in a public bar or not."

Marcus's shoulders relaxed ever so slightly. The tension that had gripped him since the man's approach eased, just enough to let him breathe.

The man extended a broad, well-kept hand across the table, the glint of a signet ring catching the dim light of the bar. As he spoke, his voice held a confidence that settled over Marcus like a warm cloak.

"Clifford Palmerston," he said, his sharp eyes flickering with interest.

Marcus hesitated for a heartbeat before clasping the offered hand. "Marcus Diarmuid," he responded firmly, knowing the instant his English accent slipped out that he had been marked for what he was, a foreigner.

Palmerston raised an eyebrow, the corner of his mouth curling into a knowing smile. "Ah, English, then. What is it that brings you to these shores, young man?" he asked, leaning back in his chair, studying Marcus with genuine curiosity.

There was a simplicity in the way Palmerston spoke, a certain ease, and something in his tone, despite its worldly edge, made Marcus decide to offer up his story. He spoke of the long voyage across the seas aboard the Otranto, the weeks of saltwater and endless horizon, and the instructions his Uncle Miles had sent him. He spoke of Quilpie, of his destination and the journey that still lay ahead, of a life begun anew in the rugged heart of Australia.

Palmerston listened intently, nodding occasionally as Marcus unfolded his tale, the older man's sharp eyes never leaving his face. When Marcus finished, the silence hung between them for a moment before Palmerston rose to his feet, tilting his empty glass towards Marcus with a knowing smile.

"What are you drinking, Marcus?" Palmerston asked, his tone light, almost conversational.

Marcus glanced at his nearly empty pint, feeling a sudden wave of self-consciousness. "Not sure," he admitted, shrugging. "I just asked for a beer, and she poured this for me."

Palmerston chuckled softly, a rich sound that seemed to fill the space between them. He strolled to the bar, disappearing briefly into the crowd, only to return moments later, placing a fresh drink in front of Marcus.

"There you go, lad." Palmerston raised his glass slightly before taking a sip. "Welcome to Australia… Cheers!"

Marcus mirrored the older man's casual ease, lifting his glass with a faint smile, though the weight of his unfamiliar surroundings still lingered at the edge of his awareness. The two clinked their glasses together, the sound echoing in the clamour of the bar, as Marcus, still new to this strange land, found himself feeling, just for a moment, as though he had found something solid to hold onto in a world that was rapidly shifting beneath his feet.

As the evening stretched on, Clifford Palmerston, clearly enjoying the young man's company, insisted on treating Marcus to dinner. It was a gesture of appreciation for their conversation, though Marcus, still wary of the man's intentions, hesitated. Eventually, the warmth of Palmerston's presence won him over, and with a reluctant nod, he agreed. The two made their way to the hotel's dining room, a quiet, refined space that felt like a sanctuary after the raucous noise of the bar.

Seated at a table near the window, the soft glow of the evening sun casting shadows on the table, they dug into a feast of Moreton Bay Bugs, Mangrove Jack fillets, and crispy potato chips. The rich flavours were a welcome departure from the bland shipboard fare Marcus had subsisted on for weeks. He savoured each bite, grateful for the taste of real food, as Palmerston spoke with ease, revealing a bit about himself.

"I live up in Maryborough," he said, gesturing vaguely to the north with his fork. "About a hundred and sixty miles from here. I come to Brisbane regularly for business, nothing terribly exciting, but it keeps me moving."

He sipped his drink, then leaned back in his chair, his tone shifting slightly as he continued. "I usually stay at The Shamrock, just around the corner. But, I must say, the service there's been slipping. The food's not what it used to be, and the accommodation… well, I've certainly had better."

Marcus listened politely, his attention now focused on the older man as Palmerston's voice grew more critical. The older man's expression grew thoughtful for a moment before he turned his gaze on Marcus, almost casually asking, "How are the rooms here? Decent enough?"

Marcus didn't even think before responding. "Rather excellent, but then, I've been cooped up with three other fellows in a small ship's cabin for the last two months."

Palmerston's short laugh was rich with amusement, but there was something in his expression that Marcus couldn't quite place, a flicker, maybe, of something darker beneath the surface.

"That sounds like fun!" Palmerston remarked, his tone light, but Marcus couldn't shake the nagging feeling that there was more to it than just a casual comment.

Marcus simply shrugged, taking another bite of his meal. The sensation of solid ground beneath him, both literal and figurative, was enough to allow him to forget for a moment the journey that lay ahead.

Swirling the amber liquid in his glass, Palmerston regarded Marcus with a keen interest. His voice was as smooth as the whisky he held, the words slipping out casually, as if they were a natural extension of their conversation.

"I say, would you mind terribly if I were to take a look at your room? I might just start staying here rather than The Shamrock."

Marcus, still too naïve to pick up on the subtle shifts in Palmerston's demeanour, nodded without hesitation. "Of course, I don't mind," he said with a polite smile. "It's nothing fancy, but if you're looking for a change, you might find it decent enough."

Palmerston smiled, tipping his glass towards Marcus in a gesture of camaraderie. "Splendid."

The words hung in the air between them, though Marcus remained blissfully unaware of the deeper currents swirling just beneath the surface of their conversation.

Marcus turned the key in the lock, the soft click of the mechanism echoing in the quiet hall as he pushed the door open. He stepped aside to allow Palmerston to enter, watching as the older man strolled in with that characteristic air of casual authority, his gaze sweeping the room with the practiced eye of one who had seen countless spaces like this before. There was a quiet appraisal in his eyes, as though he was mentally weighing the quality of the modest furnishings, as if it was beneath him to be here at all.

Marcus followed him in, closing the door behind him with a soft thud that seemed too loud in the stillness.

Without warning, Palmerston turned abruptly, his expression shifting in a way Marcus couldn't quite interpret. There was something unsettling in the change, a flicker of something darker, more calculating. The older man's eyes glinted, and then his voice dropped to a low, assured murmur.

"I know what you want, young man."

Before Marcus could react, Palmerston lunged at him, his arms stretching wide in a movement that was meant to pull him into an embrace. The suddenness of it, the invasive force of the gesture, left Marcus frozen for a heartbeat.

Then, instinct took over.

A surge of revulsion ripped through him, and he shoved Palmerston away with every ounce of strength he could muster. His palms connected with Palmerston's chest, and with a force that surprised even him, he pushed the man back, sending him stumbling away.

Palmerston didn't expect such a violent reaction. His heel caught the foot of the bed, and for a fleeting moment, he looked like a child who had lost his balance. He flailed his arms, trying to catch himself, but it was too late. The momentum carried him backward, and with a sickening crash, his skull slammed into the corner of the heavy wooden chest of drawers at the foot of the bed.

The sound was jarring, a sickening crack that seemed to reverberate through the room.

For a heartbeat, everything was still. The air, thick with the tension of the moment, held its breath. Palmerston lay there, slumped in a way that was far too still, his body contorted unnaturally on the floor.

Marcus stood frozen in place, his chest heaving with panicked breaths, his mind scrambling to understand what had just occurred. His hands trembled at his sides, and he felt a cold sweat break out across his brow.

Then, the horror of it sank in.

Palmerston wasn't moving.

He was dead.

The realisation crashed over Marcus like a wave, drowning him in a sea of disbelief. His gaze locked on the motionless form at his feet, unable to tear away from the grisly sight of the older man's lifeless body. The air in the room felt thick, suffocating, as Marcus struggled to comprehend the chaos of the moment.

What had he done?

Marcus had not slept. Not a single moment. He sat on the edge of the bed, his hands clenched so tightly together that his knuckles had turned white. His gaze, wide and unblinking, remained fixed on the lifeless form sprawled across the floor. The dim glow of the streetlamp outside filtered through the thin curtains, casting long, shifting shadows that seemed to dance across the still figure of Clifford Palmerston.

His mind was a battlefield of colliding thoughts, confusion, panic, dread. What in God's name was he supposed to do? Go to the police? Tell them it had been self-defence? But the moment the idea formed, an icy claw of fear raked through his stomach. Who would believe him? A seventeen-year-old, fresh off the boat, caught drinking illegally in a bar, now standing over a dead man in his room? There were no witnesses, no proof. Just his word against the grim finality of the corpse before him.

No. He could not go to the police.

The more he turned it over in his mind, the more certain he became. If he stayed, he would be arrested. And then what? A trial? A prison sentence? The noose? His breath came short and sharp, panic clawing at his throat. He had no friends in this city, no allies. No one to vouch for him. The authorities would see only a frightened boy and a dead body.

There was only one option.

He had to leave.

The plan, or whatever passed for one, formed rapidly in his mind. Take his bags. Walk out the door. Disappear. If he kept moving, if he could reach Quilpie before the body was discovered, then he might just have a chance. No one here knew where he was headed. No one in Brisbane, at least.

At precisely four-thirty in the morning, Marcus took a deep breath and reached for his bags. His fingers wrapped around the worn leather handles, his pulse hammering in his ears. He had one foot out the door when something caught his eye, a small detail that sent a fresh chill slicing through him.

From this new angle, just as he turned to leave, he saw it.

A sliver of black leather peeking out from the breast pocket of Palmerston's coat.

Marcus hesitated, his breath coming in short, uneven gasps. His hands were trembling. His whole body felt taut, ready to snap. Slowly, deliberately, he eased the door shut again, his fingers barely making a sound on the brass handle.

Forcing himself to breathe, he set his bags down.

Then, moving with careful precision, he reached for the wallet. His fingers brushed the fine leather, still warm from the man's body. He hesitated only a moment before pulling it free and flipping it open. The scent of aged leather mingled with the lingering trace of cigar smoke, an oddly intimate reminder of the man now lying dead on the floor.

Inside, gleaming in gold letters, was the name:

Clifford Palmerston.

Tucked neatly into the wallet's inner fold were four business cards, each immaculate, the name embossed in elegant gold lettering. Clifford Palmerston. Beneath it, in stark black print, was the company name: Palmerston Timbers – Maryborough. A single line of text followed at the bottom, Tel. 4453.

Marcus swallowed, his throat dry as dust. His fingers moved to the next section of the wallet, and what he found there made his breath hitch. Stacked in perfect order, crisp and untouched, were seventy-six one-pound notes and six ten-shilling notes.

A fortune.

More money than he had ever held in his life. More than enough to get him to Quilpie, to vanish into the sunbaked interior where no one would ever find him. Compared to the pitiful sum in his own pocket, it was a king's ransom.

For a fleeting moment, guilt stirred in his chest. Was he really going to take it?

But what choice did he have?

With a swift, decisive motion, he pulled the notes free and shoved them into his own pocket, alongside his meagre coins. The business cards he left in the inner fold. The wallet, now disturbingly light, remained in his hands as he hesitated.

Common sense told him to leave it. Discard it. Burn it.

And yet, he slipped it into his coat pocket. Why? He wasn't sure. Perhaps to avoid suspicion. Perhaps because leaving it behind felt too much like evidence.

Straightening, he exhaled slowly, his decision made.

Picking up his bags once more, Marcus stepped into the dimly lit corridor and walked away without a backward glance. The door clicked shut behind him, sealing the past in that room, along with the body of Clifford Palmerston.

The streets were silent, the city still gripped in the hush of early morning. A low mist clung to the ground, curling around the street lamps, diffusing their glow. By the time Marcus reached Roma Street railway station, the first tendrils of dawn stretched across the sky, casting long, skeletal shadows on the empty platform.

Five o'clock.

The train to Toowoomba wouldn't leave until one in the afternoon.

He lowered himself onto a wooden bench, his bags at his feet, arms folded against the lingering chill. His breath misted in the crisp air, dissipating as quickly as his fleeting sense of safety. He had done it. Walked away. Stepped out of that hotel a free man. No one had called after him. No alarm had been raised. He was just another traveler now, another faceless figure waiting for a train.

Slowly, his muscles uncoiled. He forced himself to relax, to appear composed, natural. If anyone looked at him, they would see a young man weary from travel, not a fugitive running from a corpse.

Then he saw them.

Two uniformed police constables stepped onto the platform.

Marcus stiffened.

They weren't searching, weren't scanning the crowd for a suspect. They moved at an unhurried pace, deep in conversation, their boots clicking against the stone platform.

But still, Marcus felt the sweat bead on his brow. His heart pounded, a hammer against his ribs. They were coming straight toward him.

His fingers tightened on the bench, nails pressing into the wood. This was it. The moment he had feared since the instant Palmerston hit the floor. If they were here for him, there was nowhere to run.

The constables drew closer, their voices a low murmur. Then, just as they were about to pass, one of them glanced up. His eyes met Marcus's.

A nod. Brief. Polite. Nothing more than a passing acknowledgment of another man on the platform.

Marcus nodded back automatically, his muscles loosening as the constables continued walking past without a second glance.

Relief crashed over him in a wave so strong he had to grip the edge of the bench to keep from sagging. He exhaled sharply, breath shuddering, whispering to himself,

Relax, Marcus. Relax.

At 10:20 a.m., the housekeeper made her way down the dimly lit hallway of the Terrace Hotel, her cart of fresh linens and cleaning supplies rattling softly over the threadbare carpet. She stopped at Room Seven, balancing a small stack of towels in one arm as she rapped lightly on the door.

"Housekeeping!" she called in a bright, practiced tone.

Silence.

Her eyes flicked to the room list. Room Seven was due to be vacant today. Check-out was at ten, and guests were expected to have left by now. With a slight shrug, she reached for the master key hanging from the chain at her waist, slid it into the lock, and turned the handle.

The door swung open.

A peculiar stillness met her.

The curtains were drawn, allowing only a sliver of daylight to pierce the gloom. The air inside was heavy, stale. She stepped forward, the soft tread of her shoes swallowed by the silence. Then her eyes fell on the motionless figure sprawled at the foot of the bed.

Her breath hitched.

For a fraction of a second, her mind refused to process what she was seeing. The towels in her arms slipped free, landing in a soft, forgotten heap at her feet. Then, as the grim reality sank in, a scream ripped from her throat, raw and primal, shattering the hush of the hallway and echoing down into the lobby below.

At the reception desk, the young clerk on duty jolted, his pen slipping from his fingers, clattering onto the ledger. A second later, the manager and a bellboy burst from the office, their footsteps thudding against the carpet as they rushed toward the commotion.

By the time the police arrived, the housekeeper was sitting in the hallway, trembling, her fingers gripping a handkerchief offered by a concerned colleague. Guests had gathered nearby, muttering in hushed voices, their curiosity barely restrained by the grim tension in the air.

Inside Room Seven, the scene was stark.

The dead man lay sprawled awkwardly on the floor, his limbs splayed at unnatural angles. His eyes were open, fixed in a vacant, unseeing stare. No blood. No immediate signs of struggle. Just a lifeless body, alone in the gloom.

Two uniformed officers moved about the room, methodical, searching. But after a few minutes, it became clear, there was no wallet, no identification, no papers. Whoever he was, he had been cleaned out.

One of the officers, Sergeant Ross Gillard, turned toward the nervous young receptionist, who stood wringing her hands in the doorway.

"Who was staying in this room?" His voice was calm, clipped, businesslike.

The receptionist swallowed, fumbling with the leather-bound hotel register. She ran a finger down the list of names before stopping at the entry for Room Seven.

"Mark Dawson," she said, her voice barely above a whisper. "From London, England."

Gillard jotted the name down in his notebook, exchanged a glance with his partner, then snapped the book shut.

"Well," he murmured, rubbing his jaw. "It's about smoko time. The saloon bar open?"

The train pulled into the platform at 12:45, a behemoth of steel and steam, hissing as it settled into place. Fifteen minutes until departure.

Marcus hoisted his bags, weaving through the throng of passengers as they jostled for position. A blast of steam curled around his legs as he climbed the metal steps, gripping the cold brass railing. Inside, the carriage smelled of polished wood, worn leather, and the faint tang of coal smoke that drifted through the open windows.

He found his seat near the window and settled in, his bags tucked securely beneath his feet. Outside, porters shouted, their voices rising over the hiss and clang of railway men preparing for departure. Passengers called hurried goodbyes, hands grasping through open windows for one last touch. From the refreshment room, the rich, savoury aroma of fresh-baked meat pies drifted through the air, mingling with the acrid scent of burning coal.

Then, with a deep, mechanical groan, the locomotive shuddered to life. The great wheels bit into the steel rails, and with a shriek of metal on metal, the train began to roll forward, sluggish at first, then faster, pulling free from the station like a beast unleashed.

The cityscape blurred past, the streets, the buildings, the people, until the suburbs of Brisbane took their place. Milton, Indooroopilly, Oxley, the names rolled by like chapters in a book. Timber houses on stilts dotted the landscape, their corrugated iron roofs glinting under the midday sun. In backyard gardens, children dashed to their fences, their arms flailing in excitement as they waved at the passing train. The whistle screamed, cutting through the air like a bird of prey.

Marcus barely saw them. His eyes tracked the world outside, but his mind was locked in the events of the previous night. The weight of it sat heavy on his chest, a dull pressure he couldn't shake.

He inhaled slowly.

No. He couldn't dwell on that now.

The city fell away behind him, swallowed by the endless expanse of open countryside. The greens of farmland rolled past, vast and untouched, stretching toward the horizon. The rhythmic clatter of the wheels against the rails set a steady, hypnotic tempo, a lulling beat that seeped into his bones.

For the first time since leaving Room Seven, Marcus allowed himself to loosen up and to try to relax.

The train lurched and groaned, steel and steam battling against the incline as it pressed inland, carving its way through the rugged Queensland countryside. At every small station, Rosewood, Laidley, Gatton, it slowed, brakes screeching, as the platforms sprang to life. Farmers, townsfolk, and railway men moved with quiet efficiency, hauling crates of fresh produce into the freight cars, bundles of cabbages, sacks of potatoes, wooden boxes brimming with apples, the scent of earth and ripened fruit filling the air.

Vendors threaded through the press of travellers, their baskets laden with warm meat pies, sticky currant buns, and glass bottles of sarsaparilla, the hiss of escaping gas as they popped their corks punctuating the murmur of conversation.

Marcus had little appetite, but he bought a bottle of sarsaparilla from a barefoot boy barely older than himself, handing over a shilling with a nod. The spiced, honeyed drink was cool against his throat, its taste momentarily distracting him from the gnawing unease in his gut. Around him, passengers leaned from open carriage windows, exchanging hurried farewells, collecting parcels, or simply watching the world pass them by.

Then, with a shrill blast from the conductor's whistle, the train heaved forward once more, leaving behind the clutter of the station and pressing deeper into the wilderness.

Beyond Helidon, the journey became a battle. The Great Dividing Range loomed ahead, and with it, the climb. The air thinned, cooler now, carrying the scent of damp earth and eucalyptus, mingling with the ever-present sting of coal smoke. The locomotive groaned under the strain, metal joints grinding, steam hissing as it clawed its way upward.

Marcus felt the effort in his bones, the strain of steel against gravity rattling through his seat. The train snaked through deep rock cuttings, walls of raw stone flashing past, while beyond them, the valley stretched below, patchworks of farmland, the white specks of distant homesteads, windmills turning lazily in the breeze.

Then came the tunnels.

Black voids swallowed the train whole, their soot-streaked interiors thick with the stink of burning coal. The world narrowed to pitch blackness, the thunder of the locomotive reverberating off stone, the air heavy and choking. Marcus pulled his collar to his nose, feeling the grit of soot settle on his skin. Around him, others did the same, some pressing handkerchiefs to their mouths, others simply enduring. Seasoned travellers didn't flinch, their eyes fixed ahead, waiting for daylight to return.

And then it did.

They emerged, blinking, onto the crest of the range, and before them, the Darling Downs unfurled in an endless sea of golden grass, rolling plains stretching to the horizon, swaying in the afternoon breeze. The worst of the climb was behind them. The train gathered speed, gliding across the plateau with renewed ease.

At last, Toowoomba Station loomed ahead, its red-brick facade, arched windows, and iron railings standing firm and unyielding, a place of motion and permanence in equal measure. The platform bustled with life, porters unloading luggage, drovers in wide-brimmed hats shaking hands, families clasping one another in tight embraces.

With a final, shuddering sigh, the train hissed to a halt, four hours and sixteen minutes since departing Roma Street.

Marcus took a slow breath, steadying himself.

He had arrived in Toowoomba.

The next step of his journey awaited. And with it, the desperate hope that he could finally leave Brisbane, and the ghost of Clifford Palmerston, far behind.

The ticket clerk barely glanced up, his fingers mechanically punching Marcus's fare, one way, all the way through to Quilpie. Marcus folded the ticket between his fingers, his eyes flicking to the departures board.

The next train to Charleville, the last stop before Quilpie, was set to depart at 7:49 p.m., a long, overnight haul through the endless vastness of the Queensland interior. Nine hours and twenty minutes of black, unbroken land rolling past in the dark, the steady clack of wheels on rails the only constant.

With time to spare, Marcus eased the weight from his shoulders, depositing his bags in the baggage shed. The relief was fleeting, but he took it where he could.

He drifted toward the tea room, drawn by the glow of yellow lamplight spilling across the station floor and the scent of freshly baked bread and meat pies curling in the air. The small café hummed with life, passengers in transit, railway workers grabbing quick meals before returning to their duties.

Marcus joined the queue at the counter, hesitating only a moment before ordering a meat pie. He wasn't hungry, food had been an afterthought all day, but he needed to keep his strength. Balancing the hot, flaky pastry on a plate, he moved to the self-serve tea station, where steam curled from battered tin teapots, their handles blackened by years of service. He poured a cup, the rich, bitter liquid swirling as he added a splash of milk. The act of it, the simple, familiar motion of stirring, settled him, if only slightly.

The tea room felt too crowded, the press of bodies, the murmur of conversation, the clatter of crockery setting his nerves on edge. Instead, he took his meal out onto the platform, settling onto a wooden bench in the cool evening air. The first bite of the pie sent peppery gravy spilling onto his tongue, its warmth pushing back the chill creeping into his bones.

The station buzzed with quiet anticipation. Porters wheeled heavy trolleys, their boots thudding on the wooden planks, while announcements crackled over the loudspeaker, voices tinny and distorted. A steam engine rumbled in the yard, the metallic chuff of its breathing rising above the restless stir of departing travellers.

Marcus sipped his tea, letting the heat seep through his fingers.

He tried not to think.

Tried not to picture Palmerston's body lying crumpled on the floor.

But the thought coiled in his mind like a snake, tightening with each passing second. By now, the body would have been discovered. Perhaps even by midday, when the hotel staff had gone about their rounds. A knock at the door, unanswered. A key turned in the lock.

And then, the silence breaking.

A gasp. A cry of alarm.

The police would have been called. An investigation would be underway. And someone, a porter, a waiter, a passing guest, would surely remember seeing them together. Walking to the room. Sharing a meal in the dining hall.

Would they remember his face? His accent? His name?

Marcus's pulse kicked against his ribs.

He had to leave.

He had to be gone before the trail turned hot.

For a moment, a single, desperate moment, he considered going to the police himself. Walking into the station house, sitting across from a sergeant with tobacco-stained fingers, and telling them everything. That it had been self-defence. That he hadn't meant to kill Palmerston.

But would they believe him?

Or would they see only a young man on the run, a foreigner with no alibi, no proof, and nothing to his name? Would they assume he had robbed Palmerston?

His fingers twitched against his knee.

No. He couldn't risk it. Not yet. Not here.

He needed distance.

He needed Quilpie.

He needed to disappear.

God help me.

He had been in this blistering country for less than a day, and now, just look at him. A fugitive. A man on the run.

Despair clawed at his chest, tight as a noose. His hands clenched in his lap, his breath coming in short, ragged bursts. He wasn't a murderer. He wasn't some bloody outlaw hiding from the gallows. And yet, here he sat, alone on a dusty train station bench, waiting for a train that would drag him deeper into the unknown.

His self-pity swallowed him whole, so much so that he failed to notice the man who had taken a seat beside him, watching him with the lazy curiosity of a man with nowhere to be and all the time in the world.

"You all right there, mate?" The voice came thick with an Aussie drawl, slow and easy like a summer afternoon. "Looking' a bit pale-ish."

Marcus jerked upright, his pulse slamming against his ribs. He hadn't even heard the man approach, hadn't sensed him, hadn't felt the shift of the bench beneath his weight. His nerves were razor-thin, stretched so tight he thought they might snap. The feeling of exposure sent a cold shiver through him.

He pulled back slightly, his stiffness bordering on rudeness.

"Oh… I'm fine, thank you," he muttered, trying to force the words out steady. "It's just that…"

Just that what? That he had killed a man last night? That he had spent the entire day waiting for the cold press of a constable's hand on his shoulder and the words, You're coming with us, son.

The thought choked him.

"I was miles away, that's all." He waved a hand vaguely. "Didn't even realise what I was thinking."

Finally, Marcus forced himself to look at the stranger properly. The man wasn't young, but not old either, perhaps mid-thirties. Broad-shouldered and stocky, his skin tanned deep from long hours beneath a merciless sun. His clothes were the kind of practical, hard-wearing gear meant for a man who spent more time under open skies than beneath a roof, a faded denim shirt, khaki trousers, a wide-brimmed brown felt hat pulled low against the evening light.

But it was the boots that caught Marcus's eye.

Elastic-sided. Cuban heels.

Riding boots.

A horseman, then. A stockman. A man used to hard work and harder country.

The stranger nodded, unbothered by Marcus's hesitation. "Fair enough," he said easily. "We all get lost in our heads sometimes."

Marcus exhaled, willing his body to loosen the iron grip of tension.

Perhaps… just perhaps… talking to this man wouldn't be the worst idea.

The stranger stretched out his legs, boots scuffing against the platform, and glanced at him sideways. "Where you headed, mate?"

Marcus hesitated.

He had spent the past twenty-four hours second-guessing every word, every decision. But before he could consider a lie, the truth slipped free. His mouth had decided before his brain.

"Quilpie," he said.

The man's eyebrows lifted slightly.

Marcus swallowed, his voice firmer this time. "Quilpie."

He didn't know why saying it felt important, as if giving the place a name would somehow make it more than just an escape route.

The stranger let out a chuckle. "Well, I'll be buggered." His grin flashed, white teeth bright against sun-darkened skin. "That's where I'm headed too. Not much to see there if you're a tourist, though. Just red dirt, cattle, and the odd pub."

He shifted slightly, then stuck out a hand, rough, calloused, strong.

"Name's Jack. Or 'Jacko,' as most blokes call me."

Marcus looked at the offered hand for a fraction too long before clasping it. The grip was firm, a working man's handshake.

"Marcus."

Jacko nodded, seemingly satisfied. "Well, Marcus, looks like you and I are in for a long ride. Most of these blokes, probably all of 'em, will be off at Charleville in the morning. Should have Quilpie in our sights before smoko."

He slapped his knees, stretching his legs out even further.

"So," he said, flashing another grin. "What's a bloke like you headed for a place like Quilpie for?"

Before Marcus could answer, Jacko reached into his pocket and pulled out a crumpled pack of Woodbines, shaking one loose with a flick of his wrist. He held it out without a word, his rough fingers stained from years of work, tobacco, and sun. Marcus hesitated, then took it, feeling the dry paper between his fingers. A moment later, Jacko produced a battered Zippo, the metal worn smooth by time and use. He thumbed it open with a sharp clink, struck the flint, and a small, wavering flame licked at the darkness.

Marcus leaned in first, drawing deep as the tobacco caught, then exhaled slowly, the acrid smoke curling up into the cool night air. Jacko did the same, inhaling with the satisfaction of a man who had earned his vices.

"I'm off across the street," he said, tapping his cigarette against his thumbnail. "Grabbin' a half dozen Fourex and a few packs of Smith's crisps for the trip." He took another drag, squinting at Marcus through the smoke. "Might wanna get some for yourself, mate. Nothing worse than a long train ride with an empty belly and nothin' but your own bloody thoughts for company."

Marcus hesitated, an instinctive wariness coiling in his gut. He had trusted men before. It had cost him. And yet, something about Jacko's easy manner, his lack of prying questions, made him seem different.

Jacko shrugged, as if he'd already made up his mind not to give a damn either way. "Suit yourself." He stubbed his cigarette out beneath his heel and started toward the station exit.

Marcus sat there, frozen in indecision. But then, as if some unseen hand shoved him forward, he pushed himself up.

"Wait for me," he called, striding after him.

Jacko glanced back, a grin tugging at the corner of his mouth. "Sensible lad. No point sittin' around starvin'."

They found the pub at the end of Railway Street, where it met Russelll Street, its weathered facade cast in the amber glow of a flickering streetlamp. The sign above the door read The Railway Hotel, the paint peeling in long, curling strips, as if the building itself had given up fighting the brutal Queensland sun.

Inside, the place reeked of stale beer, wood polish, and sweat. A handful of men leaned against the bar, their work shirts stained with the dust of a hard day's labour. From somewhere in the back, a radio crackled to life, the voice of a race announcer rolling through the room like distant thunder.

Jacko walked to the bar with the easy swagger of a man who belonged. Marcus followed, stiff-backed, trying to blend in.

"Two schooners of bitter, love," Jacko called out, rapping his knuckles on the counter.

The barmaid, a sharp-eyed woman with auburn hair, gave Marcus a slow, appraising look. "Has your mate got ID?" she asked, her lips curving into a smirk. "Looks like he's still in nappies."

Marcus stiffened, but Jacko scoffed, leaning against the bar with a grin.

"Aw, pull yer head in, darlin'," he said. "Just get the beers." A heart beat. Then, with a flash of teeth, "Please."

The barmaid snorted, shaking her head as she reached for two schooner glasses, tilting them under the tap with the skill of someone who had poured more drinks than she cared to count. The golden liquid foamed high before settling, rich and amber.

She set them down with a smirk. "Don't let him drink too fast, or he'll be needing nappies."

Jacko chuckled, lifted his glass, and clinked it against Marcus's. "Welcome to Australia, mate."

Marcus took a cautious sip. The bitterness hit first, then the smooth malt. Stronger than what he was used to, but warming, grounding. He took another.

The pub grew livelier as the night deepened, voices rising in a familiar chorus of drink and laughter. Jacko kept an eye on the time, though, and when their second schooners were drained, he tapped the bar with his knuckles and nodded toward the door.

"Time to move, mate. Train won't wait for us."

They stepped back into the cool night, the scent of rain lingering in the air, and made their way to the station's bottle shop. Jacko grabbed a carton of XXXX Bitter to share, twelve massive, 27-ounce bottles. Marcus had never seen beer in bottles that big before, but Jacko just grinned.

"You'll be bloody glad for 'em," he assured him. "Long ride ahead."

They threw in three packets each of Smith's crisps, good for soakin' up the grog, as Jacko put it, and made their way back to the station, the weight of their supplies pressing comfortingly against their sides.

The train loomed in the distance, a steel serpent coiled and waiting, its windows dark except for the occasional flicker of movement.

Marcus swallowed hard, the reality of it settling in his gut like a stone.

Back at the station, Marcus retrieved his bags from the dimly lit baggage shed. The night air was thick with the scent of coal smoke and oil, the quiet hum of the railway broken only by the distant murmur of voices and the occasional clang of metal on metal.

The train loomed before them, a hulking beast of steel and shadow, its carriages stretching into the darkness. A soft hiss of steam curled along the platform, dissipating into the cool night.

Jacko moved with the easy confidence of a man who had done this a hundred times before. He climbed aboard first, stepping lightly into the narrow corridor. Marcus followed, glancing into compartments as they passed, each one dimly lit, some already occupied by passengers settling in for the long journey ahead.

At last, they found an empty compartment. Jacko tossed his canvas bag onto the overhead rack with a practiced flick of the wrist, then reached down for Marcus's suitcases. With a grunt, he heaved them up beside his own, then crouched to slide the carton of beer beneath the seat.

"There," he said, brushing his hands off on his trousers. "That should keep us sorted."

The compartment was small but serviceable, with two long cushioned bench seats facing each other, a fold-down table beneath the window, and an air of faded comfort. The lingering scent of old leather mixed with the sharper tang of coal smoke from the engine.

Then, with a sharp whistle and a jolt, the train lurched forward, the heavy carriages shuddering as the wheels bit into the steel rails. At exactly 7:49 p.m., they pulled away from the station, the rhythm of the tracks settling into a steady, hypnotic clatter.

Jacko stretched out lazily, crossing one ankle over his knee. He reached into the carton, plucked out a bottle, and with a practiced motion, popped the cap off against the edge of the seat frame. The cap hit the floor with a dull metallic plink. He passed the bottle to Marcus before cracking open one for himself.

"To Quilpie," Jacko said, raising his beer with a grin.

Marcus hesitated for only a moment before clinking his bottle against Jacko's. "To Quilpie," he echoed, then took a long pull of the bitter, malty brew.

Outside, the lights of Toowoomba flickered past and faded into the vast blackness of the Queensland interior. The train picked up speed, the iron rails stretching ahead of them like veins through the heart of the land.

Then, the overhead speaker crackled to life.

"The eight o'clock news, brought to you by ABC Queensland."

Marcus barely registered the first few lines, his mind drifting with the gentle rock of the train. But then,

"Brisbane police believe that the body of a man found in a room at the Terrace Hotel this morning may have been the victim of a robbery, as no bags or wallet were found in the room. The man has been identified as arriving from the ship Otranto yesterday morning. Police have not yet released the name of the deceased as they are currently seeking his next of kin in England."

Marcus felt the blood drain from his face.

His fingers, wrapped tightly around the neck of his beer bottle, tensed until his knuckles whitened. His pulse hammered against his ribs.

He had expected this. Of course, he had.

But hearing it spoken aloud, cast out over the airwaves for the entire state to hear, made it all too real.

Jacko, his beer held loosely in one hand, turned his head slightly towards Marcus. His expression was unreadable, his sharp eyes narrowing as he took in the news. "Huh," he muttered, his voice low and rough. "Poor bastard. City's getting rougher these days."

Marcus, his throat as dry as dust, forced a nod. He focused on keeping his face impassive, taking a slow sip of beer to steady the tremor in his fingers.

The announcer moved on to the next story, but Marcus's mind stayed locked on the words that had just echoed through the carriage. No bags, no wallet found. The police weren't treating it as an accident. They were looking for someone.

And then the name of the ship Otranto. The same vessel Marcus had boarded in England. The hair on the back of his neck prickled as the implications settled in. The man had arrived from the Otranto, and the police were seeking his next of kin in England. Could they possibly believe he was the dead man?

He forced his mind to stay sharp, to push aside the creeping unease.

Jacko, sensing the silence, broke it with a deep, rumbling chuckle. "So, tell us about yourself, young Marcus. You're obviously a pommy, but what's the bloody go with Quilpie? Why the hell would you want to go to bloody Quilpie?"

Marcus snapped back to the moment, his hand gripping his beer tighter. "My uncle... My uncle Miles. He has a property near Quilpie."

Jacko's brow furrowed in thought. "Miles… Miles... No way... Do you mean Mr. Diarmuid... Miles... Diarmuid?"

Marcus felt a rush of relief flood through him, his heart picking up its pace. "You know him?" The question tumbled out, and his voice cracked slightly. The thought of arriving in Quilpie only to find that his uncle had never existed, that he had been chasing ghosts, had been gnawing at him ever since he left Brisbane.

Jacko's eyes widened in surprise. "Yeah, I've seen him a few times. One of those blokes you notice. Stands out. Tall, wiry, always dressed sharp for a bushman. Doesn't say much, but when he does, people listen. Old-school type. Been out there forever."

Marcus absorbed the description, trying to force the image into the fragments of memories that clung to his mind. His mother had never spoken much about Uncle Miles, but when she had, her words had been laced with a grudging respect. A man who had carved out a life for himself in the vast, unforgiving expanse of the Australian outback.

Jacko took another swig of beer, then shook his head slowly, a rueful smile tugging at his lips. "Stratheden, mate... that place used to be legendary. Biggest sheep station in the district back in its heyday, thousands of acres, head stockmen, shearers, the lot. Times have changed though. Lot of places have folded, swallowed up by bigger outfits. But, Diarmuid's still holding onto it, he must be one tough old bastard."

Marcus hesitated. "Do you know if he still lives there?"

Jacko gave a firm nod, his voice rich with approval. "Yeah, he does. Stratheden's still going, just a lot smaller than it used to be. But old Diarmuid? He's still out there, running what's left of it." He paused, then turned his gaze back to Marcus, his curiosity piqued. "So, is he meeting the train to pick you up?"

Marcus rubbed the back of his neck, his mind flicking to the vague instructions he had. "I have a telephone number to call when I arrive. Someone's supposed to pick me up… I suppose." The words felt hollow, uncertain. What if his uncle had forgotten? What if no one came?

Jacko's grin was broad, almost mocking. "Ah, well, welcome to the bush, mate. Nothing runs to a schedule out here." He finished his beer with a long swallow and stretched his legs out in front of him, the creak of his boots loud in the quiet compartment. "Better hope the old fella hasn't forgotten about you."

Marcus forced a laugh, but it sounded thin, unsure. The warmth of the beer was making him drowsy, and the gentle sway of the train rocked him like a lullaby. His eyelids grew heavy, and he slouched deeper into the seat, the rhythmic clatter of the wheels on the track lulling him into a haze.

Through the fog of sleep, he caught snippets of Jacko's voice, something else being said, but it faded quickly, the sound lost in the distance as the world around him blurred and darkened.

Marcus woke with a start, the world around him shifting as the sounds of movement filled the air, the shuffle of boots on the floor, low voices murmuring, and the distant clang of railway carriages being shunted. He blinked against the dim light filtering through the train windows, his senses clouded with the fog of sleep. For a moment, he forgot where he was.

Then, with a rush, it all came back, the long, relentless journey, the endless stretch of the outback rolling by, the conversation with Jacko, and the weight of his uncertain future pressing down on him. He straightened up, rubbing his face, trying to dispel the remnants of sleep.

Jacko, already up and stretching like a man used to early mornings, gave a grunt of effort and yawned. "Rise and shine, mate. We're in Charleville. Last big stop before Quilpie." He nodded toward the window, where station workers were bustling about, loading crates and tying down cargo. The air was thick with the acrid scent of coal smoke and dust. Outside, a few passengers shuffled off the train, adjusting their coats against the crisp bite of the early morning chill.

Marcus ran a hand through his disheveled hair and exhaled a slow breath. A few more hours, and he'd be in Quilpie. He reminded himself again to steady his nerves, to hold onto the hope that soon, answers would come, and his future would begin to take shape.

Outside, the first light of dawn broke over the horizon, spilling a soft orange glow across the vast, unbroken plains. The train jerked into motion again, its wheels clanking rhythmically as it gathered speed. A conductor, his face impassive, strolled past their compartment, nodding a greeting as he went.

"Only three and a half hours to go, fellas," the conductor said with a casual tone. "Just need to pick up three freight trucks at the yards."

Marcus barely registered the words, his mind still mulling over Jacko's cryptic comments from the night before. Now seemed as good a time as any to ask the question that had been simmering in his mind.

"So, where do you live in Quilpie?" he asked, turning to Jacko. "Are you out on a property, or do you live in town?"

Jacko stretched again, his arms reaching high above his head, his muscles rippling beneath his rough shirt. He yawned. "North of town, out on the Adavale Black Track, about fifty miles out. I live with my old man on the place. We run cattle."

Marcus watched him casually shove his last bottle of beer into his bag. He wondered if Jacko was saving it for later, or if it was simply a memento of the trip, a token from this fleeting part of his life.

Jacko caught his eye, then added, "Your place is south of town, down towards Thargomindah. About sixty-five, maybe seventy miles out. Right on the Bulloo."

Marcus frowned, mulling over the unfamiliar name. "What's the Bulloo?"

Jacko let out a surprised laugh. "The Bulloo's the river, mate. The only thing that keeps those towns alive. No river, no water, no water, no life."

Marcus nodded, trying to picture the landscape Jacko described, a river carving its way through the arid outback, a precious lifeline in a land where water was as scarce as gold. He wondered what kind of life his uncle led in this remote place. What kind of place was it, really? Would they get along? And was his uncle even expecting him?

His thoughts shifted to his aunt. What was her name again? Verity. His mother had spoken about her once, in passing, mentioning that she and Uncle Miles had lost their only son, Simon, in the war. Marcus could barely remember the mention of Simon, but now, as the memory surfaced, it sat heavy in his chest. Eighteen years old, dead in the war, six years ago now.

The train rocked gently, its wheels thundering across the rails as the wide expanse of the land stretched out in all directions. The farther they traveled, the more the earth dissolved into an endless, sun-scorched sea of red dust and scrub. Marcus stared out at it, torn between excitement for what lay ahead and unease about what he might find when he arrived.

After a moment, he turned to Jacko, his voice quieter this time. "Jack, did you know my cousin, Simon?"

Jacko glanced at him, then nodded slowly. "Yeah, I met him a couple of times. He was a bit older than me, though." He paused, rubbing the back of his neck. "Pretty bloody sad, him getting shot in the war. My dad reckons that was the turning point for Stratheden. Says that's when things really started to go downhill."

Marcus absorbed this in silence. The decline of Stratheden had begun long before his arrival, it seemed. But what exactly had changed after Simon's death? What had been lost?

Jacko shot him a sideways glance, his face now shadowed with something close to sympathy. "I suppose you'll find out all about it when you get there. If it's not what you're after, well, you can always become a traveler. Plenty of blokes do. Move around, take work where you can, until you find something that fits, or at least something that suits you for a while."

Marcus wasn't sure if that reassured him or made him more anxious. The thought of drifting, of being adrift in a country as vast as Australia, felt foreign to him. He'd spent so long clinging to the hope that Stratheden would be his new beginning, the place where he could make something of himself. The idea that it might not work out, that he might arrive to find he didn't belong, was unsettling, to say the least.

But Jacko had a point. If Stratheden wasn't the place for him, he wasn't stuck. Australia was a vast land, a place where opportunities, like the horizon, stretched out endlessly. The idea of becoming a traveler, of taking his chances on the open road, felt uncomfortable, but perhaps it was a road he might have to walk, if Stratheden didn't welcome him.

Quilpie

Marcus's gaze fixed on the endless expanse of land rolling past, a vast, unforgiving stretch of earth that seemed to stretch on forever. The sun now hung high in the sky, its relentless heat casting long, angular shadows across the cracked, parched soil. The train's wheels squealed as it began to slow, the rhythmic clatter fading to a distant hum. His pulse quickened, a knot of anticipation tightening in his chest. Quilpie, his new home.

Leaning out the window, Marcus strained to catch his first real glimpse of the place. The station came into view, a weathered platform clinging to the edge of the outback like a forgotten relic. Its corrugated iron roof offered little respite from the sun, casting a mere sliver of shade onto the dusty ground below. A handful of figures stood waiting, their faces as weathered as the land itself. Stockmen in sweat-streaked hats, their shirts clinging to their backs, a woman in a faded dress whose eyes seemed as weary as the earth, and a pair of barefoot children, their feet kicking up dust as they chased each other across the barren platform. The heat shimmered in the air, thick and oppressive, even though the morning was still young.

As Marcus swung his legs over the edge and jumped down to the ground, the sharp scent of dry earth and scorched grass filled his nostrils. The dust rose in a cloud around his boots as he hit the ground, and the heat slammed into him like a furnace door flung wide open. He squinted against the harsh glare of the sun, his eyes scanning the town ahead, trying to take it all in.

Quilpie was smaller than he had imagined, much smaller. The town was little more than a collection of buildings, their edges softened by the dust and the years. The main street was lined with low, single-story structures, most made of timber, some of rough-hewn stone, each one worn and faded by the relentless sun. A hotel stood at one end of the street, its sign long since bleached white, a relic of better days. Beside it, a general store with a wide awning stretched its shadow across the uneven ground, while a handful of tin-roofed shops stood like sentinels, their surfaces glinting under the heat.

A row of gum trees, their bark peeling and leaves stiff with the dry air, lined one side of the town, offering what little shade could be found in this arid land. Beneath their branches, the stillness was almost suffocating, the only movement the lazy swaying of their leaves in the faintest whisper of wind.

Beyond the town, the land stretched endlessly in every direction. A sea of red dirt, dotted here and there with clumps of spinifex and low, scrubby bushes. The horizon seemed to shimmer, a distant, hazy line where earth and sky met in a blur of heat. There was no mistaking it now: this was the outback, raw and untamed, a place where the land demanded respect, and survival was never guaranteed.

The town was nothing like England. Nothing like the hustle of London's crowded streets, the rolling green fields, or the damp, overcast skies. This was raw, untamed, Quilpie, a stubborn settlement clinging to the edge of the unforgiving outback. Yet, there was something in the air, something that pulled at him. A toughness. A quiet, steadfast resilience, as though the land itself had forged the people here into something tougher than the heat and dust that surrounded them.

Jacko clapped Marcus on the back, his rough hand making a solid connection. "Well, mate, welcome to Quilpie! Not much to look at, but she grows on you. Give it time."

Marcus scanned the street again, his gaze drifting over the few sparse buildings and the slow-moving figures of the townsfolk. His eyes fell on a sign that stood out in the morning heat, CBC. The Commercial Banking Company of Sydney. It wasn't the Bank of New South Wales, but it would do for now.

Turning to Jacko, he asked, "Is that the only bank in town?"

Jacko gave a lopsided grin, a glint of amusement in his eyes. "The one and only, my friend. If you're looking for the Bank of New South Wales, you're better off heading back to Charleville. This one will have to do for now."

Marcus felt a knot form in his stomach. He didn't relish the idea of leaving Jacko's easy company behind, especially now that he stood alone in this strange place. The town felt small, insular, a world away from everything he had known. But he had come here to make a life, and he needed to take the first step.

"Well, thanks, Jack," Marcus said, offering his hand. "For your help and the good company. I'll head over to the bank, then see if I can find a phone to call my uncle."

Jack grasped his hand firmly, shaking it once. "You'll see me around for a couple of days, I reckon. I'm off to find my old man at the pub, and we'll be picking up supplies tomorrow before heading out to the property. You'll be fine here. Quilpie might be small, but it's got a way of growing on you."

Marcus nodded, relieved to have made the decision. "Alright, then. Until next time."

Jack slung his bag over his shoulder with a careless ease, his grin widening. "See you 'round, young fella. And good luck with your uncle."

As Jacko strode off down the street, Marcus turned toward the bank, his mind still whirling with the enormity of it all. The sun beat down mercilessly, but he squared his shoulders, took a deep breath, and picked up his two suitcases.

The bank was silent, a stillness that seemed to hang in the air, broken only by the occasional rustle of paper from the lone teller behind the counter. The man looked up from his work, his eyes meeting Marcus's, and with a casual wave of his hand, he called out, "We'll be open soon, mate. Not quite ten o'clock yet, another ten minutes, thanks."

Marcus gave a brief nod, adjusting the grip on his bags. He had no reason to linger, so he stepped back out into the heat of the street, the sun already fierce above. His gaze drifted to the post office across the road on Brolga Street. He had noticed it earlier in passing, and now, with the faintest spark of purpose, he decided to make use of the two public telephone booths sitting in front of it.

The heat seemed to radiate off the cracked pavement as he crossed over, his boots scraping lightly against the dust. He set his bags down beside the nearest booth and stepped inside. The faint scent of sun-warmed Bakelite and dust lingered in the small metal box as he lifted the receiver, his fingers brushing against the cool plastic.

The operator's crisp voice came through the line, as if she had been waiting. "Number, please."

Marcus fumbled for the small scrap of paper he had tucked into his pocket, unfolding it with a slight rustle. He read the number aloud. "Quilpie 382, please."

A brief silence followed, the only sound the soft hum of the line. Then the operator returned, her voice neutral. "You won't get them until about lunchtime today. They're out until then."

Marcus's stomach tightened, the brief hope he'd felt sinking into disappointment. "Right. Thanks," he muttered, his words a quiet breath before he replaced the handset in its cradle.

Stepping back out into the sun, he squinted upward, feeling the heat intensify as it rose higher in the sky. It was only going to get hotter from here, but his thoughts were already turning inward, weighing his next move. The day was young, but time had already begun to slip away.

Marcus collected his bags, the weight of them a constant reminder of the long journey ahead. He crossed the street once more, the midday heat pressing down on him like a heavy cloak. As he entered the bank, he found the once-quiet interior now buzzing with activity. The line had grown, a handful of locals talking in low voices as the tellers worked to keep the pace moving. At least now there were two tellers behind the counter, which meant the line would move faster, though it hardly made the wait feel any shorter.

Marcus shifted his weight from one foot to the other, his patience thinning with every passing minute. The rhythmic shuffle of feet and the murmur of voices seemed to stretch time, and finally, after what felt like an eternity, it was his turn.

He stepped forward, placing his letter of introduction and his bankbook on the counter. The book, a relic from the London Bank, displayed a balance of £12,000, money he hoped would buy him the fresh start he desperately needed. The teller, a middle-aged man with wire-rimmed glasses and an air of quiet efficiency, picked up the documents. His sharp eyes scanned them carefully before meeting Marcus's gaze.

"This letter is addressed to the Bank of New South Wales," the teller said, his voice neutral. "And your bankbook is only valid at the

Institutional Bank of London or a branch of the Bank of New South Wales."

Marcus's frown deepened. "So, if I open an account here, can you transfer the money into it?"

The teller's expression didn't change, but his response was swift. "Afraid not. You can certainly open a savings account with us, if you have money to deposit, but we can't transfer funds from an account with another bank. You'd need to handle that at a branch of the Bank of New South Wales."

Marcus exhaled sharply, the frustration creeping up on him. It was more complicated than he'd expected, but at least there was a way to keep some of his cash safe. With a resigned nod, he made the decision. He opened an account with the CBC and deposited £50. Not much, but enough to start, and perhaps the rest could be sorted later.

After thanking the teller, he gathered his bags once more, the weight of them a constant companion, and turned back towards the street. His mind was already shifting toward the post office, the next stop on his journey, but something told him the hardest part of the day was still ahead.

The heat of midday had settled over Quilpie like a heavy cloak, the town still and quiet, save for the distant rumble of trucks stirring the dust on the road. It was almost as if time itself had slowed to a crawl in the unforgiving outback. Marcus sank onto a weathered wooden bench outside the post office, his bags resting at his feet. He leaned back, his hands clasped behind his head, and let his eyes drift lazily across the street, watching the world go by. The dry, cracked earth stretched out before him, the sun hanging high and unforgiving in the sky.

By 11:45, the stillness had become almost unbearable. He stood up, brushing the dust from his trousers, and walked back to the telephone booth. The sound of his boots on the ground was the only noise to break the silence. Inside the booth, the air smelled faintly of dust and the warm plastic of the receiver. He lifted it and dialled the number again, his fingers a little less sure this time. When the operator answered, there was no mention of "try again later." Instead, there was a brief click, and then the line opened.

The ringing tone stretched into what seemed like an eternity, but then, at last, a woman's voice answered, a voice full of warmth and energy, as bright as the sun overhead.

"Hey loo, Verity speaking!" she greeted, her voice lilting and light.

Marcus had prepared for this moment, rehearsing his words a hundred times in his head, but now that the moment was here, his thoughts faltered. His mind went blank, the words slipping away like water through his fingers. All he could manage was a hesitant, "Hello… Auntie Verity?"

There was a brief silence on the other end of the line, as if she was trying to place him. Then, her voice returned, cautious, as if she was unsure of who was calling. "Who is this, please?"

Marcus swallowed hard, his throat suddenly dry. "It's… Marcus, Auntie! Oliver and Doreen's son, Marcus." His words tumbled out in a rush, and he added the last part quickly, afraid she might not recognise him.

The pause on the other end seemed to stretch for an eternity. But then, with a sharp intake of breath, Verity's tone shifted. The suspicion vanished, replaced by something softer, surprise, and perhaps a touch of delight.

"Oh, good God, child!" she exclaimed, her voice filled with genuine warmth. "Where are you? You're not here, are you? You're in Quilpie? My God!"

Marcus's heart lifted at the relief in her voice. "Yes, I'm in Quilpie. I just arrived this morning."

"Oh, we were expecting you, sometime this week or next. I wasn't sure when exactly, but I knew you'd be turning up!" Verity's voice bubbled with enthusiasm now, animated and full of life. "Oh, but today's Wednesday, isn't it? That means you've missed the mail truck."

"The mail truck?" Marcus repeated, confused.

"Yes, love, the mail truck, it runs only on Wednesdays and Saturdays. It would've taken you out to Stratheden. You'll have to wait until

Friday when Patrick, one of our workmen, comes into town for supplies. He'll be able to pick you up then."

Marcus's spirits sank for a brief moment, a flicker of disappointment settling in his chest. Two more days in town felt like a lifetime in this barren stretch of the world, but he quickly steadied himself. At least he had made contact. He wasn't stranded in this dusty town alone.

"Alright," he said, forcing a smile into his voice. "Friday it is."

"We'll let Patrick know to look out for you. Just stay in town, and we'll see you soon, darling."

As Marcus hung up the receiver, a mixture of relief and unease settled over him. He'd made it this far, but now the waiting began. Two more days in Quilpie, two more days to test the patience that had already been worn thin by the harsh landscape. But at least now, there was a plan. And in this wild, isolated place, that was something to hold onto.

With a quick glance at the relentless sun beating down, Marcus hefted his bags and made his way to the hotel, determined to secure a place to rest for the next few days. The building stood as a weathered sentinel to the passing years, its timber verandah offering a sliver of respite from the midday heat. Inside, the air was cooler, thick with the scent of beer, tobacco, and aged wood, a smell that spoke of time spent in the shadows of long conversations and hard days.

The man behind the busy counter looked up with a casual grin, his face sun-browned from years under the harsh sky. "Two nights, mate? Not a problem." He turned to a small wooden cupboard, each shelf lined with brass keys, and plucked one from the array. With a swift motion, he slid it across the counter. "What brings you to Quilpie Central?" he asked, the corners of his mouth lifting in a knowing smirk.

Marcus accepted the key, shifting the weight of his bags to his other hand as he spoke. "I've come to stay with my aunt and uncle," he said, then added, "at Stratheden. Patrick is coming into town on Friday to pick me up."

At the mention of Stratheden, the man's brows arched, recognition flashing in his eyes. "Stratheden, eh? Diarmuid? You're Miles's nephew?" His grin broadened, and he gave Marcus a once-over, appraising him with a look that seemed to weigh more than just his clothes. "Well, welcome to Quilpie, my boy."

The man paused for a moment, as if struck by an afterthought, before chuckling. "You'll need the room for three nights, though. Paddy usually stays here on Friday nights when he's in town, so you won't be heading out until Saturday morning. That's seven shillings a night, includes brekky."

Marcus hesitated for a moment, weighing the offer, then nodded in agreement. "Alright then, three nights it is." He handed over a pound note and a floren. The man returned the change with a single shilling and gave him the directions to his room. "Room three's upstairs, halfway down the corridor. Bathrooms on either side of the hall."

Marcus took his bags and ascended the creaky stairs to the second floor. The room was simple, but it offered a sense of calm after the long morning. He placed his bags down on the small bed and then, with a glance at the clock, decided it was time for some lunch. The hotel's rough-hewn charm had a welcoming pull, and Marcus felt the hunger of the road in his bones. With a stretch, he turned and made his way downstairs, ready to sample what the hotel could offer a newcomer to this isolated outpost.

The bar was lit by the filtered sunshine coming through the Louvre blinds on the windows, the scent of beer, cigarette smoke and old wood heavy in the air. A low hum of conversation buzzed around the room, punctuated by the occasional burst of laughter or the clink of glasses. Marcus paused in the doorway, letting his eyes adjust before scanning the faces within.

At the right-angled corner of the bar, he spotted Jacko, deep in conversation with an older man with a sweat stained brown felt hat pushed back on his head, broad-shouldered and weathered, with the hard edges of a man who had spent his life under the Australian sun. The resemblance was unmistakable. Marcus didn't need to guess; this had to be Jacko's father.

Jacko looked up then, spotting Marcus in the entrance. His face split into a grin, and he lifted his glass in greeting. "Marcus! Over here, mate!"

Marcus made his way over, weaving through the clusters of drinkers, feeling the warmth of the place seep into his bones. He had barely reached them when Jacko turned to the older man and gestured in his direction.

"Dad, this is Marcus. Marcus Diarmuid, Miles's nephew."

The older man, Ben Southwell, turned sharply at the name. His eyes locked onto Marcus, and for a fleeting moment, he seemed frozen, as if he'd seen a ghost.

Then, with a start, he exhaled through his nose, his brow furrowing as he studied Marcus with keen intensity. "By the jingies," he murmured, his voice roughened by years of smoke and whisky. "He looks just like Simon…"

Marcus felt a strange shift in the air, as if unseen threads had suddenly tightened between them. He extended his hand, and Ben clasped it in a firm, calloused grip.

"How are you, young fella?" Ben asked, his tone softer now, filled with something Marcus couldn't quite place.

Ben's grip remained firm, his calloused fingers pressing into Marcus's palm as if trying to draw something out of him, something buried deep in the past. His sharp, searching eyes lingered on Marcus's face, scrutinising every detail, as though looking for traces of someone else in his features. Then, with a slow nod, he released his hold and leaned back against the bar.

"Has Verity seen you yet?" he asked, his voice rough but laced with something softer, curiosity, perhaps, or the faint stirrings of old ghosts.

Marcus shook his head. "No, they weren't coming in to meet me." He hesitated for a moment, watching Ben's expression, then added, "Patrick is coming to Quilpie on Friday, and I'm going to Stratheden with him on Saturday."

He paused then, before tilting his head slightly, his gaze narrowing as he studied Ben's reaction. "Apparently," he added, his voice carrying a note of uncertainty, an unspoken question hanging between them.

Ben's lips curled at the corners, though it wasn't quite a smile. He took a slow sip of his drink before setting the glass down with deliberate care.

"Well, then," he said, his tone unreadable. "That'll be something, won't it?" Ben pushed himself up from the bar with the slow, deliberate ease of a man who had nothing to prove and all the time in the world. He adjusted his hat, his weathered face unreadable, though there was a flicker of something, approval, perhaps, or nostalgia, as his gaze lingered on Marcus for a fraction longer than necessary.

"Well then," he said, voice steady but edged with finality. "No doubt we'll see you around from time to time. Take care, young fella." With that, he turned toward Jacko, giving a brief nod, silent instruction to finish up and get on with their business.

Jacko drained the last of his drink and clapped Marcus lightly on the shoulder. "Have a good trip out to Stratheden, mate," he said with a grin, though his eyes carried something else, something that Marcus couldn't quite place.

And then, just like that, father and son strode out of the bar, their boots sounding a measured rhythm against the wooden floorboards. Marcus watched them go, feeling there was yet another story to be gleaned from Ben. He settled at the bar to finish his drink, and he thought, maybe another.

Sergeant Gillard flipped through the final page of the Otranto's passenger list, his lips thinning as he exhaled sharply. Every name had been scrutinised, every detail checked against the manifest from the ship's last voyage that had ended in Brisbane. Not a single Mark Dawson, nor anything remotely close to it, appeared. Every last passenger had either a forwarding address or an agent's contact, and the authorities were busy confirming that all 478 male passengers had reached their destinations. So far, only seven were still unaccounted for.

But Gillard was certain. Whoever the dead man in Room Seven of the Terrace Hotel was, he was not Mark Dawson from the RMS Otranto.

He rubbed his hand across his face, frustration creeping in, before standing and grabbing his hat. Another trip to the Terrace Hotel was in order. He needed to speak with the receptionist, the same woman who had checked Mr. Dawson in on Monday.

The hotel lobby greeted him with its musty scent and faint sounds of murmured conversation. At the reception desk, Gillard leaned in, fixing the receptionist with a hard, unwavering stare. "Did you notice if he had luggage? A bag, perhaps?" Her tone was patient, but the steel underneath was unmistakable.

The receptionist shifted uncomfortably, her hands fumbling nervously. "I… uh… honestly don't remember checking him in," she admitted, looking flustered. "And we're not even full, so it's not like we've been run off our feet. Maybe he arrived during my break? One of the other staff might've handled it."

Gillard's eyes narrowed, the suspicion in his gut growing like a slow burn. "That usual?"

The receptionist hesitated, then shook her head. "Not really… unless he arrived early, before reception opened. If that was the case, maybe one of the bar girls checked him in."

The sharpness in Gillard's gaze was like a brand, burning into the woman's conscience. His patience had run out. His jaw tightened, and his voice came out like a whip crack. "Well, how about you get off your arse and ask them?"

The receptionist flinched, her face flushing red, and for a moment it seemed like she might try to protest. But under the weight of Gillard's stare, all protest vanished, swallowed by the force of the sergeant's presence. With a stifled grunt, the woman nodded quickly and disappeared through a side door leading to the public bar.

Gillard stood there for a moment, hands clasped behind his back, staring out the window at the bustle of Brisbane. The answer was still out there, somewhere. And he was going to find it, no matter how long it took.

Gillard's fingers drummed against the counter, the sharp sound echoing in the quiet hotel lobby, his irritation simmering just beneath the surface. This should have been settled yesterday, yet here he was, still grasping at half-formed leads.

A moment later, the receptionist returned, flanked by a younger woman with auburn hair tied back in a loose ponytail. She crossed her arms with an air of quiet defiance, studying Gillard with an expression more curious than fearful.

"This is Jess," the receptionist explained, voice tinged with haste. "She remembers checking a young bloke in on Monday, around lunchtime."

Jess gave a nod, her tone casual but with a certain sharpness. "Yeah. Young fella, carrying two suitcases. Can't remember his name, but I know it was Room Seven, because the key tag had a burnt corner."

Gillard's pulse quickened, a flicker of something stirring within him. Finally, a detail worth something.

"No moustache?" he asked, his voice sharp, clipped.

Jess shook her head, her face momentarily scrunching in thought. "Nah. He was only a kid." She paused, as if something from the back of her mind was trying to claw its way to the surface. "Come to think of it… yeah. I reckon I poured him a beer later that evening."

Gillard's jaw tightened as he studied her. "I thought you said he was a kid?"

She blinked, then shrugged, unbothered. "Well, he certainly looked to be over eighteen." Her frown deepened slightly as she reconsidered. "But yeah, he wasn't exactly a baby."

Gillard exhaled sharply, rubbing the back of his neck. "You didn't check?" He waved a hand before she could answer. "Doesn't matter. Was he alone?"

Jess pursed her lips, brows knitting together in concentration. "Hmm... think so…" She hesitated for a beat, then her eyes widened with a hint of recollection. "No, wait. He was sitting with some bloke. Wearing a suit."

Gillard straightened slightly, the hairs on the back of his neck prickling. "Go on."

Jess's gaze drifted, her mind sifting through fragments of memory like sand through a sieve. "Yeah…" she murmured, her voice distant, more to herself than to him. "I think he was with a fat fellow… yeah, a fat fellow in a suit."

Gillard's mind snapped into focus, each word ringing with significance. "That's all you remember?"

Jess shrugged again, her face apologetic. "Sorry. Not real sure."

Gillard didn't waste another second. He reached into his coat pocket and pulled out the photograph, the stark, black-and-white image of the body found in Room Seven. Holding it up, he placed it directly in front of Jess.

"Is this the young bloke you checked into Room Seven?"

Her reaction was immediate. Jess went pale, her face draining of colour as her eyes widened in horror. She recoiled from the photo as if it had struck her, her body jerking back instinctively.

"No! No way!" she shrieked, her voice high with panic, shaking her head furiously. "That's not him! But…" Her breath quickened as she stared at the image, her voice faltering as uncertainty crept in. "I think... I think that might have been the other guy at the table with the kid."

Gillard's heart rate spiked. Now we're getting somewhere. The game had changed.

Gillard gave Jess a curt nod, his hand slipping the photograph back into his pocket with a practiced movement. Without another word, he turned sharply on his heel and strode out of the hotel, his boots echoing on the floorboards as he made his way toward the door.

The dry heat of the midday sun hit him like a wall as he stepped out onto the street, but he paid it no mind. His thoughts were already spinning, each new piece of the puzzle falling into place with unnerving precision.

The more he considered it, the clearer the picture became. This wasn't just some random traveller or a misunderstood identity. No, this was something bigger. Something that had more layers than he cared to admit.

He moved quickly, his pace steady as he made his way back toward the station. The weight of his conclusions hung heavy on his shoulders, but Gillard was no stranger to a challenge. This had the markings of a case that would need more than just a local constable's eye.

This looks like a job for the 'dee's, he thought grimly. The detectives. And with them, the wheels would begin to turn in ways they hadn't yet. The real hunt was just beginning.

Sergeant James Gallagher leaned back in his creaky wooden chair at the Quilpie police station, his fingers tapping absently on the edge of his desk as he studied the telex from Brisbane. The request was simple enough: confirm that a Mr. Marcus Diarmuid, a passenger aboard the Otranto, had safely reached his intended destination, Stratheden. Gallagher knew Stratheden, a sprawling and remote property tucked far out along the Quilpie-Thargomindah Road.

Gallagher's brow furrowed as he scanned the message. That road was no place for the faint of heart, a gruelling eighty miles of rock and dust that swallowed vehicles whole and offered no mercy to the unprepared. He knew it well, every twist and turn of the unforgiving landscape. No point driving all the way out there just to return with a 'yes, he's arrived, or a 'no, he hasn't, not when he could be checking in with the Diarmuid's from town.

With a sigh, he reached for the phone and dialled the number for Stratheden. After a few moments, the call was answered by a pleasant, woman's voice. The lady of the house, Mrs Diarmuid confirmed that Marcus had indeed made it to Quilpie, but wouldn't be heading to Stratheden until Saturday, when Patrick would be bringing him out. For now, she thought he was staying in town at either the Imperial, or the Railway Hotel.

Gallagher glanced at the clock, noting it was just past noon. Well, that made things easier. No need to waste half a day in the dust, chasing down a man who wasn't even at his destination yet. With a grunt of satisfaction, he hung up the receiver and stood. He might as well head over to the Imperial Hotel, check in with this Marcus Diarmuid, if he's there and, while he was at it, grab some lunch. It wasn't the worst way to spend an afternoon in Quilpie.

Marcus sat uneasily on a worn barstool at the Imperial Hotel, his hands wrapped tightly around a glass of warm beer, the smell of sizzling T-bone steak drifting from the kitchen. He wasn't hungry, his nerves had seen to that, but the thought of something solid in his stomach gave him a faint sense of normalcy. That was, until the door swung open, and a policeman stepped inside.

Marcus's heart skipped a beat as he watched the officer, a tall, broad-shouldered man with an easy, almost lazy smile, approach the bar. His eyes narrowed, studying the officer's every movement, and he felt his stomach churn in response. The barman and the policeman exchanged a few casual words, but Marcus's focus was locked on them, every muscle in his body tensing. Then, with an unsettling calm, the barman turned and pointed directly at him.

Marcus froze. A cold sweat broke out on his brow, his pulse quickening. Why are they looking for me? What do they know? The questions pounded in his head, his thoughts spiralling into panic. His throat felt tight, and his palms turned clammy. The officer started walking toward him.

The man's voice was deep, friendly, and disarmingly casual. "G'day," he said. "Are you Marcus Diarmuid?"

The words barely registered as terror gripped Marcus's chest. In a wild, uncontrollable rush, he blurted out, his voice cracking under the strain, "It was an accident! He was going to assault me!" His breath came in ragged gasps, the words tumbling out like a confession. "I only pushed him away from me!"

For a heartbeat, the officer's face remained unreadable. Then the smile slid off his face, replaced by a steady, assessing look. It was clear now that this wasn't some casual conversation, this was something far more serious.

"Alright, son," the policeman said, his tone firm but not unkind. "You'd better come with me to the station."

Marcus's mind spun, his body still trembling from the shock. He opened his mouth to protest, but the words caught in his throat. He simply nodded, too rattled to argue, as the midday crowd in the bar fell into a heavy silence, every eye trained on the scene unfolding before them.

Gallagher, sensing the unease in the air, gave a reassuring gesture. "Don't worry," he said, his voice softening just a touch. "It's just a short walk down the street."

As Marcus stood and followed him out into the blistering Queensland heat, Gallagher's mind churned. What the hell have I walked into? The questions gnawed at him, but he had learned to trust his instincts. And right now, his instincts were telling him there was more to this than a simple check.

Marcus sat across from Sergeant James Gallagher, the weight of his journey pressing against his shoulders like a leaden cloak. The air in the small office was thick with tobacco and old paper, the scent of law and order, though Marcus knew all too well how easily both could be twisted to suit a man's intent.

Gallagher leaned back in his chair, arms folded, his eyes sharp and assessing. He was a man accustomed to reading truth and falsehood in the flicker of an eyelid, the hesitation of a breath.

Marcus took a deep breath and began, his voice steady but laced with the raw edge of exhaustion. He started at the beginning, back in London, when he had first stepped aboard the ship, still blind to the storm that lay ahead. He walked Gallagher through each moment, every turn of fate that had led him here, across oceans and continents, to this very room.

When he reached the events at the Terrace Hotel in Brisbane, his voice faltered only slightly, the memory of that night still vivid, still heavy. He described the moment he had been attacked by Palmerston, the sickening dread that had coiled in his gut, the sheer, unrelenting panic that had gripped him when he realised how damning it all looked.

"I was terrified," he admitted, his fingers curling into fists on the table. "I didn't know what to do. I knew how it would seem, how it would all line up against me. So I ran."

Gallagher didn't speak right away. He simply watched Marcus, his face giving nothing away. Then, slowly, he exhaled through his nose and reached for his pen.

Gallagher kept his expression hard, unreadable, but inside, his gut twisted like a coiled snake. He listened to Marcus speak, his voice steady yet laced with something raw, something that struck a chord too deep for comfort. He had a son, not much younger than this lad, a boy with the same restless fire in his blood, the same vulnerability hidden beneath a layer of hard won confidence. His boy was off at boarding school in Roma, sheltered for now, but Gallagher knew all too well how quickly a young man could find himself in the jaws of trouble.

The thought gnawed at him like a rabid dog. If his son had been in Marcus's place, alone, hunted, would he have had the sense to fight, and would he have done just as Marcus had, fled into the night, trusting no one? He knew the answer. A frightened young man, blindsided by the ruthless cunning of men like Palmerston, would do exactly what Marcus had done. He would run. And in running, he would seal his own fate.

Gallagher had seen it too many times before, and the bitter taste of it still lingered at the back of his throat. Justice, as it was supposed to be, was an ideal, a noble concept preached in the halls of law but rarely practiced where it mattered most. In reality, the courts in Australia had an unsettling habit of favouring the cunning, the seasoned criminals who knew how to play the game, while men like Marcus, young, inexperienced, and naive enough to believe the truth would set them free, were left to rot behind bars.

He had no illusions about what was coming. Marcus's life, as he had known it, was about to come crashing down around him. Whether he was guilty or not would mean little when he stood before a judge who had grown deaf to cries of innocence. The prosecution would be ruthless, twisting facts, manipulating evidence, painting Marcus as the villain they needed him to be. The jury, a collection of strangers with their own prejudices, would see only what they were shown.

Gallagher leaned back in his chair, his gaze heavy on the young man sitting across from him. Marcus had no idea what was waiting for him in that courtroom. He still held onto hope, clinging to the belief that the truth would be enough to save him. Gallagher wished he could believe it too. But he had seen too many innocent men condemned, too many liars walk free with smug grins on their faces.

Marcus was heading into a storm, and Gallagher knew there was little he could do to stop it. The law was a blunt instrument, and more often than not, it struck the wrong man down.

Gallagher clenched his jaw, his fingers tightening around the pen he held. Men like Palmerston were the filth of the earth, predators who thrived on the weak and the unsuspecting. They needed to be stopped, rooted out like the vermin they were. Locked up, yes, but hanging would be better. A clean rope and a swift drop, that was justice for a man who built his power on the ruin of others.

Suspect Found, Charged and Tried

It is often said that the law has a way of finding its quarry, but in this case, it was nothing but sheer fortune that had brought Sergeant Ross Gillard's investigation to its boiling point. A string of coincidences, or fate, perhaps, had led them straight to their suspect, and the Brisbane Police were now hot on the trail.

Gillard, his mind sharp as ever, sat in his cramped office at the Brisbane Police Station, reviewing the latest update on the case, the dead man found in Room Seven at the Terrace Hotel. The suspect was now in their custody, in Quilpie. But the revelation that the man had a leather wallet bearing the name Clifford Palmerston was what had truly piqued his interest.

Without hesitation, Gillard scanned the contents of the telex and found the part referring to the wallet.

Among the mess of papers were four business cards, all identical, each bearing the name:

Palmerston Timbers
Maryborough
Tel 4453

A solid lead, but it didn't end there. The wallet held no money but Gillard felt that theft was not the motive here. Gillard's pulse quickened. There was something about this that didn't sit right. He reached for the telephone, his fingers moving with purpose. The weight of the situation hung in the air like the promise of a storm.

The phone rang twice before a soft, polite voice answered. "Good afternoon, Palmerston Timbers. May I help you?"

"I need to speak with Mr. Palmerston," Gillard's voice was steady, though a sense of urgency lurked beneath it.

"I'm afraid Mr. Palmerston is not available," the voice replied, cool and collected, but Gillard could sense a subtle edge of finality in her tone.

"Can you tell me when Mr Palmerston will be available?" Gillard wasn't about to be dismissed so easily. "Can you also confirm the business address?" His words came out sharp, commanding.

"Yes, sir. We're located on South Street, Maryborough."

That was all he needed. He hung up the phone without another word, his mind racing as he formulated his next move. He snatched a pen and began drafting a telex to the Maryborough Police, his hand moving swiftly across the paper.

Request an urgent background check on Mr. Clifford Palmerston, Palmerston Timbers, South Street, Maryborough.

The trap was closing in, and Gillard could feel the heat rising. This case was about to unravel in ways he hadn't anticipated.

The pieces of the puzzle were beginning to snap into place, like the shifting of stones in an ancient ruin. Sergeant Ross Gillard could feel the weight of the investigation bearing down on him, but now, at least, there was a thread to follow. The question remained, was Clifford Palmerston the key to unlocking the mystery of the dead man in Room Seven?

Gillard's patience was tested further when the return telex from Maryborough Police arrived, carrying the grim confirmation he had been hoping for. Clifford Palmerston was indeed missing. His last known whereabouts were the City Crest Hotel on Turbot Street in Brisbane, where he had checked in on Monday afternoon. Since then, there had been no word from him, a disappearance as quiet and unsettling as the stillness that often followed a violent storm.

As if on cue, the situation took another sharp turn. News arrived that Palmerston's wife had traveled from Maryborough to Brisbane. There was no mistaking her sorrow, the kind of grief that sears itself into a man's soul. She positively identified the body found in Room Seven at the Terrace Hotel, it was her husband, Clifford Palmerston. The confirmation was like a cold slap to Gillard's face, but he steeled himself, knowing it only pushed the case forward.

With the identity of the victim now beyond doubt, the investigation accelerated, gathering speed like a river that had finally broken free of its dam. Marcus Diarmuid, the young man whose name had been swirling in the air like smoke, was formally charged with the murder of Clifford Palmerston.

Gillard's thoughts swirled with questions, what had driven Diarmuid to kill? What had transpired between these two men, and who, or what, had truly been behind it all? But there was no time for answers yet. For now, the wheels of justice were turning, and Marcus Diarmuid would have to face the consequences of his actions.

Saturday arrived under the unforgiving sun of the Queensland outback, the heat pressing down like a hammer upon the earth. It was the day Marcus Diarmuid would turn eighteen, a day that should have been filled with the promise of a new chapter in life. But fate, it seemed, had other plans. Just three days after Marcus's arrival in Quilpie, the courthouse became the unlikely stage for a drama that would stain the town's quiet history forever.

A magistrate from Charleville made the long journey to Quilpie, his dusty car a sign of the distance he had travelled. The brief hearing was over almost before it had begun. Marcus, the young man caught in the grips of an investigation that spanned hundreds of miles, stood in silence as he was remanded in custody. His fate, like so many others before him, was now in the hands of the law. He would be transferred to the Brisbane City Watch House, where he would await trial for the brutal murder of Clifford Palmerston.

For Quilpie, it was an event as rare as a tropical storm in the desert. The small, isolated town had rarely seen anything so grand, so explosive. Yet now, the sleepy streets buzzed with whispers and rumours. Quilpie had become the unexpected epicentre of a murder investigation that stretched across the vast and unforgiving expanse of western Queensland, from the bustling streets of Brisbane to the remote cattle stations far out in the bush.

The Trial of Marcus Diarmuid

The trial of Marcus Diarmuid opened in the Brisbane Supreme Court in December 1951, drawing a crowd eager to witness the spectacle of a young man standing trial for the death of a well-respected businessman. The case quickly gripped the public's attention, as the courtroom became a battleground for two starkly opposing narratives. On one side stood the Crown, led by the relentless Senior Crown Prosecutor James Hargreaves, and on the other, the defence, with Marcus's fate hanging on the words of his barrister, Henry Calloway.

The Crown's case was straightforward, yet brutal. Hargreaves painted Marcus Diarmuid as a man who had intentionally caused the death of Clifford Palmerston through a violent confrontation. Witnesses from the Terrace Hotel testified that Palmerston had been seen drinking heavily with a younger man matching Marcus's description on the night of his death. The prosecution seized on the fact that Palmerston's wallet was found in Marcus's possession when he was arrested in Quilpie, suggesting a robbery after murder. Little, or no consideration was taken as to the statement submitted by Sergeant Gallagher from the Quilpie Police.

The pivotal moment came when the pathologist, Dr. William Carter, took the stand. He confirmed that Palmerston had died from blunt force trauma to the skull, likely the result of a fall. But in a twist that would prove crucial to the defence, Carter also testified that Palmerston's blood alcohol level was exceedingly high, leaving open the possibility that his intoxicated state contributed to his inability to break his fall or defend himself.

The defence, led by the shrewd and eloquent Henry Calloway, painted an entirely different picture. Calloway argued that Marcus was a frightened, naïve young man, barely seventeen at the time, who had acted in self-defence when Palmerston, much older and larger, had become aggressive.

In a moment of raw emotion, Marcus Diarmuid himself took the stand. Nervously, he recounted the events of that fateful night in Room Seven at the Terrace Hotel. He described Palmerston as belligerent and intoxicated, confronting him in a way that made him feel trapped.

"I didn't mean to hurt him," Marcus insisted, his voice cracking under the weight of his own guilt and fear. "I just wanted to get away."

As the courtroom listened in tense silence, Marcus explained that in his panic, he had pushed Palmerston away to escape, but the older man had stumbled backward, his head striking the sharp edge of a wooden dresser before he collapsed to the floor.

Calloway further bolstered Marcus's defence by presenting character witnesses, including a statement from his aunt and uncle from Stratheden, who testified to Marcus's quiet, well-mannered nature, far removed from the picture of a violent criminal the prosecution sought to portray.

The trial spanned three intense days, with both sides presenting their arguments with skill and passion. Finally, the jury retired to deliberate. Five long hours later, they returned with a verdict that spared Marcus from the gallows but left him with a sentence that would change his life forever. He was found guilty of manslaughter, with the jury rejecting the more serious charge of murder. The verdict acknowledged that while Marcus's actions had led to Palmerston's death, there had been no intent to kill.

Justice Reginald Thornton, in his sentencing remarks, struck a balance between sympathy and responsibility. "You are young, and I believe you did not set out that night with the intention to take a man's life," he said, his voice steady and measured. "However, your recklessness and your failure to seek help afterward weigh heavily against you."

The sentence was handed down: ten years in prison, with the possibility of parole after serving 80%, eight long years.

As the gavel struck, the courtroom fell into a hushed silence. Marcus Diarmuid stood motionless, his fate sealed. In that moment, the full weight of the trial hit him, the struggle of a young man who had been thrust into a world of violence and fear, with the burden of one fatal night now etched into his soul.

Handcuffed, he was led away from the courtroom, bound for the notorious Boggo Road Gaol, where he would serve his sentence in the harsh reality of Queensland's prison system. His life had been irreversibly altered, his freedom shattered by one moment of panic, and the consequences would follow him for the rest of his days.

By 1950, Boggo Road Gaol had earned its place as one of the most notorious prisons in Australia, a brutal testament to the harsh conditions that its inmates endured. Originally built in the late 19th century, the gaol had become an institution marked by overcrowding, rotting stone walls, and rusted iron bars. The very architecture of the place seemed to suffocate its occupants, as if the walls themselves held a deep, abiding grudge against those forced to live within.

The cells, small and stifling, were meant for one but often crammed with two, sometimes three prisoners. The stale air was thick with the smell of sweat, human waste, and the ever-present stench of decay. Prisoners were given little more than a thin straw mattress to lay on the cold, unforgiving concrete floor, while the steady scurry of rats and cockroaches echoed in the dark. Solitary confinement was meted out for the smallest of transgressions, an angry word, a stubborn look, and men could spend days, weeks even, in the darkness of a single cell, their only company the biting insects that crawled over their skin.

The food, if it could be called such, was barely fit for animals. Breakfast consisted of second grade processed meat or watery thin porridge, lunch offered bread and vegetables with poor quality meat, often goat or rabbit. While dinner was nothing more than a watery soup, or stew that barely filled the belly. Hygiene was an afterthought; prisoners were expected to wash with cold water, and showers were a rare luxury, perhaps once or twice a week. Skin infections, malnutrition, and tooth decay became common afflictions for those unlucky enough to be trapped in the prison's iron grip.

The guards who ruled the prison were men of iron, and poor education using their batons and fists to enforce order. The slightest mistake was met with violence. Any attempt to defy the system resulted in brutal punishment, solitary confinement in "the black hole," a windowless cell so dark and airless that the very act of breathing became an agony. Men were left to rot in that hellish void for days, sometimes weeks, with nothing but their own thoughts for company. Floggings were still an occasional form of punishment, though the real torment often came from the guards themselves, who regularly beat prisoners into submission, or from the other inmates, who ruled the yard with knives and cruelty.

The work was gruelling, a ceaseless cycle of labor meant to break the spirit as much as the body. Prisoners spent up to ten hours a day engaged in exhausting tasks, cleaning, stitching prison uniforms, or toiling in the bakehouse. The unrelenting Queensland heat, combined with the lack of drinking water, made the days a haze of sweat and dust. And in the yard, violence lurked in every corner. Fights were constant, fuelled by frustration, fear, and a desire to assert dominance. Stabbings and intimidation were everyday occurrences, as survival meant showing no weakness.

Medical care was a distant dream, and the poor excuse for a hospital was a luxury afforded to very few. Injuries, whether from a fight or a labor accident, often went untreated, and the prisoners were left to suffer in silence. Mentally ill inmates were treated no better. Rather than receiving the care they needed, they were often shoved into solitary confinement or subjected to untested, inhumane treatments. The pain of the place was so unbearable that suicide became a tragic, common escape. Bedsheets, shoelaces, and makeshift weapons became tools of finality for those who could no longer face the darkness of their existence.

By 1950, Boggo Road Gaol had gained a reputation as a place where only the strongest or the most ruthless could survive. It was a prison of brutality and despair, where the very air felt like it was trying to choke the life from you. It had become an institution of fear, a symbol of a system that cared little for mercy or redemption. The weak withered, and the strong endured, but at a cost. Each day in that hellish place chipped away at the souls of its inmates, leaving behind only shadows of the men who had once walked free.

The iron gates of Boggo Road Gaol towered before Marcus Diarmuid as he was shoved off the prison transport truck, the weight of heavy metal cuffs biting into his wrists. The suffocating heat of the Queensland sun clung to his skin, thick and oppressive, as he was herded forward with a ragged group of fellow prisoners. The red-brick walls, towering and menacing, were lined with jagged coils of razor wire that seemed to devour the very air around them. As he passed through the main gate, Marcus felt a dark chill race down his spine. He had heard the legends of Boggo Road, the brutal prison where time crawled by and men were ground down until nothing was left but raw survival.

At the entrance, a burly, sunburned guard with a permanent scowl barked orders at the new arrivals. "Stand straight! Heads up, looking forward!" His voice boomed like thunder, echoing off the stone walls. Marcus flinched involuntarily, the sound of it slicing through his resolve like a knife. The man's eyes, cold as flint, flicked over Marcus and the others, sizing them up like cattle.

Inside the processing room, the air was thick with the stench of sweat, disinfectant, and despair. The sound of chains and murmurs echoed in the gloom, and the smell of hopelessness seemed to hang in the very atmosphere. One by one, the new prisoners were stripped of their clothes and issued the prison's uniform, a coarse grey shirt, dark shorts, and thin-soled boots that would offer no protection from the hard concrete floors.

"Diarmuid, Marcus," a guard called out, his tone a mix of disdain and amusement. He looked Marcus up and down, scribbling his name into a ledger with the casual air of a man used to dealing with the worst of humanity. "Welcome to Boggo Road, son. You're lucky, you got ten years. Some of these poor bastards will rot here."

Marcus's dry mouth barely allowed him to form a response. His throat felt as though it had been filled with sand, his stomach twisting into tight, painful knots. Ten years... It was a lifetime in a place like this.

The medical inspection was no better. A doctor, whose cold eyes betrayed no hint of empathy, checked him for disease, lice, and the marks of a life spent in struggle. The man's touch was clinical, efficient, like a butcher examining his stock. No care, no comfort, just a grim necessity.

With his dignity stripped away, Marcus was handed a blanket and a tin cup, the weight of them like lead in his hands. He was then led down a narrow, dimly lit corridor, the walls heavy with the scent of sweat and the grime of years. Steel doors lined either side, each one marked with the jagged, desperate scrawl of past inmates. Names, curses, and hopeless prayers were etched into the metal, the silent testimony of those who had once stood where Marcus now stood.

The clang of a door slamming shut echoed in his chest as he was thrown into his cell, a small, claustrophobic space barely six feet by eight, with an iron bedframe and a mattress that offered little more comfort than the bare floor. The faint smell of urine and stale air hung heavy, and the walls were covered in the faded graffiti of men who had long given up counting the days. A bucket sat in the corner, the only privacy afforded to him.

As the guard's boots faded down the corridor, the metallic echo of the cell door ringing in his ears, Marcus sank onto the edge of the thin mattress. His eyes wandered over the peeling paint on the walls, trying to make sense of it all, but it was impossible. The weight of the place pressed down on him, suffocating, relentless.

The first lesson Marcus learned in Boggo Road Gaol was simple: survive. Keep your head down, keep your mouth shut, and never, ever show weakness. It was a game of endurance, and in this place, only the strong or the ruthless lasted.

The first morning in Boggo Road Gaol began with the violent crash of metal batons against cell bars, the sharp sound cutting through the stillness like a gunshot. "Up! On your feet! Get ready for muster!" The guards' voices rang out, harsh and commanding, reverberating through the concrete corridors. Marcus jolted awake, his muscles stiff from the thin mattress, the reality of his new life sinking in like a cold, relentless tide. His body ached, and for a moment, he forgot where he was. Then the memories of the night before came rushing back, and he pushed himself up, his legs unsteady.

He shuffled out into the central yard, the sun beating down like a hammer on an anvil, its fiery heat nearly unbearable as the prisoners were forced to stand in rigid lines for the morning headcount. The guards, khaki-clad and grim-faced, strode past, their eyes scanning the men with a blend of disinterest and disdain, their steps heavy and authoritative. The air was thick with the stench of sweat, dust, and the desperation of men trapped in a place that had long since stopped offering any kind of hope.

After muster, Marcus was assigned to the prison workshop, a grim building where the stench of oil and sweat hung in the air. He was placed in the tailor's section, a small, dimly lit corner where men toiled away, sewing prison uniforms with grim efficiency. The men barely acknowledged his presence. Some had eyes that were dull, lifeless, as though they had seen too much suffering to care about anything anymore. Others cast quick, sharp glances his way, sizing him up like a piece of meat, wondering if he was a friend, a foe, or simply another victim waiting to be claimed.

By the third day, Marcus had drawn the attention of 'Big Ernie' Callaghan, a hulking brute of a man whose massive body was covered in crude tattoos and old scars, a living map of violence and survival. Ernie's voice was a low growl as he leaned in close, his breath rank with the stench of unwashed skin and tobacco. "Fresh meat," he sneered as Marcus passed him in the yard, his eyes glinting with a dangerous gleam. "Try not to piss anyone off, boy." The words hung in the air like a warning, a threat that Marcus could feel deep in his gut.

The food, if it could be called that, was barely fit for human consumption. Watery porridge or pressed processed meat greeted him in the mornings, tasteless and thin. Lunch and dinner were no better, gristly meat and stale bread that left a bitter taste in his mouth, if it even stayed down at all. Some men ate in silence, their eyes vacant, while others jostled and fought over the smallest scraps of food, as if it was the only thing left worth fighting for. Marcus quickly learned the harsh truth of life in the gaol: the strong took what they wanted, and the weak were left to scrape by with whatever was left.

By Thursday, Marcus had witnessed his first prison beating. A young inmate, no older than Marcus himself, had made the fatal mistake of owing a favour to the wrong man. In the shadow of the laundry block,

Marcus saw two men drag the boy behind a stack of dirty sheets. The sounds of fists striking flesh echoed through the yard, muffled by the rustling of fabric. When the boy re-emerged, his face was a swollen mess, his nose broken, and his eyes cast down in silent defeat. Marcus couldn't tear his gaze away, the brutality of it sinking deep into his bones.

At night, Marcus slept fitfully, every sound outside his cell door making his heart race. The clang of metal doors, the murmurs of men plotting in the darkness, the occasional scream from a man being attacked in his cell, it all became part of the rhythm of life behind bars. He had no choice but to grow accustomed to it. Survival in Boggo Road Gaol was a brutal thing, and Marcus had already learned that the only way out was to keep his head down, endure the violence, and hope that one day, somehow, he would find a way to make it through alive.

By the end of his first week, Marcus Diarmuid had learned one grim truth: if he hoped to survive the next ten years in Boggo Road Gaol, he would need to harden himself in ways he'd never thought possible. The conditions in this prison were nothing short of medieval, he could scarcely believe it was 1950. The damp, oppressive air, the stench of sweat and grime, the clanging of chains and metal, it was like being thrown back in time to a forgotten age. Only the heavy iron bars and the ever-watchful guards reminded him that this wasn't some colonial outpost, but a supposedly modern institution of law and order.

But Marcus had no time for outrage or disbelief. He needed to adapt, or he wouldn't last a week longer.

It was during his grim, solitary first weeks that Marcus stumbled upon an unexpected ally in Joseph Rascher, a towering, broad-shouldered Austrian who carried himself with the quiet grace of a man who had learned to endure the worst. Joseph's eyes were calm and steady, but there was a steel to them that told you not to underestimate him. Despite his intimidating size and rugged appearance, there was an undeniable gentleness to the man, something that set him apart from the violent, bitter men who populated the prison.

Joseph had arrived in Australia in 1939, just as the storm clouds of war began to darken Europe's skies. A locksmith by trade, he had come to this faraway land with hopes of forging a new life, leaving behind the ever-tightening grip of conflict. The gentle giant had worked hard to build a modest but respectable business in Brisbane, repairing locks and safes for a living. But the reality of Australia's lax security culture quickly shattered his dreams.

Australians, it seemed, took little care with their security. Many families left their doors unlocked, blissfully unaware of the risks lurking in the shadows. Even commercial properties were shockingly vulnerable. Joseph, trained in the art of security by the esteemed Carl Richter Safe Company in Dresden, Germany, knew better. He had learned his craft the hard way, spending years perfecting his trade, unlocking the most intricate safes and designing some of the most formidable security systems in Europe. But when he came to Australia, he was appalled to find that while English-made safes were built to last, many of the American imports were subpar, with faulty locking mechanisms and weak, easily bypassed doors.

Joseph's business, which had once seemed promising, soon foundered as the quality of his work was undermined by the simplicity of the local security standards. With the economy faltering and business opportunities dwindling, the temptation to exploit the weaknesses in Brisbane's security systems grew too strong. Using his finely honed skills, Joseph discovered that he could crack open any number of commercial strongrooms, which were little more than doors that could be picked with the right tools. What had started as a quiet, almost innocent exercise in testing his craft soon spiraled into something far more dangerous.

Breaking into businesses in Brisbane became shockingly easy. Most stores and shops had no alarm systems to speak of, and those that did were often poorly maintained or left switched off altogether. Joseph had even crafted his own set of precision tools, each one designed for the sole purpose of unlocking the city's myriad safes and strongrooms. His secret enterprise thrived, and soon, Joseph found himself walking away with vast sums of money, cash that flowed easily and silently into his hands. For a time, it seemed as though nothing could stop him.

But as always, all good things come to an end. Joseph, too confident, too bold in his quiet mastery of Brisbane's weak security, had overreached. The very skills that had brought him riches, his ability to crack safes and bypass locks, had led him into a trap. One careless mistake, one job too many, and the law had caught up with him. Now he found himself in the very place where no lock could be picked, no door forced open: Boggo Road Gaol.

Joseph's past crimes, though grim, did little to diminish the man's inherent likability. His calm, measured demeanour was a rare thing in the brutal, anarchic world of the prison. His towering frame and forbidding presence, tempered by a quiet, almost philosophical manner, made him a figure not to be trifled with. His reputation within the prison walls was one of respect, and though he kept to himself, few men dared challenge him. And so, Marcus, the young and vulnerable newcomer, found himself under Joseph's protection. It was an unspoken bond, formed in the harshest of environments, but one that would see him through the days ahead.

Marcus had been put to work in the prison's clothing workshop, where uniforms were made for the inmates. The work was gruelling, and the conditions, as expected, were harsh. The uniforms themselves were a cruel mockery of comfort: made from rough, unyielding calico and wool, dyed a drab blue-grey, and designed for one purpose only, to be uncomfortable. The fabric was itchy, the seams rough, and each uniform was as poorly fitted as it was utilitarian. A loose shirt, baggy trousers, and a thick, heavy jacket, each piece deliberately crafted to restrict movement and ensure no inmate could ever feel at ease.

Marcus, who had never once touched a needle or thread in his life, now found himself at the mercy of a rickety old sewing machine. The foot-powered treadle machine seemed as stubborn and unforgiving as the guards who paced the workshop, their eyes ever-watchful. The machines were ancient, creaky things that resisted every attempt to function properly. Prisoners spent more time wrestling with the machines than actually working, constantly adjusting the tension, unjamming threads, and replacing snapped needles, which was no easy feat. To replace a needle, Marcus would have to beg for permission from the overseer, a surly man who cared nothing for the frustrations of the prisoners, and even less for their attempts at doing their jobs.

The fabric, too, was a cruel adversary. Thick and stiff, it fought against the needle, often causing the machines to jam. The tension was so tight that it felt as though the thread itself would snap before it ever passed through the needle's eye. The constant struggle of forcing the material into the machine left Marcus' hands raw, his patience worn thin. And when a mistake was made, when a sleeve was sewn backward, or the trousers were cut too short, the punishment was immediate. The uniform had to be undone, every seam pulled apart, every stitch unravelled, and the task redone from scratch. It was a cruel cycle that doubled the workload, turning every mistake into a reminder of the prison's unforgiving nature.

The workshop itself was little better than the cells. The air was thick with dust from the fabric and the musty smell of sweat and old machinery. The dim, grimy windows let in barely enough light to see what they were doing, and the sound of creaking machines and breaking thread was a constant backdrop. The prisoners worked in near silence, save for the occasional grumble or curse when a machine jammed or a needle snapped. The heat was oppressive, and the cramped space made every movement feel like an effort.

For Marcus, each day in the workshop was a battle, a battle against the machines, against the fabric, and against the weight of the reality that surrounded him. But there was something else at play, something that had become clear as the days wore on. Joseph Rascher, though no saint, had become something of a mentor to him. His quiet strength, his ability to weather the harshest of storms with an almost calm resolve, was a stark contrast to the madness of the prison. And as Marcus sat at the sewing machine, struggling with his work, he found that Joseph's presence was a steadying influence, a reminder that even in a place like this, survival was possible, if you had the right allies.

Joseph Rascher, with his seasoned hands and years of experience in welding, fitting, turning, and metal fabrication, had found himself assigned to the prison's maintenance workshop, where his skills were finally put to good use. The clang of steel against steel, the hiss of the welding torch, and the rhythmic hum of the machines were sounds Joseph knew well. Unlike the soul-crushing monotony of stitching uniforms, here, he could breathe life into the aging, rusted machinery that had been left to decay within the grim confines of Boggo Road Gaol.

There was a certain satisfaction in the work. Amid the decay, the rust, and the stifling air of the prison, Joseph found a small, silent peace in the act of keeping the machinery running. The grinding gears, the sputtering engines, and the heavy presses that could crush a man with a single misstep, they all had to be maintained, and Joseph took pride in ensuring that they would not break down at the worst possible moment. It was, after all, the only place he could assert control over his environment.

But the satisfaction Joseph found in his work was often clouded by his assistant, Domnino Gabretti. A squat, wiry man with an ever-suspicious glare and a permanent air of unease, Gabretti was about as useful in the workshop as a broken tool. He had little to no interest in mechanical work, preferring instead to deal in hashish and opium, using his position as Joseph's assistant to traffic illicit goods within the prison walls. It was clear to Joseph that Gabretti had no intention of learning the trade or of lending a helping hand. He was more interested in making connections, securing deals, and feeding the addiction that ran through the veins of the prison like a poison.

Joseph, with his stoic nature and deep knowledge of metalwork, tolerated him with thinly veiled contempt. Gabretti, for his part, seemed to resent Joseph's expertise, his calm, precise manner, and the way he could take a broken piece of machinery and turn it into something useful again. The two men rarely spoke, and when they did, the air was thick with mutual irritation. Gabretti, with his suspicious, calculating eyes, seemed constantly on the lookout for an opportunity to exploit whatever he could, while Joseph kept his distance, focused solely on the task at hand.

Marcus, having spent more time than he cared to admit in the sewing room, had grown increasingly frustrated with the daily struggle of fabric and thread. Watching Joseph wield his tools, taking apart engines and fixing broken machines with the deftness of a master, Marcus couldn't help but envy him. There was power in his work, real, tangible power that he could see, feel, and touch. The hum of machinery was far more appealing than the stifling silence of the sewing room.

One afternoon, as the two men sat together in the prison yard, their lunch meagre and tasteless as always, Marcus could no longer hold back his desire to switch positions. He eyed Joseph warily, careful to phrase his words just right.

"If Domnino ever… stops being your assistant," Marcus said carefully, his voice low, "maybe you could put in a word for me?"

Joseph's pale blue eyes flickered with understanding. A slow, knowing smile spread across his face, the first real sign of warmth Marcus had seen from him in days. There was a glint in Joseph's eyes, one that told Marcus he had not only heard the request, but also that he had already made up his mind.

"Ja," Joseph replied, his voice low but firm. "I can do this for you. It will happen. Just give me a couple of days."

Marcus was taken aback by Joseph's eagerness. The man's response was not one of mere tolerance or reluctant agreement, it was as if Joseph had been waiting for this moment, as though he had been ready to offer Marcus this lifeline from the moment they first met. It was a bond, unspoken but clear, forged in the fire of shared survival within the prison's walls.

However, Marcus was about to learn a lesson that would shape the next few days of his life. Joseph's eagerness, his willingness to help, came with a price far heavier than Marcus could have anticipated. It would not be a simple matter of words and kindness. The brutality of the prison world had a way of turning the most innocent actions into something far darker, and Joseph, with his quiet authority, was about to reveal the true cost of survival in Boggo Road Gaol.

The next morning, as the sun beat down relentlessly on the grey stone walls of Boggo Road Gaol, the workshop was filled with the usual clatter and grinding noise of machines. The air was thick with the acrid scent of oil and rust, a constant reminder of the prison's decaying machinery. Domnino Gabretti, as usual, was too distracted by his own thoughts to pay attention to the work at hand.

He had been walking too close to the leather pulley strap that connected the overhead drive wheel to a distributor wheel bolted to the floor. One moment, he was fumbling with something, his hands moving absently over the rough materials, and the next, there was a sickening snap, sharp, like the crack of a whip.

The strap whipped out, catching Domnino's arm with a brutal force. Marcus froze, eyes wide, his breath hitching in his chest. In the span of a heartbeat, the leather strap yanked his arm forward, twisting it with a horrific, unyielding power. The scream that tore from Domnino's throat was primal, a guttural wail of pain that sliced through the air like a blade.

The sound of snapping bone and tearing flesh followed, and Marcus's stomach churned. The arm was severed cleanly at the elbow, leaving behind a grotesque mess of blood, shredded skin, and splintered bone. It was an image that would stay with him for the rest of his life, a stark reminder of the unforgiving brutality of life behind these walls.

The workshop erupted into chaos. Prison guards rushed in, shouting orders, their boots clanging against the stone floor as they scrambled to contain the scene. Inmates turned away in disgust, some gagging, others too stunned to move. But not Joseph.

He stood there, a silent figure amidst the frenzy, watching with a cool, detached gaze. His eyes, pale and unblinking, betrayed no emotion. He had seen it all before. Death, injury, the endless tide of suffering that came with life in this place.

Marcus's heart pounded in his chest. He had expected Domnino to be removed from his post, perhaps reassigned to a less dangerous job, but not like this. The sight of the severed limb, the blood pooling around it, was enough to make his stomach churn, but it was the indifference of Joseph's gaze that unsettled him the most.

Joseph's face remained unreadable, his posture relaxed as ever, even as the chaos swirled around him. Marcus could feel the tension in his own body, the tremor in his hands as he fought to steady himself. This was a world where anything could happen, a world where survival depended on much more than skill or luck.

On that day, Domnino had been carted off to the prison hospital, his career as a workshop assistant permanently ended. The accident would be remembered by those who had witnessed it, but in the harsh, unfeeling world of Boggo Road, it would soon fade into the background, overshadowed by the endless grind of prison life.

Later, as Marcus walked across the prison yard, he spotted Joseph. The big Austrian was moving with his usual purposeful stride, his shoulders broad and his face set in that calm, unreadable expression. As he passed Marcus, Joseph gave him a slow, deliberate nod.

Marcus felt a chill crawl up his spine. He had no idea whether the accident had been pure misfortune or whether something else entirely had been at play. All he knew was that the world within these walls was a place of ruthless survival, and in this place, the weak were left to perish while the strong continued to carve out their existence.

The next morning, as Marcus stepped into the maintenance workshop as Joseph's new assistant, he understood one thing with stark clarity: there were things better left unsaid in this place. And so, without a word, he rolled up his sleeves and got to work, knowing better than to ask too many questions.

Marcus was keenly aware of his vulnerability when Joseph wasn't by his side, a grim truth that gnawed at him every day. The sheer brutality of life at Boggo Road Gaol made every moment a potential threat, and Joseph, ever the pragmatist, saw this too. The big Austrian knew that physical fitness, though necessary, was not enough. Survival here demanded far more.

Joseph's voice was firm as he laid out the plan: daily, gruelling exercises to build Marcus's strength and endurance. "You will be stronger, faster, and tougher, or you won't last long," he said, his tone leaving no room for argument. But Joseph also knew that brute strength alone couldn't ensure Marcus's survival in a prison where the rules were written in blood.

It was then that Joseph introduced Marcus to Rahman bin Osman, a quiet yet formidable figure who exuded an air of quiet danger. Rahman was a Malaysian man, his presence calm but charged with an undercurrent of raw power. He had mastered the ancient art of Silat, a martial discipline that, while rooted in Southeast Asia, was as effective in the brutal confines of a prison as it was in the jungles of Malaysia.

Silat was a way of life, a philosophy, not just a fighting style. Rahman moved with the fluid grace of a river, each motion calculated yet flowing, the strength in his limbs masked by the elegance of his form. To him, Silat was not merely self-defence, but a system for survival, honed through years of practice and unwavering focus. It was a blend of strikes, joint locks, deceptive movements, and throws, a weapon in its own right, meant to cripple, incapacitate, and kill.

Marcus listened intently as Rahman explained the intricacies of the martial art. "It is not only about strength," Rahman said, his voice low but certain. "It is about using the enemy's force against them, understanding their movements before they even make them. You must learn to think ahead, move faster, and strike with precision."

Marcus knew the danger of this place all too well, and with grim resolve, he threw himself into the training. Each day, after the mandatory exercise routines, he dedicated at least an hour to practicing Silat under Rahman's watchful gaze. His body, stiff and uncoordinated at first, slowly grew accustomed to the fluidity of the movements. His initial awkwardness was replaced by the sharpness of instinct, his reflexes quickening with each passing lesson. The pain in his limbs became a reminder of the power he was forging, not just in his body, but in his mind.

Every strike, every lock, every throw left him stronger, more aware of his surroundings. His confidence grew with each passing day, and though the physical changes in his body were evident, it was the mental clarity that began to set him apart. In a place like Boggo Road, where every day was a fight for survival, that mental edge could be the difference between life and death.

But no amount of training could fully shield Marcus from the harsh realities of the prison. Strength, speed, and skill could only take him so far. The gangs, the violence, the endless threats, it was a landscape where even the most trained men were sometimes overwhelmed. Marcus learned quickly that in Boggo Road Gaol, the price of survival was steep, and strength alone was never enough to guarantee safety. No, survival was about more than just being able to fight, it was about knowing when to fight, when to yield, and when to disappear into the shadows.

The evening air was thick with the stench of sweat and mildew as Marcus stood beneath the meagre trickle of cold water in the prison's grim ablution block. The cold droplets stung his skin, a fleeting respite from the heat that clung to his body, but his thoughts were far from the discomfort of the shower. He was weary, his muscles aching from the training, his mind constantly alert to the dangers of the unforgiving world of Boggo Road Gaol.

Then, from the shadows, a presence loomed, massive, looming like a storm on the horizon. Konstantin Alexopoulos, known to all inmates and prison guards alike as "The Animal," appeared in the doorway. At nearly sixty, his skin was as hardened as the crimes he had committed, yet there was no mistaking the predatory gleam in his eyes.

A man serving twenty years for embezzlement, Alexopoulos was a legend, one that filled both prisoners and guards with dread. But it was not his white-collar crimes that made him infamous; it was the terrifying reign of cruelty he had unleashed within the iron walls of the prison. The very mention of his name was enough to make hardened men flinch. Alexopoulos was not just feared, he was hated, his brutality known to all. Inmates whispered of the horrors he'd inflicted on those unlucky enough to cross his path, his reputation as a sadist and tyrant spreading like wildfire through the ranks.

Tonight, Marcus had been chosen as the prey.

Alexopoulos stood, a cruel smile twisting his lips, flanked by two hulking figures. His henchmen, each one as ruthless and calculating as their leader, hovered close by, their dark eyes fixed on Marcus with cold, malevolent intent.

The guard on duty, like most of the guards, was a man who had long sold his conscience for opium, had been conveniently bribed to take a thirty-minute stroll. It was a cruel joke, a mockery of the supposed authority that lay within the prison's walls.

Marcus saw them approach, his pulse quickening as the reality of the situation set in. His training had prepared him for a fight, but this was no ordinary fight. The odds were impossibly stacked against him.

Before he could react, the three men descended upon him like wolves on a wounded animal. Alexopoulos's fist struck first, a brutal, unrelenting blow to his midsection that knocked the wind from his lungs. He staggered back, trying to regain his footing, but it was no use. The larger of Alexopoulos's men grabbed him by the hair, yanking his head back, while the other pummelled him mercilessly.

Marcus fought back with everything he had, his training surging to the forefront of his mind. He threw a swift elbow at the nearest assailant, landed a kick to Alexopoulos's knee, but they were relentless. The blows rained down with bone-crushing force, each strike driving him further into the filth of the prison floor.

Blood welled from a split lip, and his ribs cracked under the weight of their fists. Dazed, gasping for breath, Marcus felt his body begin to give way. The world around him blurred, fading into darkness as the pain became too much to bear. Every ounce of resistance drained from him as his vision went black.

When the guard finally returned, strolling back from his leisurely walk, he found Marcus lying unconscious, broken and bloodied, in a crumpled heap beneath one of the showers. The faint hiss of the water continued, indifferent to the scene of carnage beneath it, washing away Marcus's blood as though it were nothing more than a stain on the floor. The murky water swirled down the drain, mixing with the grime and decay of the prison's soul.

There were no witnesses to the beating, no cries for help, only the silence of the ablution block, where justice had no place, and mercy was a word long forgotten. The world outside continued on, oblivious to the brutality that unfolded in the shadows. But for Marcus, a new chapter of suffering had begun, and it was one he had not yet begun to understand.

Marcus drifted in and out of consciousness for three days, lost in a fog of pain and fevered dreams. When he finally awoke, the dim light of the prison hospital greeted him with cruel indifference. His skull throbbed with the remnants of a severe concussion, his face was a tapestry of bruises and swelling, and every breath sent daggers of agony through his shattered ribs.

The doctors had considered transferring him to intensive care at Brisbane Community Hospital, but by some grim twist of fate, his body had begun to respond to treatment. Instead, he was kept within the confines of Boggo Road's prison infirmary, where he endured two long weeks of painful recovery. The sterile walls and the stench of antiseptic did little to distract from the storm raging inside him.

Marcus knew exactly who had done this to him. He could still see the cold, sneering face of Konstantin Alexopoulos, could still feel the weight of the bastard's fists breaking his body. The rage that smouldered within him was not the blind fury of a beaten man, but something darker, sharper. This was not just about vengeance. This was about reclaiming his pride, his dignity.

When he was finally released from the infirmary and allowed to return to the prison's routine, Marcus sought out the one man he could trust, Joseph Rascher. The two sat in the workshop, surrounded by the hiss of welding torches and the metallic clang of tools striking iron. The air smelled of oil and sweat, thick with the heat of the day.

Marcus spoke in a hushed, furious tone, his knuckles white as he clenched his fists. "They have to pay, Joseph. I won't let them walk away from this."

Joseph exhaled heavily, setting down the metal file he had been working with. His pale blue eyes met Marcus's, cold and steady. "Forget about it," he said bluntly. "They got what they wanted. They'll move on to someone else now."

"That's not good enough," Marcus snapped. His pulse pounded in his temples. "I can't just let this go."

Joseph studied him for a long moment, then shook his head. "Listen to me, Marcus. Revenge in this place is a fool's game. You make your move, you get caught, and then what? Solitary? More beatings? Or maybe the screws let it happen again, just to teach you a lesson." He leaned forward, his voice a low growl. "No one here is going to save you. Not the guards, not the system, and sure as hell not me if you go about this like a hot-headed idiot."

Marcus swallowed hard. The logic was sound, but it didn't ease the fire in his gut. He wanted justice. He wanted to see Alexopoulos suffer.

Joseph wiped the sweat from his brow, his face hardening. "You want payback? Fine. But you need to be smart. There's more than one way to break a man. And for that… you need to speak with Rahman bin Osman."

Marcus exhaled sharply, forcing himself to accept the bitter truth, Joseph was right. Revenge would come, but timing was everything. It had to be precise, calculated. Yet, as he soon discovered, Rahman bin Osman saw things differently.

Rahman had been watching him, reading the storm that raged beneath his skin. He understood war. He knew that some battles could not be delayed. That evening, as the two men sat in their usual quiet corner of the yard, Rahman spoke at last, his voice a whisper against the hum of prison life.

"The longer revenge is delayed, the less its purpose is remembered," Rahman said. His dark eyes remained fixed on Marcus, unblinking. "Justice must be swift, or it risks fading into weakness."

Marcus frowned, the words unsettling him. He had expected Rahman to preach patience, just as Joseph had. But instead, the old fighter was calling him to arms.

"Tell me," Rahman continued, his voice as sharp as a honed blade. "Who is this man that violated you?"

Marcus hesitated, feeling the weight of the moment press down on him. Then, in a quiet murmur, he spoke the name that had haunted him since the night of the attack.

"Konstantin Alexopoulos."

Rahman gave the slightest nod, as if he had already known. His gaze never wavered. "I thought as much."

Then, leaning in ever so slightly, he said, "Tomorrow, we will end this."

A shiver ran through Marcus, not of fear, but of something darker. Anticipation.

"Do not hesitate to do as I ask," Rahman continued. "'The Animal' will not harm you in the canteen tomorrow. And after he leaves that canteen, he will never harm you, or anyone else, again."

Marcus swallowed hard. "What do I have to do?"

Rahman's lips curled into something that wasn't quite a smile. "Simple. Meet me at the canteen entrance in the morning. We will wait until 'The Animal' is seated, just as he is about to eat."

He paused, ensuring Marcus was listening.

"Then you will walk past him, and once behind him, you will insult him. Loudly. Challenge him in front of everyone."

Marcus tensed. "And then?"

Rahman's expression remained unreadable. "And then," he said quietly, "you will say these words: Katapausis meta tou Theou."

Marcus frowned. "What does it mean?"

Rahman's gaze darkened. "It is not for you to understand. Only to say."

Marcus hesitated, but Rahman's voice cut through his doubt.

"Practice those words tonight," he ordered. "Say them until they come as naturally as your own name."

Marcus gave a slow nod, his pulse hammering in his ears. Rahman had already turned away, sinking back into his silent meditation, as if nothing more needed to be said.

But Marcus knew the truth. He had just stepped into a war he did not yet understand.

That night, Marcus barely slept. His mind churned with anticipation, uncertainty, and a simmering rage that refused to cool. He lay rigid in his bunk, staring at the cracked ceiling, whispering the foreign phrase over and over again.

"Katapausis meta tou Theou."

He repeated it softly at first, then with more conviction, rolling the syllables over his tongue like a blade he was sharpening in the dark. The words became second nature, flowing effortlessly from his lips.

"Katapausis meta tou Theou."

But as the phrase grew more familiar, another thought took hold of him, he had no idea what it meant.

Marcus awoke to the pale light of dawn creeping through the dust-streaked slit of a window. A heavy weight pressed against his chest, an oppressive sense of unease that made the air in his cell feel thick and stifling. His limbs felt leaden, his stomach a twisted knot of ice.

What the hell am I doing?

The confidence that had burned in him the night before, the fire that had kept him muttering Rahman's words like a battle hymn, had shrivelled in the cold light of morning. In its place was a gnawing, clawing dread. A voice inside him, bitter and craven, begged him to find a way out.

Tell Rahman it's too soon. Tell him you're not ready. Tell him Alexopoulos won't even remember what he did.

But even as the thoughts formed, Marcus knew they were coward's lies. He wasn't looking for wisdom, he was looking for an escape. He was afraid. Afraid of provoking The Animal, afraid of what Rahman's game truly was, afraid of what might happen if things went wrong.

He sat up, his breath slow and unsteady. The cold concrete floor numbed his feet, but it was nothing compared to the chill that settled deep in his gut.

You don't have to do this.

The words whispered through his mind like a plea. He could walk away, let this go, let Alexopoulos move on to another victim.

But then another voice, quieter yet infinitely more powerful, answered back.

And what if you don't? What if he comes after you again? What if next time, there's no one left to pick you up off the shower floor?

Marcus's jaw tightened. His hands curled into fists at his sides.

There would be no next time.

He forced the air from his lungs, steadying himself. Then, in a voice stronger than before, he whispered, "Katapausis meta tou Theou."

He cleared his throat and said it again, louder this time. "Katapausis meta tou Theou."

The words rang through the cell like the first strike of a war drum.

And yet, the question still gnawed at him.

What did it mean?

As Marcus approached the canteen that morning, he spotted Rahman standing near the entrance, his posture relaxed, hands clasped behind his back. His face was unreadable, his expression giving nothing away. The morning air was cool, but Marcus felt a trickle of sweat snake down the back of his neck. His stomach churned, a sickly mix of nerves and the remnants of a restless, fear-ridden night.

He swallowed hard and stepped closer, lowering his voice so only Rahman could hear. "What do those words actually mean?" he asked. "Katapausis meta tou Theou. What is it, that I am really saying to him?"

Rahman turned his head slightly, his dark eyes locking onto Marcus's. For a long moment, he said nothing. It was as if he were weighing something, considering whether the answer was worth giving. Then, finally, he spoke.

"The words themselves," he said carefully, mean only 'Rest with God'."

Marcus frowned. He had expected something more ominous, something that would strike fear into Alexopoulos the moment it left his lips. But Rahman wasn't finished.

"The true power of those words," he continued, his voice lowering to something almost conspiratorial, "is not in their meaning, but in their timing. Alexopoulos's two henchmen, Nikos and Stavros, they are Greek, just as he is. And when they hear you say those words to him, just before their fearless leader meets his end later today, they will not see you as a man seeking revenge."

Rahman leaned in slightly, his breath calm, steady. "They will see you as the man who foretold his death."

A chill ran down Marcus's spine.

"They will not come after you," Rahman assured him. "They will fear you."

Marcus swallowed, his throat suddenly dry. This was bigger than revenge. This was power. A message, written not in words, but in blood and fear.

Rahman studied him, reading the storm behind his eyes, then gave a small nod toward the canteen doors.

"Now," he said softly, "let us begin."

As they entered the canteen, side by side, the murmur of prisoners' conversations faded into the background, drowned out by the relentless pounding of Marcus's heartbeat. He scanned the room until his eyes found him, Konstantin Alexopoulos.

The Animal sat exactly where Marcus knew he would: second seat from the end of the fifth bench on the first aisle. Even before Marcus had stepped into the room, Alexopoulos had been watching. His dark eyes, sharp and calculating, locked onto them. A smirk curled at the corners of his lips, as though he already knew something they didn't.

Flanking him were his two lieutenants, Nikos and Stavros. Their relaxed postures belied the quiet menace beneath the surface, their eyes flicking between Marcus and Rahman, watchful, measuring. A silent warning to anyone foolish enough to challenge their leader.

Marcus's throat tightened. He tried to swallow, but his mouth was dry as sand. Rahman, sensing his hesitation, leaned in just slightly, his voice a breath of air against Marcus's ear.

"Just say the words when he turns toward you."

Calm. Steady. The way a man speaks when he already knows the outcome.

Marcus nodded, forcing his legs forward, though they felt like lead. As they reached the table, Rahman stopped, but Marcus kept going. His pulse roared in his ears.

Alexopoulos turned his sneer toward Rahman, his mouth opening,

Marcus struck first.

"Hey! …Animal!"

The canteen froze. Conversations died mid-sentence. The scrape of utensils against metal trays ceased. Alexopoulos stiffened, startled by the sudden challenge. Slowly, he turned, his henchmen mirroring his movement. Nikos and Stavros's faces darkened with irritation.

Marcus inhaled. Deep, steady, just as he had practiced. Then, in a voice that cut through the silence, he spoke.

"Katapausis meta tou Theou."

For a heartbeat, nothing.

Then the Greeks burst into laughter. Harsh, barking, mocking. Nikos shook his head, grinning. Stavros wiped an imaginary tear from his eye. Alexopoulos chuckled, the sound thick with amusement.

Their laughter was misplaced.

Unnoticed by all, Rahman had already completed his work. As Alexopoulos had turned to face Marcus, Rahman's fingers had moved with the precision of a surgeon. A light dusting of finely ground Cerbera odollam seed extract had vanished into the man's breakfast, indistinguishable from the black pepper already sprinkled on his food.

A death sentence, delivered in silence.

Rahman clapped Marcus on the shoulder. His voice, light and amused, carried across the canteen.

"Come along, Marcus. Get over it."

Behind them, Alexopoulos laughed again. The sound followed them as they moved to the servery, collecting their breakfast trays.

It would be his last.

By the time the sun dipped beneath the horizon, Konstantin Alexopoulos was dead. The official cause, as recorded by the prison hospital, was a heart attack. A routine tragedy, barely worth a footnote in the daily operations of the penitentiary.

Only two men knew better.

Rahman bin Osman was from Malaya, a land where the jungle whispered its secrets to those patient enough to listen. Among its countless mysteries were the poisons, silent, deadly, and honed over centuries by those who wielded them. The indigenous tribes of the Malay Peninsula, like their distant cousins in the Amazon, had perfected the craft of extracting toxins from the living world, distilling nature's venom into the most effective weapon of all: a death that came without warning.

Rahman had learned this art from his father, Osman, in the way such knowledge had always been passed down, through quiet observation, through patience, through the meticulous discipline of those who dealt in death. Their family's particular expertise lay in the Cerbera odollam tree, known in hushed whispers as the "suicide tree." It was nature's own assassin, a plant that killed without leaving a trace.

The process was a lesson in precision. The seeds, deceptively unremarkable, were first ground into a fine paste using a mortar and pestle, each motion slow, deliberate. The grinding took hours, for the toxins within were stubborn, demanding patience. Water was then added, binding the crushed pulp into a thick, viscous sludge. From that murky mixture, the lethal element emerged. As the paste dried, a delicate crystalline crust formed at its surface, a whisper-thin film that contained death itself.

Rahman would scrape it away, grinding it once more, repeating the process until the extract reached its purest, most potent form. It was a ritual of refinement, each step removing the weak, leaving only what was deadly.

Once complete, the poison mimicked the venom of the Malayan pit viper. It worked swiftly, thickening the victim's blood into a gel-like sludge that the heart could not pump. Circulation ceased. The heart spasmed, seized, and then failed, silent, final. A perfect death, swift and undetectable.

In the cold, sterile light of the prison hospital, the doctors found nothing unusual. No wounds, no struggle. Just another unfortunate inmate whose heart had given out.

Rahman bin Osman had done his work well.

The Greeks had ruled the prison with an iron grip. Konstantin Alexopoulos, Nikos, and Stavros, three men who had built their empire on violence and fear. Others had learned long ago that to cross them was to invite ruin. But now, their world had shifted. Their foundation, so solid for so long, had cracked beneath them.

Alexopoulos was dead.

It wasn't the death itself that unsettled them. Men died in prison all the time. A shank in the yard, a beating in the showers, those were deaths they understood. Predictable. Logical. But this? This was something else. Alexopoulos had been alive and laughing over breakfast. By sundown, he was gone. No fight, no struggle, no sign of an enemy's hand.

Only the words.

Katapausis meta tou Theou.

Marcus had spoken them that morning, staring Alexopoulos down with an eerie calm. Hours later, the man had collapsed, his heart seizing in his chest as though those words had summoned some unseen force.

It was coincidence, surely. It had to be. And yet, Nikos and Stavros could not shake the weight of those syllables. A phrase spoken, a man fallen. No blade, no poison, just words. And what words they were. A resting with God. A final sleep. A decree from something beyond human understanding.

Superstition took hold, cold and unrelenting. The Greeks were men of blood and bone, but they were also men of old stories, of whispered fears that stretched back beyond memory. And in their minds, the whisper of a name took shape.

Thanatos.

The god of death, the silent hand that carried souls beyond the veil. Or perhaps Hypnos, his twin, whose touch pulled men into eternal sleep.

They began to fear Marcus, not as a man, but as something else. Something other.

They would not cross his path. They would not meet his gaze. They would not speak his name more than necessary, and when they did, it was in hushed voices, their eyes darting over their shoulders as though he might hear. Their men followed suit. A shift rippled through the prison, subtle at first, then undeniable. The Greeks, once the predators of these halls, had found a new master.

And Rahman, watching from the sidelines, allowed himself the faintest smile.

A Free Man

By the time Marcus had endured five years behind the thick stone walls of Boggo Road Gaol, he was no longer the man who had first walked through its rusted gates. The prison had reshaped him, chiseling away at the excess, hardening him into something leaner, sharper. He had learned the unspoken rules of survival, when to stand his ground, when to disappear into the shadows, and when silence was the most powerful weapon of all.

Through those years, Joseph Rascher had been his guide, his mentor in a world where weakness was fatal. The older man had seen something in Marcus, something worth preserving. But even Rascher's time had an end. The day came when the guards led him through the gates, back into the world beyond the prison walls. Marcus watched him go, knowing he should feel something like relief for his friend. Instead, there was only the dull ache of absence.

Yet prison had no patience for sentiment.

With Rascher gone, Marcus inherited his position in the maintenance workshop, a role that came with privileges most inmates could only dream of. A measure of freedom, access to tools, and the ability to shape his own routine, however limited. In a place where every aspect of life was dictated by the whims of men in uniform, such advantages were worth more than gold.

Marcus wasted no time in securing his next move. He made his request in careful, measured words, ensuring that it appeared practical rather than personal. Rahman bin Osman would be his assistant. He cited the man's discipline, his skill, his unwavering reliability, qualities that made him an asset. The request was granted without question.

It was the right decision.

Together, he and Rahman formed a partnership built on quiet understanding. Trust, in a place like this, was rarer than diamonds, and infinitely more valuable. They had seen each other's true natures. They had survived together before. They would do so again.

Marcus also had one other thing: a friend on the outside. Joseph had promised to be there when he got out. And in the back of his mind, in the place where the walls of Boggo Road did not exist, Marcus held onto that promise.

The next three years passed with a sense of purpose that Marcus had never known before. Though he remained locked within the unforgiving walls of Boggo Road Gaol, he no longer saw himself as just another inmate struggling to survive. Instead, he treated his time as an opportunity, a forge in which he could temper his body, his mind, and his will.

A great deal of this transformation was due to Rahman bin Osman. More than an ally, more than a friend, Rahman became the older brother Marcus had never had. Their days revolved around their work in the maintenance workshop, but beyond those hours, Marcus committed himself to an even greater discipline, one that would shape him into something far deadlier than the man who had first walked into prison.

Rahman had introduced him to Silat in the early days of their friendship, a dance of death passed down through centuries. What began as simple movements, repetitions of strikes and counters, soon became an obsession. Marcus trained with the relentless focus of a man who had no choice but to master every technique. His muscles grew lean and strong, his reflexes sharpened, his body honed into a weapon as efficient as any blade.

Rahman rarely gave praise, but one evening, after a gruelling session in the shadows of their cell, he studied Marcus in silence, then nodded.

"Your skill is now that of a warrior," he said. "You have learned well."

The words carried more weight than Marcus had expected. For the first time since entering Boggo Road, his achievements were not tied to survival alone, not to brutality or fear. He had risen beyond the prison's grim realities. He had become a fighter, a man in command of his own strength, his own fate.

No matter how high the walls around him, they could not contain what he had become.

The day Marcus had long awaited had finally arrived, his parole had been granted. Eight years inside Boggo Road Gaol, eight years of blood, sweat, and silent battles, and now the gates stood open before him. Yet as he walked toward them, the feeling he had imagined, elation, triumph, never came. Instead, a strange hollowness settled in his chest, a weight that refused to lift.

Freedom was within reach, but as he stepped forward, he found himself looking back. Against all odds, this place had forged him into something more than a prisoner. It had given him purpose. And more than that, it had given him Rahman bin Osman, a mentor, a brother, a man whose presence had shaped him in ways Marcus could never put into words.

Their farewell had been brief, spoken in hushed tones as the first morning light slanted through the iron bars of their cell. Rahman had never been one for sentimentality, and Marcus had known better than to expect it.

"When you walk through those gates, do not look back," Rahman had said. "You have earned your freedom. Do not carry this place with you."

Marcus had nodded, his throat tight. "We'll meet again."

A faint smile had touched Rahman's lips. "If parole finds me one day, perhaps."

For years, Marcus had wondered what crime had sealed Rahman's fate in this place, but his mentor had never spoken of it, and Marcus had never asked. It did not matter. The man who had taught him discipline, resilience, and the art of survival was not defined by the past that had condemned him.

Now, beyond the gates, the outside world felt too bright, too open. The city stretched before him, loud and restless, a beast he no longer knew how to tame. Freedom, once a dream, now felt like an abyss.

But a promise had been made. And if fate was kind, he would see Rahman bin Osman again.

For now, there was only one certainty. He was heading to Fortitude Valley, to the home of the one man waiting for him, Joseph Rascher.

The bold, weathered sign hanging over Ballow Street caught Marcus's eye: Rascher Lock Co. The shop, though modest in size, stood with an undeniable presence, its unassuming frontage hiding the quiet strength within. The display window showcased a massive Chubb office safe, its steel body imposing, a silent sentinel to the notion of security. The glass reflected the soft amber light from inside the shop, where a sturdy wooden counter stood, lined with neatly organised key wallets and key ring displays.

Behind the counter, a vast wall-mounted keyboard stretched from one end to the other, filled with every conceivable key blank, each one organised with the meticulous precision that only a craftsman like Joseph Rascher could achieve. Below it, a well-worn workbench was home to three key-cutting machines, each one specialised for a different key profile. Shelves along the walls held an assortment of locks, padlocks, deadbolts, and complex security mechanisms, each one tagged with a description of its function and price.

Beyond the shopfront, the real heart of Rascher Lock Co. lay in the expansive warehouse and workshop area. This was where Joseph's mastery took form. Against the far wall stood a well-maintained metal lathe, a pedestal drill, and a milling machine, tools of precision and craftsmanship. Nearby, oxyacetylene torches and an electric arc welder rested, silent but ready, symbols of Joseph's skill in both the design and restoration of high-security fixtures.

A narrow, creaking staircase led from the warehouse to the living quarters above, humble yet comfortable. The two-bedroom unit was warm and inviting, filled with simple furnishings that bore the marks of years lived and memories made. The kitchen, though small, was thick with the scents of freshly brewed coffee and the lingering aroma of home-cooked meals, a stark contrast to the sterile and grim reality Marcus had left behind.

In the cozy living room, Marcus sat with Joseph and Hilda, a cold beer in hand, as they reminisced about the harsh days inside Boggo Road Gaol. Laughter echoed through the room, and more than once, Hilda's surprised voice broke in: "I didn't know that. You didn't tell me this?" Her words were met with knowing smiles and chuckles, a camaraderie born of shared experience. Time had softened the jagged edges of those memories, making them easier to recount than to endure.

Hilda had assured Marcus that he was welcome to stay in the spare room for as long as he needed. No rush. No obligation. Just the warmth of shelter and the quiet comfort of knowing he wasn't alone. But despite the generosity, Marcus's mind was already elsewhere. He longed to reconnect with his uncle and aunt in Quilpie, wondering if they would still welcome him after the years of silence and the dark circumstances of his departure. The years had passed, but the uncertainty of his reception hung heavy on his thoughts.

Before making any decisions, Marcus felt it prudent to assess his financial standing. The prospect of beginning anew weighed heavily on his mind, and so he made his way to the local branch of the Commercial Banking Company of Sydney (CBC). It was there that an unpleasant truth awaited him. The account he had opened on the day of his arrest, so many years ago, had long since been closed. The clerk's detached tone made the revelation sting all the more.

The £50 he had deposited, a small sum but a symbol of a life he had once hoped to build, had been slowly eroded by a relentless tide of fees, each one gnawing away at the balance until nothing was left. The account had been consumed by the very system that was meant to protect it. The clerk, without a flicker of empathy, confirmed the worst: there was nothing left in the account. The years had not been kind.

Marcus could have left then, burdened with the bitter sting of defeat, but he had one last financial lifeline. The £22 he had had in his pocket at the time of his arrest, tucked away with his personal belongings by the prison authorities, had been returned to him upon his release. It was a small sum, but at least it remained untouched, the crumpled notes and scattered coins a reminder that not everything had been stripped from him.

His next stop, the Bank of New South Wales, promised more hope. With the now, aged and slightly yellowed letter of introduction in hand, Marcus approached the teller's counter. He unfolded the letter with deliberate care, the paper crackling as it revealed the contents that confirmed his identity and detailed the funds that had been transferred to the bank from the Institutional Bank of London all those years ago.

The teller, a woman in her early fifties with steel-rimmed glasses perched precariously on the edge of her nose, took the document in hand. Her eyes scanned it, her face unreadable. For a moment, Marcus held his breath, watching as she studied the letter with the concentration of someone weighing the worth of an unfamiliar treasure. Finally, she pursed her lips, excused herself, and disappeared through a side door, leaving Marcus standing in suspense.

When she returned, her expression had shifted into the polite professionalism that Marcus had come to recognise from those in positions of power. She spoke calmly, as if reading from a script, "You will need to speak with the manager regarding this matter, which I have briefly explained to him. He is available later today. I can schedule an appointment for you."

Marcus felt a flicker of hope stir within him. This was it, the moment he had been waiting for. The chance to recover what was his, to piece together a future from the remnants of the past. He thanked the teller, took the appointment slip with a steady hand, and stepped out of the bank. The streets of Fortitude Valley stretched before him, and for the first time in a long while, he allowed himself a moment to breathe, to contemplate the next steps of his uncertain journey.

When Marcus returned for his scheduled meeting, he was ushered into an office that exuded authority and old-world charm. The room was lined with dark mahogany shelves filled with leather-bound books, and a thick Persian rug covered the polished wooden floor. Behind an imposing mahogany desk sat the bank manager, a man in his sixties, with sharply combed silver hair and the kind of dignified bearing that came from years of experience. He motioned for Marcus to sit, and without a word, he carefully unfolded the letter Marcus had presented, his eyes scanning the contents with a professional, almost detached air.

"The Institutional Bank of London," the manager mused aloud, his sharp eyes flicking over the document. "A most reputable establishment. However…" He tapped a finger against the top of the letter where the date was printed. "This letter is over eight years old."

Marcus remained composed, his gaze unwavering as he spoke. "Yes, sir. I understand. But it remains proof of my original banking reference, as well as the funds transferred to this institution."

The manager exhaled slowly, his brow furrowing slightly as he leaned back in his chair, considering. "And your identification?" he asked, his voice cautious but not dismissive.

Without hesitation, Marcus reached into his coat and placed his remaining documents on the desk. First came the well-worn passage ticket from the Otranto, the ship that had carried him to Australia all those years ago. Then, his expired passport, yellowed and creased with time. Next, a bank book from his now-closed CBC Bank account. Finally, he placed his certificate of release from HM Gaol Boggo Road, the last tangible link to the life he had left behind.

The manager's gaze lingered on the certificate for a long moment, his eyes narrowing slightly as he absorbed its significance. Then, he lifted his gaze to meet Marcus's. "You've had quite the journey since your arrival," he remarked, his tone neutral but not unkind.

Marcus met the man's steady gaze without flinching. "I have, sir. And I've served my time. I am simply looking to rebuild my life."

The manager considered him for a moment longer, his fingers steepled together as if contemplating a decision of great weight. Finally, he set the letter down on the desk and spoke, his voice measured. "The letter does confirm that funds were transferred here. And while your identification is less than ideal, I believe we may be able to verify your claim through our records." He paused, his expression turning thoughtful. "However, it will take time. In the meantime, I suggest you obtain an official, up-to-date form of identification."

A sense of cautious relief washed over Marcus. There was no immediate resolution, no windfall of riches, but there was hope. It was a commodity Marcus had almost forgotten existed. The manager, with a businesslike efficiency, suggested that Marcus consider renewing his British passport or applying for Australian citizenship. The decision, of course, was his to make. But either way, obtaining proper identification was now an urgent matter.

Determined to move quickly, Marcus made his way to the British Consulate, housed in a grand sandstone building in the heart of

Brisbane's corporate district. The structure seemed imposing, with its polished brass plaques and an air of quiet authority. As he stepped inside, the weight of the place made him pause for a moment, as though the history of countless travellers and expatriates hung heavy in the air. After a brief wait, he was ushered into an office where a consular officer, a middle-aged man with neat, parted hair and a crisply pressed navy suit, examined the documents Marcus presented.

The officer took the Otranto passage ticket, the expired passport, the old bank book, and even the release certificate from Boggo Road Gaol. Marcus expected questions, perhaps skepticism, even a lecture. But the officer simply nodded, tapping his pen against the desk in a thoughtful rhythm.

"Well, Mr. Diarmuid, your passport is indeed expired, but as you are still a British subject, renewal is straightforward," the officer said with the kind of efficiency Marcus had come to expect from men in positions of power. "There is, of course, the renewal fee of fifteen shillings."

Without hesitation, Marcus placed the required fee on the desk, the weight of it a small but significant step forward. The officer took the coins with a professional nod, then began filling out the necessary paperwork, accidentally omitting the section that asks for any recent criminal activity. When he disappeared into a side room, Marcus allowed himself a moment to reflect on how far he had come, from the dark days of his imprisonment to this simple transaction that would restore a measure of his identity.

When the officer returned, he handed Marcus a fresh, navy-blue British passport. The document was pristine, its pages filled with the promise of renewed legitimacy. The officer slid it across the desk, his tone still businesslike but with a hint of finality.

"Here you are," he said, "This should serve you well. If you decide to apply for Australian citizenship in the future, you'll need to meet the residency requirements and demonstrate good character. But for now, this will suffice."

Marcus took the passport with a steady hand, the weight of it grounding him in a way he had not expected. For the first time in years, he felt the stirrings of something like freedom, a tangible sense of possibility. He thanked the officer, slipped the passport into his coat pocket, and stepped back into the streets of Brisbane, the city now seeming less like a foreign land and more like a place he might one day call home.

The journey was far from over, but for the first time in a long while, Marcus felt the unmistakable pull of hope.

The following day, Marcus returned to the Bank of New South Wales, his heart beating with cautious optimism. He had spent the night turning over every possibility in his mind, weighing the prospect of success against the fear of rejection. This time, with the weight of his freshly renewed British passport and the letter of introduction in hand, he was determined to face whatever came next.

As he approached the counter, the bank manager, still the distinguished figure he had been the day before, looked up and acknowledged him with a nod. "Excellent, Mr. Diarmuid," he said, taking in the sight of Marcus's new passport. His eyes flicked to the letter, and he scanned it with approval. "This certainly satisfies our identification requirements."

The manager turned toward his assistant, who wasted no time slipping through the door into the records room, disappearing from view. A quiet tension hung in the air, but Marcus held his ground, his gaze fixed on the manager as he waited. His fingers, still cold from the morning's chill, gripped the edge of the counter, but he didn't allow himself to show his nerves.

Minutes later, the assistant returned, carrying a freshly printed savings book that looked so new it might have been plucked from the bank's own vault. The manager took it from him, flipping through the pages with a practiced hand before turning it toward Marcus.

"As per the records," he said, his voice cool and professional, "your account remains active." He paused, his finger hovering over a particular line in the ledger. "And I am pleased to inform you that your balance is £12,000."

Marcus's heart skipped a beat. He stared at the figure, his mind struggling to absorb the reality of it. £12,000. It was more than he had ever imagined having again, more than he had hoped for in all the years he had been separated from his past life.

A fortune, a sum that could change everything, and yet it felt almost too good to be true. The memories of his time in gaol, the hunger, the struggle, the cold nights without a future to look toward, seemed so distant now. And yet the scars of those years lingered.

His hand, trembling ever so slightly, reached for the bank book, and he slipped it into the inside pocket of his jacket. The bank manager extended his hand, his grip firm and reassuring as he offered a smile that didn't quite reach his eyes.

"I trust this will help you make a fresh start," the manager said, his tone polite, but there was something almost calculating beneath it.

Marcus shook his hand. "Thanks," he murmured, his voice steady despite the rush of emotions that were threatening to break free. He turned and walked toward the door, stepping out into the bustling streets of Brisbane.

The midday sun was high in the sky, and its warmth contrasted with the lingering chill of uncertainty that still gripped his chest. He had the money now, the passport, the chance to rebuild his life. But something gnawed at him, an unease that seemed to be rooted deep within, a reminder of the years lost, of the life he had once known but was now too far removed from.

Determined to take action, Marcus made his way down the busy street, his eyes scanning for the nearest public telephone. The city buzzed with life around him, but his mind was elsewhere, focused on one thing: calling home.

He found a red phone booth on the corner, and the hum of the city faded as he stepped inside. The air was thick with the smell of dust and stale wood, and the glass walls provided a strange sense of isolation. He fished a few coins from his pocket and dropped them into the slot, his fingers trembling ever so slightly as he dialled the number he hadn't called in years.

The phone rang twice before the frail, uncertain voice of his Aunt Verity crackled through the receiver. "Hello, Verity speaking," she said, her tone hesitant.

Marcus swallowed hard, his throat dry. "Hello, Auntie… It's Marcus,… Marcus Diarmuid."

There was a long, drawn-out silence. For a moment, Marcus thought the line had gone dead, but then Verity's voice returned, shaky and breathless, as if she were trying to make sense of the words she was speaking.

"Oh, good heavens… Marcus…" Her voice wavered. "Oh dear… We heard… we heard all about you. The court case, the trial… It was in the papers, you know. And, well… we still have your bags here from the Imperial Hotel." She paused, the hesitation thick in her voice. "Oh, good heavens, are you calling for your bags? Do you want us to send them somewhere?"

Marcus closed his eyes for a moment, the weight of his aunt's words pressing down on him. It felt like being thrust back into the past, a past he had hoped to leave behind, and yet here it was, sitting in the present.

"I was rather hoping to come and stay with you and Uncle Miles," he said quietly, each word feeling heavier than the last. The silence that followed stretched between them, fragile and taut.

Another long pause. When Verity spoke again, her voice was distant, hesitant, almost apologetic. "I… I don't really know if that's possible… after… well, you know?"

The meaning was clear enough. She had not expected to hear from him again, perhaps, on some level, she had hoped she never would.

"I will have to ask your uncle when he comes in tonight," she added, her voice betraying discomfort. "Can you call back then?"

Marcus's throat was dry, his mouth suddenly parched. "Yes, I'll call around six."

There was a final, faint click as the line went dead. He slowly placed the receiver back into its cradle, his hand lingering on it for a moment longer than necessary.

Stepping out of the phone booth, Marcus stood in the bright afternoon light, the noise of the city pulsing around him. He inhaled deeply, the warm Brisbane air filling his lungs, but it did little to dispel the tight knot of uncertainty that had settled deep in his chest. He had expected hesitation, yes, but hearing it in Verity's voice, feeling the distance between them, stung more than he cared to admit. Still, he had made the call. And now, it was a matter of waiting.

Marcus set off toward the railway station, a grim determination in his step. Quilpie was a destination, but it held no promise of welcome. His only goal now was to retrieve the two suitcases he had left behind. They were the last physical remnants of the life he had once known, the life that had been cruelly ripped away from him, piece by piece.

But as he reached the intersection and stood waiting for the traffic to thin, a sudden thought struck him like a bolt from the blue. Why should he settle for a train ticket to a place that held no comfort, no hope of redemption? What if he could buy a motor car?

The idea took root and began to grow, turning over in his mind as he stepped onto the pavement. He had the money now, £12,000, safely tucked away in his account. A fortune, a tool of freedom. A car. It would be the key to independence, to movement without restriction, to choosing his own direction for the first time in years. He had been at the mercy of others for far too long, judges, wardens, and the cold, oppressive walls of Boggo Road Gaol.

A car would mean freedom. It would mean control. The ability to escape the suffocating grip of fate and choose his own path.

His decision was made. The train station could wait. His next stop was going to be a car dealership.

Trevor, the salesman at Eager's General Motors Holden Dealer, extended his hand with a grin so wide it could have split his face. "How's it going, mate? What are we looking at today?… I'm Trevor," he said, his voice dripping with confidence, the kind only someone who'd sold more cars than they could count could muster. "You've come to the right place if you're after a new FC Holden, plenty of 'em in stock right here!"

Marcus shook Trevor's hand firmly, but the mention of a Holden threw him off balance. He frowned, unsure of what he was hearing. He had expected names he recognized, Austin, Morris, maybe even a Vauxhall. He didn't know a thing about a Holden. "What's a Holden?"

Trevor's grin faltered for just a moment, his expression shifting to one of mild disbelief. "Are you serious, mate? Or are you pulling my leg?" He eyed Marcus for a beat before it seemed to click. "Ahhh, I get it now, you're a Pom, right? No worries, mate. Lemme tell ya, Holden is the way to go. This FC model just hit the market this year, 1958, brand new! It's got a 2,300cc engine, seventy horsepower, three-speed column shift, and synchromesh between second and third gears." He slapped the side of a nearby vehicle with enthusiasm. "Australian-made, mate! Built tough for Aussie conditions. You can't go wrong with a Holden."

Trevor gestured for Marcus to follow him, and they moved through the showroom, the bright lights gleaming off the polished chrome and sleek lines of the cars. Marcus's eyes swept over the lot, but one car, in particular, caught his attention, a long-bodied vehicle that stood out amongst the rest.

"I like the look of that… the Estate Car," he said, pointing toward it.

Trevor froze mid-step, looking confused for a moment before realisation set in. "Ah! You mean the station wagon!" He laughed. "Yeah, I get it, you Brits call 'em estate cars. Well, you're in luck! I've got two colours, blue or green."

Before Marcus could respond, Trevor launched into his sales pitch, a well-practiced spiel. "This here's the FC Holden Special Station Wagon, the best in the range. Loads of space, stylish as hell, and reliable as they come. All yours, on the road, for £1,214. Drive away, no more to pay."

Trevor didn't even have time to take a breath before Marcus simply nodded and said, "I'll take the blue one, thank you."

Trevor blinked, his mouth opening and closing as if he'd just been struck dumb. "You… you'll take it?" he stammered. "No haggling? No 'I need to think about it'?"

Marcus shrugged, his voice calm and steady. "No need. I need a car, and I like that one."

Trevor let out a short laugh, clapping his hands together. "Well, bloody hell, mate, you just made my day! Let's get the paperwork sorted, and we'll have you behind the wheel in no time!"

Marcus's heart, still heavy with the weight of his past, gave way to a surge of anticipation. He was taking control of his future now, one mile at a time. The open road stretched before him, as vast and unknown as the life he was about to forge for himself.

Everything was swiftly arranged. For the vehicle registration, Trevor, ever the smooth operator, suggested using the address of Marcus's mate, the locksmith, Joseph Rascher. "No worries, mate," he said with a knowing wink, "just put down your mate's place. Plenty of blokes do it when they're between digs."

Marcus hesitated at the mention of a driver's license. "There's just one problem, I don't actually have one."

Trevor, however, wasn't phased. He waved a dismissive hand, as if the matter were a mere trifle. "Ah, no dramas, mate! I've got a mate who's a driving instructor. He'll have you road-ready in no time. A couple of lessons, a quick test, and you'll have your license sorted in a few days. Easy as."

Marcus raised an eyebrow. He had no intention of rushing into it. Learning to drive wasn't something to take lightly, not when it involved a brand-new car. "I appreciate the offer, Trevor," he said firmly, "but I'll have my friend teach me. He'll come with me to collect the car, and I'll bring a bank cheque for the payment."

Trevor blinked, clearly a little taken aback, but he quickly recovered. "No worries, mate. She'll be ready for you anytime after lunch tomorrow."

With that, the deal was sealed. Marcus shook hands with Trevor, his mind racing with excitement. By this time tomorrow, he would own his very first car. But there was one thing left to do, learn to drive.

Behind Joseph's workshop, there was plenty of space for Marcus to park his newly acquired FC Holden station wagon, right next to Joseph's Volkswagen Kombi van. It was the perfect spot to familiarise himself with the vehicle before hitting the open road. Joseph, ever patient, took Marcus under his wing, teaching him the art of driving. From handling the column-shift gears to smooth braking, and learning how to navigate Brisbane's busy streets, Marcus quickly grasped the basics. Within a week, he was ready for the driving test. It was a victory that filled him with pride, and anticipation. With his driver's license in hand, he was one step closer to the next chapter of his life: the long journey to Quilpie.

Later that evening, Marcus dialled the number for Stratheden again. This time, the call was answered by a man.

"Stratheden, Miles speaking."

The voice was strong and steady, with a hint of a southern British accent, authoritative, yet not harsh.

"Uncle Miles! It's Marcus Diarmuid speaking. I hope you are well?"

There was a brief pause before the reply came, measured and calm.

"I've been expecting your call, Marcus," Miles said evenly. "I think it's probably best we have a proper talk first, just to see how we might get along. No commitments on either side, just a conversation. Do you understand what I mean?"

The words were direct, but there was no malice in them, only the quiet pragmatism of a man who knew how to deal with people. Marcus understood. It made sense, better to talk first, to gauge the ground before anything was decided.

"Of course, I understand," Marcus replied. "I'll call you when I get to Quilpie. Should be about a fortnight."

"Good. I'll be expecting it," Miles responded before the call ended.

Marcus set the receiver down and let out a slow breath. The conversation had been brief, but it was clear: Miles was a man who didn't rush decisions, and that suited Marcus just fine. This would be a meeting of equals, nothing hasty, nothing forced.

Under Joseph's careful guidance, Marcus quickly became proficient behind the wheel. With each lesson, his confidence grew. The column-shift gears no longer felt foreign, and navigating Brisbane's bustling streets became second nature. Within a week, he passed his driving test and obtained his license. Now, with newfound independence, he was ready for the long road ahead.

Taking Joseph's advice to heart, Marcus joined The Royal Automobile Club of Queensland (RACQ). The membership would give him access to roadside assistance and valuable travel information for his journey to Quilpie. When he visited the RACQ office, he sat down with Robb, a knowledgeable staff member who spread out a large map of Queensland.

"It's about 630 miles to Quilpie," Robb said, tracing the route with his finger. "At the speed limits, you'll average about 40 miles per hour. That means you're looking at roughly 16 hours of driving. It's too much to tackle in one go. Best to break it into manageable legs, matched to your fuel stops."

Marcus nodded, absorbing the advice. Robb wasn't finished, though.

"Now, the FC Holden's got a nine-gallon tank, and at around 25 miles per gallon, that'll give you roughly 225 miles of range. But never push it to the limit, plan for fuel stops every 200 miles."

Marcus took mental notes, but Robb continued, "Also, carry a one-gallon petrol can as a backup. Some stretches of road out there are long and lonely, and you don't want to get stranded. Better safe than sorry."

That made sense, and Marcus made a mental note of the rest of Robb's advice: pack a spare radiator hose and fan belt, and get a water bag fitted to the front of the car. If the road out there didn't have much, it certainly had the heat. Marcus could feel the weight of it all, the preparation, the isolation. This wasn't just a drive, it was an adventure into the outback, and he had to be ready for anything.

By the time he left the RACQ office, Marcus felt more confident. He had a plan, a route, and most importantly, the right mindset for the journey ahead. With one more thing to do, buy a blanket and a pillow for the road, he was ready.

His final stop was the Fortitude Valley Police Station. He checked in and informed them of his destination. The officers hardly seemed to care, marking the information on his record with a simple note to check in with the Quilpie boys when he arrived. It was routine, and to Marcus, it felt like one more step in his journey toward freedom.

After bidding farewell to Joseph and Hilda, promising to keep in touch and return when he could, Marcus slid behind the wheel of his FC Holden and set his course for the wide open road. The engine purred to life beneath him, and a rush of excitement surged through his chest, mingling with a flicker of nervousness. This was his first real journey across Australia, a long-distance drive that would take him far from the familiar streets of Brisbane. It was a test, one that he intended to pass with flying colours.

Navigating the streets of Brisbane proved to be more of a challenge than Marcus had anticipated. The city's labyrinth of roads had him taking a few wrong turns, the busy traffic a constant reminder that his journey had only just begun. He had to keep his wits about him, every eye on the road and every ear attuned to the sounds of the city. But once he broke free from the urban sprawl and was heading out toward Inala and then Toowoomba, the roads opened up, stretching out like an endless ribbon before him. The FC Holden, smooth and steady, responded to his every command, its engine humming with quiet assurance, reminding him he'd made the right choice in vehicles.

By the time Marcus reached Toowoomba, he noted with satisfaction that his fuel gauge was sitting at half a tank. Though he could have continued on, the wisdom of caution prevailed. Refuelling now would save him the trouble of scrambling for fuel later in the more desolate stretches ahead. He pulled into a service station and topped up the tank, ensuring it remained full, not just for the peace of mind, but for the knowledge that the road ahead would test him, and he needed every advantage.

The journey continued for another four hours. The last seventy miles were a test of endurance, the dust swirling around him as he traversed the unsealed roads that led into Dalby. The land seemed to stretch out in all directions, a vast and rugged expanse that spoke of the hardships and the beauty of the outback. As he rolled into Dalby, the town felt like an oasis, a quiet hub of activity, its wide streets lined with weatherboard buildings, the scent of the land in the air. Here, in the Western Downs, the pulse of Queensland agriculture could be felt in the earth itself, a town born of pastoral settlers and nurtured by the coming of the railway.

Marcus found a small hotel just off the main road, the veranda stretching long in the afternoon sun. It was only three o'clock, but the heat and dust of the journey had left him parched. He entered the bar and ordered a cold beer, the liquid cool and refreshing as it eased the grit from his throat. One beer became two, and as the warmth of the alcohol settled in, Marcus decided to take a couple of longnecks with him for the road. He made his way next door to the bakery, where the smell of fresh meat pies beckoned him inside. He bought two, their golden, flaky crusts still steaming in the cool air, and tucked them away for later.

Rather than stay in town, Marcus chose to drive a little further out, following the Dalby-Miles Road until he found a quiet patch on the outskirts. The land around him stretched into infinity, the sky softening with the burnished hues of the setting sun. He pulled off onto a flat patch of ground, his wheels crunching over the earth as he parked the wagon. For a moment, he sat in the stillness, breathing in the profound quiet of the outback.

It wasn't a luxury hotel, but Marcus was content. This was his first night on the road, his first night alone in the vastness of the Australian bush. He ate his pies, washed them down with the beer, and then, with the moon beginning its climb into the sky, rearranged his gear in the back of the wagon to create a makeshift bed. Lying back with his head on a pillow, a blanket draped over him, he listened to the symphony of the bush, leaves rustling in the breeze, the occasional chirp of a bird settling for the night, and the whisper of the wind as it moved across the land. It was a sound that would stay with him, a quiet reminder that, out here, he was as much a part of the land as the stars above.

Marcus was jolted awake by a loud, thunderous bang on the roof of his car, his heart slamming into his chest like a drumbeat in the silence of the night. The world around him was pitch black, save for the faint, distant glow of the town behind him, casting an eerie light over the empty land. Blinking the remnants of sleep from his eyes, he peered out of the side window, his gaze falling on two shadowed figures standing beside his station wagon.

"Hey, you in there! Come on out!" A voice, sharp and commanding, sliced through the stillness of the night.

Marcus's instincts screamed danger. There was something wrong, he could feel it in the pit of his stomach. His hand reached for the door handle, his body tense as he slid upright, trying to make out the features of the men in the dim light.

"Who are you?" he asked, his voice steady, though his mind raced.

"Police," one of them replied curtly. "You can't camp here, beside the road."

The words didn't sit right with Marcus. He'd made a point of pulling well off the road, out of sight and far from the prying eyes of any passerby. And why were they here in the middle of the night, without uniforms or a vehicle to speak of?

Fully awake now, a flicker of unease curled in his gut. He cautiously climbed from the back of the station wagon, slipping out through the passenger-side door. Standing tall, he took a moment to size up the two men. One was stocky, just a little shorter than Marcus, with thick arms and a broad chest that hinted at a life spent in hard labour. The other was leaner, his face partially obscured as he kept his hands buried deep in his coat pockets, hanging back slightly behind his companion.

Marcus squared his shoulders, his voice cool as ice. "Let's see some identification."

The stocky man gave a smirk, a dangerous gleam in his eyes, and reached into his coat pocket. With a swift motion, he pulled out what appeared to be a police badge, flashing it before Marcus's eyes. At the same time, his right hand shot forward, grabbing a firm hold of Marcus's jacket collar, yanking him closer.

"It's a ten-pound fine, mate. On the spot," the man said, his voice low and menacing, tightening his grip. "And you're gonna pay it right now."

Marcus's blood ran cold. He had crossed paths with men like this before, thugs with no authority, who preyed on the weak and the unsuspecting. His mind flashed back to darker days, to the prison, to the brutal, unforgiving attacks in the shower block. The feeling of helplessness, something he had promised never to feel again, was rising up inside him.

The thug's hot breath was on his face as he barked, "Ten pounds! Or you're under arrest!"

But Marcus was already moving. Years of training in the Malayan martial art of Silat under the ruthless Mahaguru, Rahman bin Osman, had instilled in him a deadly grace that now surged through his body with instinctual precision.

With a swift motion, he slid his left wrist under and around the man's right wrist, twisting it outward in one smooth motion. At the same time, his right arm shot under the thug's elbow, locking both his hands in place with a grip of iron.

"I might get arrested," Marcus said, his voice cold and calm, "but it won't be by you."

Without another word, he leaned hard to his left, the sound of a bone snapping violently in the night air. The thug dropped to his knees with a howl, clutching his shattered forearm as the pain took hold of him. The night seemed to hold its breath, and for a moment, time itself paused.

The second man, who had been watching from the shadows, didn't hesitate. With a startled yelp, he spun on his heel and fled, disappearing into the darkness as if he had never been there at all.

Marcus stood over the fallen man, his chest rising and falling steadily, the calm after the storm. The fight had been over before it had truly begun, and now, as the man writhed on the ground in agony, Marcus felt a cold sense of finality settle over him.

He took a slow breath and looked down at the thug, who was still groaning, his face contorted in pain. "Are you really with the police?" Marcus asked undecidedly. The man saying nothing, just looked at him in fear. "Enjoy your day," Marcus murmured, his voice low and cutting, before turning on his heel and striding back to his station wagon.

The silence returned, but this time it was heavier. It was time to move on, Marcus decided. The last thing he needed was for the injured man's accomplice to come back with reinforcements. With a final glance over his shoulder, he climbed back into the driver's seat and pulled away, the engine purring to life beneath him, leaving the broken man and his shattered plans behind in the dust.

It was just past nine o'clock when Marcus rolled into the town of Roma, southwest Queensland. He had covered 170 miles of open road, the FC Holden's engine humming steadily beneath him. Roma, established in 1867 and named after Lady Diamantina Roma Bowen, the wife of Queensland's first governor, had once been a humble pastoral settlement. Over the years, it had grown into a powerful hub for cattle grazing and wool production. The discovery of natural gas in 1900 had turned the town into the site of Australia's first petroleum and gas well, a significant milestone that only solidified its importance. Even today, Roma remains a cornerstone of Queensland's agricultural industry, its legendary Roma Saleyards, the largest cattle-selling facility in the country, a testament to the town's enduring prosperity.

Marcus pulled into the Esso service station just off the main drag to top up the FC Holden's tank. He had a steady rhythm to his journey now, a comforting sense of the road beneath him. After refuelling, he parked along McDowall Street, right in front of the Paragon Milk Bar and Café. The rich aroma of sizzling sausages and fresh coffee wafted from the café's doors, drawing him in like a moth to the flame. Inside, he enjoyed a hearty meal of local beef sausages, eggs, and baked beans, the kind of meal that made the dust of the road fade away. His belly full and his spirit renewed, Marcus stepped out into the warm morning air.

As he turned to continue his journey, his eye caught a clothing shop next door. He had been wearing the same clothes for far too long, and it struck him that it was well past time for a wardrobe update. Without much hesitation, he pushed open the door, greeted by the scent of new fabric and leather. A few minutes later, he emerged with a fresh set of clothes that would make him look far more presentable when he arrived at his next destination.

By eleven o'clock, with his new attire packed away in the back of the station wagon, Marcus was back on the road. The Warrego Highway stretched ahead of him, a ribbon of asphalt leading him toward Charleville, 165 miles to the west.

The sun hung low on the horizon, bathing the endless stretch of road in a golden hue as Marcus eased off the accelerator, his eyes narrowing on the sign ahead. The Roma end of speed limit loomed into view, but something else caught his attention, a lone figure standing at the roadside, arm outstretched, thumb pointed skyward in the universal gesture of a traveler in need of a ride.

Marcus had seen them before, wanderers of the great open country, moving from town to town by the kindness of passing motorists. He slowed the car and rolled to a stop beside the man, who wasted no time pulling open the passenger door.

"G'day," the stranger greeted, his voice thick with a rugged Scots brogue. "Ye wouldn't be headin' as far as Charleville, now, would ye?"

Marcus nodded. "That's where I'm going."

"Well then, much obliged," the man said, hoisting himself into the seat.

As Marcus pulled back onto the road, the stranger offered a weathered hand. "Weetam's the name. Appreciate the lift, mate."

Marcus clasped his hand firmly but hesitated. "Weetam?" He tested the name, rolling it over his tongue, uncertain if he'd heard right.

The man let out a hearty chuckle. "Aye, aye, it's an odd one, right enough. Ye see, I'm the youngest of six beeg brothers, so back home they took to callin' me 'the wee one.' And me dear mother named me Thomas. Put the two together, and there ye have it, Weetam!" His grin was broad, his eyes gleaming with warmth. "But if ye prefer, ye can just call me Tommy."

Marcus chuckled, glancing sideways at his companion. There was something about Tommy, something solid, like an old gum tree that had weathered a hundred storms and still stood firm. He carried himself with the quiet ease of a man who had roamed far and wide, who had seen the worst the world had to offer and simply shrugged it off.

Marcus guessed he was somewhere around thirty, though the thick, unkempt beard made it hard to pin down an exact age. There was a wiry strength to him, the kind that came from hard living rather than the luxury of a gymnasium.

"Well, Tommy," Marcus said, dropping the gearstick into a higher slot, the engine responding with a smooth growl. "Let's get you to Charleville."

Tommy stretched his legs and settled into the seat with a satisfied sigh. "Much appreciated, I can tell you." He turned his gaze out to the vast plains rolling past them. "Folk seem a mite less inclined to stop for a man these days. They take one look and think, 'Aye, best not, he might be a murderer or some such villain.'"

His voice, thick with the rugged brogue of the Highlands, carried a wry amusement, but Marcus detected an edge beneath it, as though the man had known the sting of suspicion more than once.

"Lucky for you, I don't scare easy," Marcus replied, throwing him a sidelong glance. "And besides,..I thought, unlikely that you'd be a murderer. Like, what are the chances of having two murderers in my car at the same time?"

Tommy barked out a laugh, a rich, genuine sound that filled the car. "That, my friend, is good to know. A man never does well bein' afraid of his own shadow." He tapped the dashboard lightly with his fingers. "Aye, I reckon you and me'll get along just fine."

Tommy had obviously missed Marcus's attempt at humour but the strange thing was, he was telling the truth.

"What brings you to Australia, Tommy?" he asked, keeping his tone light.

Tommy shifted in his seat, running a hand through his thick beard as though considering how much to reveal. "Got a brother out here," he finally said. "One up from me in age. He came over on a company transfer to a branch in Sydney. I came out to visit him, but turns out, he's buggered off. Left the company, and no one seems to have a bloody clue where he's gone."

Marcus shot him a sideways glance. "So, you're hunting him down?"

Tommy grinned, but there was a flicker of something else in his eyes, something Marcus couldn't quite put his finger on. "Nah," he said, shaking his head. "Not worth chasin' ghosts. Figured since I'm here, I might as well see what the place has to offer." He gestured vaguely at the horizon, where the land rolled on in endless waves of gold and green. "And I don't mind tellin' you, I like what I see. The weather alone's worth stayin' for. Headin' back to Glasgow after this? I'd damn well freeze solid the moment I step off the boat." He laughed, a deep, hearty sound that filled the car, but Marcus caught the wistfulness beneath it.

A sudden thought struck Marcus like a whip-crack. He opened his mouth, ready to speak, but then hesitated, closing it again just as quickly. No, it couldn't be. The idea was absurd, too much of a coincidence. But still, the seed had been planted, and now it gnawed at him.

Scotty. That was the name he remembered, but what was his real name? Marcus frowned, sifting through the clutter of memory. Then, like a key turning in a long-rusted lock, it came to him. Connolly. Scotty had once told him, with a wry grin, how his boss had given him no choice in the matter. "Connolly, you're going to Australia."

His pulse quickened. He turned to Tommy, who was beginning to slump against the window, his head nodding slightly with the rhythm of the car.

"Tommy," Marcus said, his voice edged with curiosity. "Your surname, it wouldn't happen to be Connolly, would it?"

He barely had time to finish the question before Tommy snapped upright as if jolted by a live wire. His eyes were wide, his face a picture of disbelief.

"How in the name of all that's holy did ye know that, laddie?" he demanded, his thick Scots brogue sharpening with astonishment.

Marcus grinned. "I think I know your brother. I can't recall his first name, but we, well, I, called him Scotty."

For a moment, Tommy just stared, his mind clearly racing. Then, he let out a bark of laughter, shaking his head in amazement. "Aye! That's what everyone called him. His name's Andrew." His expression turned urgent, the drowsiness of a moment ago forgotten entirely. "I'll be buggered, you know my brother! Where is he now, then? Tell me, where's Scotty?"

Marcus exhaled slowly, feeling the weight of the moment settle around him. The world had a strange way of folding in on itself, weaving its threads together at the most unexpected times. Here he was, a mere stranger in the vastness of Australia, and yet the chance meeting with Tommy Connolly had revealed a connection that could very well change the course of his life. It was as if fate had reached out, pulling him back toward the past, toward a man who, despite the miles and years that had come between them, still lingered in Marcus's memory.

Tommy's excitement was a tangible force, his eyes sparkling with interest as he hung on every word Marcus spoke. Marcus turned his focus back to the road, his fingers gripping the wheel with a steadiness he didn't quite feel, and began to explain.

"I met your brother, Andrew, aboard the Otranto," Marcus said, his voice laced with nostalgia. "We were cabin mates, of all things. Two Australian soldiers, just back from a stint in Scotland, were with us. We all had our own share of stories, and Andrew, Scotty, I should say, was never one to hold back on his adventures."

Marcus chuckled, recalling one of their more daring exploits. "We had our hands full, particularly when we got involved in that business with the opium smugglers in Ceylon. I remember how we barely escaped being caught, thinking back, it's almost laughable, but at the time, the heat was enough to make you sweat through your shirt."

Tommy's face lit up with an infectious grin, his earlier apprehension vanishing into the wind. "Och, Aye! That's our Scotty, no doubting that! I've no doubt he made a mess of things, but what a lad!" He slapped his thigh in amusement, clearly delighted by the recounting of his brother's exploits. But just as quickly, his smile began to fade, replaced by the intensity of someone who had lived through darker moments. His posture straightened, the warmth in his eyes giving way to a more guarded expression.

"Between you and me, Marcus," Tommy said, his voice lowering, almost conspiratorial. "When our Scotty disappeared from that bank in Sydney, so did twenty thousand pounds." He let out a soft chuckle, but there was no humour in it. "Apparently, all this happened about four years ago. Of course, we in Glasgow, we heard nothing but the sound of the Scottish Bobbies asking around one day, looking for young Andrew. Had he come back home? But we had no idea. Not a clue."

Tommy shook his head, the memory of it evidently still fresh in his mind. "I didn't even hear of it until I went to the bank in Sydney myself, looking for him... Can you imagine my surprise when they told me?" His face twisted into a wry smile, but it was clear the revelation had shaken him to his core.

Marcus glanced over at Tommy, his expression shifting, the weight of the story settling over him like a heavy blanket. The world had a way of revealing itself, bit by bit, piece by piece. And now, it seemed, that revelation had taken another turn.

"And, do ye know, Marcus!" Tommy burst into a hearty laugh, his broad shoulders shaking with the force of it. "The wee mon at the bank, he says to me, 'If ye know where he is, there's a reward oot for him.'" He paused for a moment, his face twisting in amused disbelief, and then the two of them cracked up, the sound of their laughter echoing in the car.

"Can ye imagine that?" Tommy asked between fits of chuckles, wiping the tears of mirth from his eyes. "A reward, for Andrew! As if he's some kind of criminal on the run, rather than a lad who's just... well, disappeared off the map. It's a fine state of affairs, isn't it?"

Marcus's laughter mingled with Tommy's, but beneath the amusement, a sharp edge of realisation began to creep into his thoughts. A reward? For Scotty? The idea seemed preposterous, but the more he considered it, the more it started to make sense. Scotty, Andrew, he had thought at the time, may have been a bit of a rogue, a man who found trouble as easily as breathing, and yet, no one had ever thought of him as a criminal. To think, a reward for his whereabouts. It was absurd, yet somehow fitting for the kind of world they were both navigating, a world where the past had a way of catching up, no matter how far you ran.

Tommy settled back in his seat, his eyes twinkling with the kind of mischief that only someone who had lived a hundred lives could possess. "Aye, well, I'll tell ye, Marcus, this whole thing, it's like something out of a tale, but I'll be damned if I don't go after him myself. As for the reward... well, if I can find him, I'll take it, but I'll be the one laughing all the way to the bank." He shot Marcus a grin, the kind of grin that spoke of adventure, of brothers, and of stories yet to be told.

Marcus, still chuckling at the absurdity of it all, shook his head, but deep down, he had an idea that this was far from over.

Tommy, as it turned out, was more than just a wandering Scotsman with a taste for adventure. He was a civil engineer by trade, a man who had spent years shaping landscapes and bending nature to the will of steel and concrete. He had found work with the Charleville Shire Council, brought on to redesign sections of the town's aging road and bridge system, a task he spoke of with a mixture of pride and enthusiasm, as if he were a sculptor given a fresh block of marble.

His visa was still good for another year, but even as he spoke about his work, Marcus could hear the undertones of something deeper, something that ran beyond mere employment. There was an affection in his voice when he spoke about the land, a growing attachment that he hadn't quite admitted to himself yet.

"If I take to the job well enough," Tommy mused, scratching at his thick beard, "I reckon I'll be putting in for Australian citizenship. It's a damn sight warmer than Glasgow, that's for sure, and the folk here, they're my kind of people. No nonsense, straight talkers, hard workers. A man can make something of himself in a place like this."

Marcus nodded, understanding the pull. He'd felt it himself, and he still had the feeling, that inexplicable draw of Australia, a land where a man's fortune was determined by his own hands, where the past could be left behind like footprints in the dust.

"Aye," Tommy continued, his voice taking on a note of finality. "I reckon this might just be the place for me."

Marcus could see it in his eyes, the certainty, the quiet acceptance of a life that had taken a turn he hadn't quite expected, but one that felt right all the same.

Marcus told Tommy that he was staying at the Corones Hotel, from advice by the RACQ and asked where he was staying. The council had Tommy booked into the Cattle Camp Hotel. Tommy' having a map of Charleville in his backpack, now took it out and checked the locations. "They are about two blocks apart. I would love to have dinner with you tonight, but I have to meet up with a couple of the council fellows."

They had found Tommy's hotel and Marcus dropped Tommy off at the front door, saying farewells and what a great trip it had been. "Good luck finding your brother" Marcus had said, "I will be living at a property called Stratheden, near Quilpie, look me up if you are ever around that way."

Charleville, like Roma, was a town born from the rugged heart of the outback. Established in 1868 as a service town to support the region's booming sheep and cattle industries, it had quickly become a vital stop for Cobb & Co. stagecoaches, linking the isolated communities of the west to the rest of the colony. When the railway arrived in 1888, Charleville's position as a key regional hub was solidified, ensuring its growth. During the dark days of World War II, the town had served as a base for the U.S. Air Force, a crucial cog in the machinery of war. Today, Charleville was a living testament to Australia's pastoral heritage, home to the Royal Flying Doctor Service base and the famed Charleville Cosmos Centre, which drew visitors eager to gaze up at the impossibly clear skies of the outback.

But none of that mattered to Marcus at that moment. What mattered was the long stretch of hot, dusty road behind him and the promise of a cold drink ahead. As he rolled into Charleville, his eyes landed on the grand façade of the Corones Hotel, a stately building that stood out like a monument against the dry landscape. The sun blazed overhead, the air shimmering with heat, and in that moment, the Corones Hotel looked like the best part of Charleville, if only for the promise of a cool drink after the long, tiring drive from Roma.

As Marcus stepped through the grand entrance of the Corones Hotel, he was struck by the stark contrast between the dust-choked road he had just left behind and the air of refined elegance that greeted him inside. The scent of polished wood mingled with a faint trace of cigar smoke, filling the high-ceilinged space with a certain old-world charm. He paused, taking a moment to soak in the surroundings, the gleaming timber floors, the soaring pressed-metal ceilings, and the sweeping staircase that curved upwards, leading to the guest rooms on the floor above.

Still carrying the dust of the Warrego Highway on his boots, Marcus straightened instinctively, his posture a subtle acknowledgment of the grandeur before him. He adjusted his jacket, smoothing it over his shoulders, as he made his way toward the reception desk. Behind the counter stood a middle-aged man with slicked-back hair and the poised demeanour of someone who had seen it all before. His gaze was sharp, watchful, and, for a brief moment, he sized Marcus up as he approached.

"Good afternoon, mate. Are you looking for a room?" The clerk's tone was polite but measured, as though he were sizing up Marcus's place among the hotel's distinguished guests.

Marcus gave a small nod, his hands resting on the counter. "Yes, just for the night, thanks."

The clerk's face softened, and he slid a leather-bound guest register toward Marcus, his voice taking on a tone of pride. "Welcome to the Corones Hotel, the best hotel and pub this side of Brissy!" he said, as though every word was soaked in the history of the place. "Sign here, and I'll get the young fellow to take your bag up to your room. You can park your car out back. And if you're after an icy cold beer, the bar's just through there." He gestured toward a nearby doorway, above which hung a sign reading "Saloon Bar" in bold, gold lettering.

Marcus nodded in appreciation of the straightforward, no-nonsense hospitality. He placed his bag on the counter and turned to park his car in the rear carpark, the evening air beginning to cool with the promise of nightfall. The thought of a refreshing beer and a hearty steak dinner made his stomach growl in anticipation, the perfect end to the long drive from Roma.

As he returned through the entrance, the low hum of conversation and the clinking of glasses greeted him. The golden glow of wall-mounted lamps bathed the polished timber floors in warmth, and the delicious aroma of grilled meat and fried onions drifted from the dining room, mingling with the faint buzz of the saloon bar. There, the day's dust seemed a distant memory, and Marcus felt the weight of the journey lift from his shoulders, ready to settle into the comfort of the Corones Hotel for a well-earned rest.

Marcus had just placed his order for a schooner of beer when a sudden, excited voice from behind cut through the hum of the saloon.

"Gotta be kiddin' me! ...Sharkie?"

He spun around, surprised, to be met by a broad grin and an outstretched hand.

"Mate... fancy bumpin' into you... out here!"

The man standing before him was in his twenties, lean and tanned, his shirt covered in dust from the road, and his moleskins well-worn from hard use. Marcus narrowed his eyes, trying to place the face. Then, like a flash of recognition, it clicked.

"Jim… Jim Hammond?"

Jim laughed, nodding eagerly as they shook hands. Marcus's mind flashed back to their days in Boggo Road, an unspoken bond forged through mutual respect and quiet resilience. Jim had been one of the few who kept his head low, his fists ready when the time called for it.

He'd been locked up for four years on a trumped-up charge. A ridiculous conviction for assault with a dangerous weapon. Jim's side of the story had always been different: he'd shot a home intruder in the leg with a .22 rifle, only to find himself branded a criminal for protecting what was his.

"Bloody hell, Marcus! Been a while! What brings you to Charleville?"

Jim's enthusiasm was genuine, his voice alive with excitement at the sight of a familiar face in an unexpected place.

"Grab ya beer and come over here, meet me mates, Sharkie!"

Marcus's jaw tightened slightly, a flicker of discomfort crossing his features. He had no desire to revisit that old name.

"Please, Jim… drop the Sharkie. I don't use that name anymore. Never liked it, to be honest."

Jim's grin faltered for a split second, but then he gave Marcus a nod of understanding, clapping him on the shoulder in an easy, affectionate gesture.

"Fair enough, mate. Marcus it is, then. But come on, at least let me buy you a beer for old times' sake!"

Marcus had earned the nickname "Sharkie" during his time at Boggo Road, not for seeking trouble, but for the way he moved through the system. He kept to himself, avoided the politics, and made no effort to prove anything. He wasn't the type to walk tall and loud; he was quiet, watching, calculating. But when someone pushed him too far, when they cornered him or made him respond, it was swift and brutal. Like a shark, silent, precise, and without mercy.

It was a name that had clung to him, no matter how far he tried to leave it behind. But that was the past, a time he had no interest in revisiting.

Jim, sensing the shift in his friend's mood, hesitated for just a moment before introducing him to the others.

"This is Johno, Dave, and Squid…" Jim gestured to the men at the table, all of them looking up as he spoke, "and this here is Sh, " He caught himself mid-sentence, grinned sheepishly, and corrected himself, "Marcus."

The three men nodded in greeting, their faces weathered and hard, shaped by the relentless Australian sun. They pulled up a chair, making space for Marcus at the table.

And as the conversation flowed, easy, unhurried, and full of the warmth that comes with old camaraderie, Marcus allowed himself to relax, if only for a moment. The road had been long, but in the company of familiar faces, it felt like he might just find a place to rest.

Jim leaned back in his chair, tipping the last of his beer down his throat before wiping his mouth with the back of his hand. "We're shearers," he said, nodding toward the men at the table. "Part of a bigger crew working' the station circuit. We were meant to start at Warunga Station yesterday, forty miles east of here."

"What happened?" Marcus asked, swirling the amber liquid in his glass.

Jim snorted. "Bloody cook didn't show."

Johno let out a dry chuckle. "Useless bastard left us high and dry. You can't shear without a cook, blokes won't last a day without proper tucker."

"Our contractor reckons he's got another one lined up," Jim added, stretching his arms behind his head. "Says he'll meet us here at the pub later tonight."

Marcus listened, intrigued despite himself. He had no great interest in shearing, but there was something about the rough camaraderie of these men that pulled at him, their easy banter, their reliance on each other, the sheer physicality of the work. It was a different world, but a world that had its own rules, its own way of sorting men from boys.

The shearers had booked a table for ten in the hotel's dining room, a gathering for the whole crew, six shearers, two roustabouts, their contractor, and the new cook, if he decided to show. But when the contractor arrived without the man, Jim immediately turned to Marcus with a grin.

"Bugger it, join us for dinner," he said. "You can sit in the cook's seat. Food and a bed are covered by the contractor anyway."

Marcus wasn't one to turn down a free meal, especially when the alternative was eating alone in the bar.

Earlier, as the beer had flowed, he'd mentioned in passing that he was between jobs, making his way west to visit his uncle and aunt at Stratheden, near Quilpie. That had caught Bruce's attention.

The contractor, a heavy-set man with sun-leathered skin and a calculating eye, rubbed his chin. "Stratheden, eh? We'll be shearing there in about a month, after we get through three more sheds." He studied Marcus for a long moment before adding, "What are you like in a kitchen?"

Marcus lifted an eyebrow. "I can handle myself well enough. I'm no chef, but I won't let a crew starve."

Bruce gave a slow nod, weighing him up. "We need a cook, badly. If this bloke doesn't show by tomorrow, we're in a real bind." He leaned back, arms crossed over his chest. "It's simple. Three meals a day, meat, spuds, damper. Keep the tea boiling, make sure the blokes don't go hungry, and they'll treat you like a king. You interested?"

Marcus hesitated. He'd never cooked for shearers before, but he knew his way around a campfire. More than that, it was an easy way to keep busy, put some money in his pocket, and take his time heading toward Stratheden.

Jim clapped him on the shoulder. "Reckon you could do worse, mate. Beats sittin' around doing nothin'."

Marcus smirked. "I'll think about it over dinner. But if I do take it on, you'll need another cook by the time we get to Stratheden."

Bruce grinned. "Fair enough. Let's eat first, talk business after."

The dining room filled with the low hum of voices, the clink of cutlery against china. The scent of grilled steak and fresh bread wafted from the kitchen, mingling with the yeasty tang of beer.

Marcus took a slow sip from his schooner, a wry smile tugging at the corner of his mouth. This was going to be an interesting night.

By lunchtime on Sunday, it was clear as the Outback sky that the new cook wasn't coming. No word, no excuses, just a no-show. And just like that, Marcus found himself with a job he hadn't been looking for.

Bruce, true to his word, promised to stay on a couple of days to help him find his feet. It was an unusual move for a contractor, most of them kept their distance, letting the shearers and their crew run things. But Bruce had started out in the galley himself, a dozen years back, sweating over a wood-fired stove in the middle of nowhere, feeding hungry men with nothing but a sack of flour, a side of beef, and a pot of tea. He knew the grind, the long hours, the unforgiving heat, and the importance of a solid meal at the end of the day. He wasn't above rolling up his sleeves when it counted.

That night, Marcus placed a call to Stratheden. It rang twice before a deep, steady voice answered.

"Stratheden, Miles speaking."

Marcus felt a flicker of something familiar, respect, perhaps, or the quiet weight of family ties.

"Uncle Miles, it's Marcus." He paused briefly. "Just wanted to let you know, I'll be coming out to Stratheden with the shearing team. Turns out I've taken on the job as the cook."

There was silence for a beat. Then a low, knowing chuckle.

"Well now," Miles said. "That'll be a bit of a baptism by fire."

Marcus could picture his uncle, leaning back in a battered old chair, rubbing his jaw as he considered the news.

"But there's no better way to understand a shearing team than to work alongside them," Miles continued. "Good experience for you and you will learn something of sheep. Being the cook they may teach you something about butchering and breaking down a carcass, and that will come in handy for you."

There was no, real, grand approval, no unnecessary words, but Marcus could hear it in his uncle's tone. A quiet acceptance. Maybe even something close to pride.

"Anyway it sounds like you're making yourself useful."

"That's the plan," Marcus said, a small smile playing at the corner of his lips.

"Good," Miles said simply. "I'll see you when you get here."

The line went dead, leaving Marcus standing there, phone still in hand. His uncle had never been a man for sentiment, never one to offer praise freely. But there had been something in his voice, respect, maybe, or at least the acknowledgment of a man pulling his own weight.

And that, Marcus thought, was something worth holding onto.

By Monday afternoon, the shearing team had arrived and were settling into the shed, their movements purposeful, their preparations swift. The men knew their work, knew the rhythm of a shearing run, and wasted no time in making themselves at home. Now, as the last of the day's heat stretched across the land, they sprawled across the front veranda of the mess hall, longneck bottles in hand, sweat drying on their sunburned forearms. The air was thick with the smell of dust, wool grease, and the sharp bite of beer.

Marcus stood nearby with Bruce, listening as the contractor laid out the finer points of his new role.

"In most sheds, the cocky, the grazier, supplies the food," Bruce said, taking a swig from his bottle. "Now, what you get depends on the deal they've struck with the contractor. Some sheds do it right, live meat, usually lambs. Shearers like that. They want to see what they're eating. They'll judge the age of the beast themselves."

Marcus nodded. He'd heard about that. Shearers were particular about their meat. If the grazier supplied butchered mutton, there was no telling whether it had come from a prime lamb or a tough old ewe. And no man who spent his days bent over the long blows of a sheep's back wanted to chew on boot leather at the end of it.

Bruce continued, his tone casual but authoritative. "Now, if we're shearing in the cooler months, March through May, you'll usually get beef as well. It'll come as a half carcass or a couple of quarters, depending on the size of the shed. Either way, it's up to the cook to break it down into proper cuts. That's you, Marko."

Marcus took it in, filing the information away. He wasn't a butcher, but he'd slaughtered and dressed enough animals in his time to make a fair go of it.

Bruce jerked his head toward the back of the mess hall. "Veggies, too. Most stations have a patch, and the cook's welcome to help himself."

Marcus had already seen the garden, rows of spuds, onions, cabbages, maybe even some carrots. It was better than nothing. Boiled meat and damper would keep a man alive, but it wouldn't keep him happy.

Bruce clapped him on the back, the force of it nearly knocking the breath from his lungs. "You'll be right, mate. Keep the tucker coming, the tea hot, and don't let the shearers go hungry. Do that, and they'll treat you like a king."

Marcus exhaled slowly, adjusting to the weight of this new reality. He hadn't planned on this, but out here, plans shifted like red dust in the wind.

Bruce motioned for him to follow. "Come on, Marko. I'll show you how to kill a sheep and hang it proper. We'll cut some steaks off the beef side for tonight, fry up some chips from the spuds." He cast a glance toward the food store, grinning. "Might as well throw in some eggs, too. We seem to have a bloody oversupply."

Marcus followed without hesitation. This was his world now. And if he was going to do it, he was damn well going to do it right.

They strode toward the small holding yard near the shearing shed, where four sturdy hogget's shifted uneasily, their ears flicking at the low murmur of approaching boots. They were oblivious to their fate but not entirely at ease, animals always sensed when something was coming.

A few paces away, the slaughtering slab stood beneath a crude but effective gallows, built for dressing meat. Adjacent to it was the walk-in meat safe, a solid, fly-proof structure designed to keep the carcasses cool while allowing air to circulate. Inside, Marcus could see the tools of the trade: a stainless steel butcher's bench, a bandsaw for heavier cuts, a handsaw, a cleaver, and a row of knives so well-worn they looked like an extension of a man's hand, sharpened to a deadly edge through years of use.

"Bigger stations have gone soft," Bruce muttered, stepping into the yard. "Electric cool rooms, flash refrigeration. Out here, we do it the old way, same as our fathers did before us. Meat tastes better for it, too."

Marcus said nothing, absorbing every detail. He had never butchered a sheep before, but in this land, hesitation was a weakness. He would learn fast, or not at all.

Bruce moved with the ease of a man who had done this a thousand times. The sheep shrank back as he entered, instinctively pressing against the far fence. He didn't rush. Instead, he took his time, his steps slow, deliberate. Then, in a single practiced motion, he lunged, gripping one by the hind leg and dragging it backward through the gate. The others shifted but did not panic.

"You can't afford to stir them up," Bruce said, steering the animal toward the slab. "Heat 'em up, and adrenaline floods the meat, makes it tough as boot leather. No stress, no struggle."

Marcus committed the words to memory. There was a science to this, as much care as there was ruthlessness.

Bruce straddled the sheep with practiced ease, one firm hand gripping its jaw. The animal remained still, trusting, its head tilted back as far as it would go. In a single fluid motion, Bruce drew his knife, a fine-bladed Victorinox boning knife, razor-sharp, and pushed it cleanly through the throat, right to left the drew the knife downwards. The steel slid through flesh and artery with practiced precision. The sheep crumpled without a sound, its death instant.

Bruce worked fast. The carcass was hoisted in moments, two precise cuts above the hind legs allowing him to slip a hanging beam through the tendons. With a practiced heave, he lifted the body high, leaving it to dangle from the gallows.

Then came the real work. Skinning, gutting, breaking down the carcass with an efficiency honed by years of repetition. The fleece peeled back in clean, smooth strokes. Entrails spilled into a shallow tray, expertly sorted, lungs, kidneys, and liver placed to one side, nothing wasted.

Marcus watched, fascinated. There was no hesitation in Bruce's hands, no wasted movement. It was skill born of necessity, a lesson written in blood and sinew.

Bruce wiped his hands on his apron, his expression unreadable. Then he turned to Marcus, his eyes holding the weight of a challenge.

"Day after tomorrow," he said, voice flat. "You'll do the next one."

Marcus drew in a steady breath, the scent of dust and meat heavy in the air. He had come out here looking for a change, and by God, he had found one.

Back in the kitchen, the heat from the wood stove filled the space, mingling with the sharp scent of raw potatoes. A long, battered wooden prep table stood in the center of the room, scarred by decades of hard use. Marcus stood before it, a peeler in hand, a sack of spuds at his feet. Bruce had wasted no time putting him to work.

"Right," Bruce said, rolling up his sleeves, his voice carrying the weight of experience. "Rule number one when cooking for shearers, portion control. You allow one and a half to two potatoes per man. No more." He tossed a solid spud onto the table with a dull thud.

Marcus nodded and got to work, the rhythmic scrape of the peeler against potato flesh filling the silence.

Bruce leaned against the counter, arms crossed, watching him with a knowing smirk. "You feed 'em more, they'll eat more. And that just means more work for you. Remember that. It's like feeding a pack of cattle dogs, fill their bowls, and they'll lick 'em clean every time."

Marcus smirked but didn't pause, the pile of peeled potatoes growing steadily. He was starting to see that cooking for shearers wasn't just about throwing food on a plate, it was a game of endurance, strategy, and keeping the men fed without breaking himself in the process.

Bruce led him into the storeroom, where a sturdy, foot-operated chipper sat on a lower shelf, its metal frame worn but solid. He tapped it with his knuckles. "Every shed's got one of these," he said. "And if they don't, you tell 'em to get one. Fast."

There was an authority in his voice, this wasn't a suggestion. Marcus noted it, filing the information away.

Next came the eggs. Bruce yanked open the old fridge, nodding toward the neatly stacked trays inside. "Take these out well before you start cooking," he instructed. "Let 'em get to room temperature. Makes 'em easier to crack without busting the yolk. And it stops the whites from going rubbery."

Another lesson, another unspoken rule of bush cooking. Marcus was fast learning that out here, every detail mattered.

With the prep underway, they moved outside to the meat hanging room. Bruce flicked open the fly-screen door and grabbed a swatter, expertly flicking away the few lingering insects hovering near the fresh sheep carcass. The meat was hung beside a heavy quarter of beef, the cool, fly-proof space keeping everything in check.

Then, without a word, Bruce reached for the beef quarter. He wiped his hands on his apron before gripping the hefty slab, fingers sinking into the deep muscle fibres. With nothing but the strength of his hands and the knowledge of a man who had done this a hundred times over, he began pulling apart the joints, following the natural seams of the meat.

"See here?" he said, barely needing his knife as he worked open a section. "You follow the grain, not fight it. Less effort, cleaner cuts."

Once the joint was separated, Bruce reached for his twelve-inch butcher knife. He handled it like an extension of his own arm, slicing ten thick, one-inch rump steaks with the kind of practiced ease that only came with years of work. The cuts were smooth, each one a perfect replica of the last.

Then, setting the knife down, Bruce stepped outside the meat room and struck a match against his boot. He lit a cigarette, taking a slow pull before exhaling into the cooling dusk. His gaze settled on Marcus, sharp and serious now.

"One thing," he said, tapping ash off the end of his cigarette. "Never mix up the butcher knives with the kitchen knives. And don't ever smoke in the meat room or the kitchen."

Marcus gave a slow nod.

There was an order to things out here, an unwritten code that kept the whole operation running smooth. And despite Bruce's easygoing nature, one thing was clear, things were done right, or they weren't done at all.

Dinner that night was a triumph. The thick-cut rump steaks were charred to perfection, their juices running rich and deep, while the hand-cut chips came out crisp and golden. The eggs, room temperature as Bruce had insisted, were fried just right, their yolks like pools of molten gold. The shearers ate with the single-minded intensity of men who had worked their bodies to the brink. Grunts of approval and nods of satisfaction punctuated the clatter of cutlery, and by the time the plates were cleared, Marcus had secured his place in the camp.

Afterward, the roustabouts pitched in to help with the washing up, sleeves rolled back, hands plunged into steaming water. Banter flew across the kitchen as they ribbed each other about the day's work, who had dragged their feet, who had kept pace, who had let a sheep get the better of them. Marcus appreciated the extra hands. Running a shearing shed kitchen was no small task, and he was quickly learning that any help, no matter how rough around the edges, was worth its weight in gold.

With the last of the pots scrubbed and stacked, he wandered into the dining hall. A game of euchre was already underway. The shearers hunched around a scarred wooden table, cards flashing between calloused fingers. A haze of cigarette smoke hung thick in the air, mixing with the sharp tang of sweat and the occasional clink of beer bottles. Laughter rumbled through the room, deep and unrestrained, the kind shared between men who had spent years on the road together, working, drinking, gambling, moving from shed to shed like nomads with shears.

Marcus lingered at the edge, beer in hand, watching the game unfold. Euchre wasn't just a card game; it was a test of nerve, quick thinking, and luck. He studied their movements, the subtle shifts in expression, the unspoken signals between seasoned players. Eventually, one of the men jerked a thumb at an empty chair. "Reckon you're game?"

Marcus slid into the seat. "You'll have to teach me."

The hours slipped by in a blur of laughter and friendly competition, but as the night deepened, Marcus knew he had one last task before he could call it a day. At nine o'clock sharp, he pushed back from the table and strode into the kitchen. A heavy iron pot sat on the stove, and he filled it with rich, dark cocoa, stirring until the warm scent of chocolate filled the mess hall. Then, wiping his hands on his apron, he returned to the dining room and under strict instructions from Bruce, clapped his palms together.

"All right, fellas. Last drinks. Finish your hands and wrap it up."

There were a few half-hearted grumbles, but they knew the drill. By ten, Marcus had herded them out into the cool night air, locking the mess hall doors behind him. Getting into his bed, he was worried that he may not hear the alarm clock that Bruce had given him.

The next morning came early. Too early.

Marcus dragged himself out of bed at five, rubbing sleep from his eyes as he stumbled toward the kitchen. Outside, the darkness was beginning to lift, the first faint blush of dawn stretching across the horizon. A faint breeze carried the scent of dry earth and cattle dung, a stark reminder of where he was.

Bruce was already up, leaning against the doorway with a steaming mug of tea. He took a slow sip before fixing Marcus with a knowing look. "First lesson of a shearers' cook, let the bastards serve themselves. You try running around after 'em, you'll drop dead before smoko."

He stepped inside and tapped the edge of the Bain Marie with his knuckles. "Right. First thing's first. Lamb chops. Bacon. You want plenty of both, but don't be stupid about it. Keep the heat on medium, too high and the bacon'll dry out, the chops'll turn to boot leather."

Marcus nodded, already moving to retrieve the meat from the cold storage.

"And eggs," Bruce continued, cracking one deftly into a pan. "Two per bloke, standard. And make sure you eat too. Nothing worse than a cook trying to run a kitchen on an empty stomach." He flipped the egg with a flick of his wrist. "You want 'em slightly underdone. Stick 'em in the Bain Marie like this, they'll keep cooking just enough. You serve rubber eggs, you'll never live it down."

Marcus absorbed every word, setting to work. Soon, the hiss and sizzle of bacon filled the mess hall, mingling with the deep, mouth-watering aroma of frying chops. Bruce nodded in approval, clapping him on the back.

"There you go, old son. Keep the food coming, make sure the tea's hot, and you'll be right."

Bruce had already boiled two massive kettles, pouring the scalding water into a hulking teapot. The brew was dark and strong, enough to put fire in the belly of even the weariest shearer.

Next came the toast. "Keep it coming," Bruce instructed, gesturing toward the industrial toaster. "Pile it high in the basket, and keep the butter out where they can reach it. Jam and honey, too. Shearers like their sugar."

Marcus worked fast, flipping eggs, stacking chops, making sure everything ran like clockwork. The Bain Marie's gentle heat kept everything at the perfect temperature, and by six o'clock, the first of the shearers shuffled in, bleary-eyed but hungry.

They didn't wait. Shearers never did. They grabbed their plates, loaded up, and tucked in, washing down mouthfuls of food with strong, scalding tea.

"Good tucker, mate," one of the older men grunted, tearing into a chop.

Others nodded, mumbling their approval between bites.

Bruce shot Marcus a look of satisfaction. "You're getting the hang of it." He leaned in slightly, lowering his voice. "Just remember, keep the food coming, keep the tea hot, and stay out of their bloody way."

By seven, breakfast was winding down, the shearers heading off toward the sheds, ready to tackle another brutal day's work.

Marcus, wiping the last smear of grease from his hands, was already thinking ahead to morning smoko.

Tea, biscuits… maybe a batch of scones if time allowed. Bruce had advised to cook an extra chop with dinner for each of the gang, or steaks if that's what's on for dinner, and use these for smoko. They'll just lobe them.

Bruce clapped him on the shoulder, grinning. "Welcome to the world of a shearers' cook, mate. You survive this, you can survive anything."

A Stint in the Shearing Shed's

Seven o'clock was not when the men arrived, it was when the work began. The shed hands, the roustabouts, and the shearers didn't drift in lazily at the start of the day; they were already at their posts, ready for the relentless rhythm of the shearing shed.

Before the first sheep was even touched, before the roar of the shearing shed truly began, there was a ritual as old as the trade itself, the sharpening of the combs and cutters. It was a process that separated the professionals from the amateurs, for a shearer was only as good as his gear. A dull comb would pull at the wool instead of slicing clean through, slow a man down, and turn a tough day into an agonising one. Worse still, it could tear the sheep's hide, and there was no faster way to earn the wrath of the boss than to have the shed-hand constantly dabbing iodine onto bloodied flanks.

The grinding wheel stood at the ready, a worn old thing mounted on a sturdy bench, its spinning surface coated in fine emery dust. Each shearer brought his own set of combs and cutters, worn steel stained dark with years of use. The combs, wide-toothed and curved like a predator's jaw, determined how much wool was taken off with each stroke. The cutters, smaller and set atop the comb, moved with a rapid, relentless precision, slicing the wool clean as they passed.

The technique was everything. A steady hand, the right amount of pressure. Too light, and the combs wouldn't sharpen evenly, leaving dull spots that would snag in the fleece. Too heavy, and the steel would overheat, warping the edge and rendering it useless. The old hands, the veterans of the trade, had it down to an art, holding the comb against the whirring wheel with just enough pressure, moving it in slow, deliberate arcs, the sparks flying in tiny, brilliant showers. The smell of hot metal mixed with lanolin hung in the air, a scent every shearer knew well.

Each set was sharpened with meticulous care, checked against the light, edges tested against a thumbnail for that razor-sharp bite. It was a quiet moment before the storm, the last bit of preparation before the shearing began in earnest.

Because once the first sheep was dragged onto the board, there would be no time for mistakes. The pace would be furious, the work unrelenting. And a shearer with blunt combs might as well pack up his swag and go home, because out here, on the big stations, there was no room for a man who couldn't keep his gear sharp.

The shed hands were supplied by the farmer, as was the wool classer, often the farmer himself or, in some cases, one of his sons. The baler, a man with sinewy arms and a back like iron, pressed the wool into tight, dense bales for transport, his role as crucial as any in the shearing operation. These men started well before the first sheep was shorn, ensuring that the pens were full and the shed was primed for action. The shearers worked with brutal efficiency, and any delay in delivering sheep to their stands could spell disaster for the day's tally.

The first day at the shed was generally reserved for the rams. These were the most difficult to shear, only a few of the gang were qualified to shear them. Some of the gang refused to shear them. But the ones that did were paid handsomely and deservedly so!

The rams were different. A different breed of beast altogether. Shearing a ewe or a wether was one thing, hard work, sure, but manageable. The rams, though, were an entirely different proposition. They were big, thick-set brutes, muscled like prizefighters and just as mean. Any shearer worth his salt knew that handling a ram wasn't just about strength; it was about strategy, about knowing when to hold firm and when to move fast.

For one, their wool was thicker, tougher. Heavy with lanolin, dust, and God knew what else, it clogged the shears, blunted the blades faster than anything, and made the entire process a battle from the first stroke to the last. It was easy enough to nick an ordinary sheep, but a ram's hide was loose, folded over itself like layers of tough old leather, making every pass of the shears a gamble between efficiency and injury. A slip of the hand, a moment's hesitation, and there'd be blood on the board.

Then there was their temperament. A ewe might kick, a wether might struggle, but a ram fought back. A ram had weight behind it, solid, unrelenting power. He could throw his head back and break a man's nose before he even saw it coming. A well-placed kick could crack ribs, shatter fingers, or send a shearer sprawling onto the boards, winded and cursing. Some of the bigger ones, if they got loose, would charge without a second's thought, sending men diving out of the way or else ending up with their legs taken clean out from under them.

The real danger, though, was in the repetition. A single ram was a challenge. But a full day of them? That was a grind that tested even the toughest men in the shed. The constant strain on the lower back, the endless battle to keep the ram pinned and still, the sheer weight of the animal bearing down on tired muscles, it was enough to ruin a man if he wasn't careful. Hands blistered, backs ached, and more than one shearer had left the shed for good after taking a bad hit from a particularly savage ram.

Yet, there was a strange pride in it. The best shearers, the real professionals, they didn't just shear rams, they conquered them. And when a man had finished his run, stepped back, and looked down at a perfectly shorn beast, steam rising from its bare hide in the cool morning air, there was a sense of triumph in that. The ram had fought, but the man had won.

And that, in the end, was what separated the boys from the men in the shearing sheds of the Outback. In respect to sheep, of course

Weather was the eternal enemy of the shearing shed. Rain was a curse. The moment a cloud burst, the focus shifted to protecting the flock. Sheep were either driven beneath the shearing shed or huddled in makeshift shelters to keep their fleece dry. A wet fleece wasn't just a nuisance, it was a deal-breaker. If the wool absorbed too much moisture, the shearers would refuse to work. It wasn't only that damp wool was tougher to handle; the real trouble was the stench. The acrid, ammonia-like reek of wet fleece could choke a man, turning the shed into a suffocating, unworkable space. Avoiding such setbacks was the mark of a well-run operation.

Some of the bigger sheep stations had enough undercover pens for their entire flock. These would generally be located in the vicinity of the shed but in some instances may be spread around the property. These sheds were favoured by the shearers as there were seldom holdups from 'wet sheep'

At the heart of the shed was Jimmy, the gun shearer. He moved with a speed and precision that was mesmerising, his shears carving through fleece in long, clean sweeps. He was taking down 180 to 200 sheep a day, a mark of both skill and endurance. The rest of the team weren't far behind, averaging 170 each. At £7.10/- per 100 sheep, they were earning a solid wage, hard-earned, but respectable.

Not all of their pay stayed in their pockets. Each shearer contributed £2 per 100 sheep towards the cook's wages and the cost of their meals. It was a necessary system, ensuring that the food was hot, the portions were generous, and the entire shed ran with military precision. Even after deductions, the take-home pay was strong, £51 a week in 1958 was a wage that could turn a hard man into a wealthy one, if he had the grit to keep up the pace.

The schedule was unrelenting. The shearing gang worked a 54-hour week, pushing their bodies to the limit. The day began at seven sharp and finished at five in the afternoon, broken only by two fifteen-minute smoko breaks, one in the morning, another in the afternoon, and a half-hour for lunch. Every stroke of the shears was another step towards the tally, every fleece thrown onto the sorting table another measure of their toil. It was back-breaking, brutal work, but for those who endured, the rewards were well worth it.

Warunga Station had a flock of 7,000 sheep, and the shearing gang dispatched them in seven days. By the time the last fleece was packed and the shed swept clean, their thoughts had already turned to the next job. The following morning, they would set their sights on Catalina Station, out near Cooladdi on the Diamantina Road, halfway between Charleville and Quilpie.

The journey was no mere jaunt. Catalina lay 160 miles away, a full day's drive across the open country, where the roads were long and the dust settled thick on the windscreen. Warunga had been a sprint, quick work, well executed. But Catalina was another beast entirely. With 18,000 sheep waiting in the pens, they expected to be there for the better part of three weeks. If all went smoothly.

Each man was prepared for the road. The shearing gang was a travelling unit, well-equipped and self-sufficient. Every shearer had his own vehicle, except for Jimmy, who hitched a ride with Dave in his Dodge. The roustabouts shared a lift in Phil's trusty FJ Holden ute. The rest of the convoy followed, a procession of Australian road legends rolling across the outback. Bruce, the boss, led the way in his gleaming '55 Chevrolet, his pride and joy. Behind him, the line stretched out, an FJ Holden sedan, an FJ ute, a Ford Zephyr, another Dodge ute, and Marcus's FC, all kicking up dust as they carved their path towards the next shed, the next tally, the next payday.

Bruce had wired ahead to Catalina Station, making sure everything was in place before they hit the road. The journey ahead was no easy trip, 160 miles of bone-rattling, unsealed tracks, the kind that could shake a man's teeth loose if he wasn't careful. The convoy moved in tight formation, dust billowing behind them in great swirling plumes, the sun burning high and merciless in the cobalt sky.

Midway through the haul, they pulled off into the shade of a gnarled coolabah tree, stretching out stiff limbs and shaking the dust from their shirts. Lunch was simple, sandwiches hastily unwrapped, cold lamb chops gnawed to the bone, and bottles of beer pulled from eskies packed with half-melted chiller blocks. The beer was lukewarm, bordering on tepid, but no one grumbled. A man who'd spent days bent over a fleece, working in the sweat and stink of the shearing shed, knew better than to turn his nose up at a drink, cold or not.

With hunger sated and thirst temporarily dulled, they climbed back into their vehicles and pressed on, engines growling as they chewed up the miles. The convoy wound its way toward Catalina Station, where more hard, unrelenting work lay ahead.

Bruce had arranged for an extra shearer to join them at Catalina, bringing the tally to seven, one for each stand in the shed. More hands meant faster work, but it also meant more mouths to feed, and Marcus felt the weight of it settle on his shoulders. He was already working at full tilt, and the thought of stretching supplies and rations even further set his mind racing.

Bruce must have caught the look on his face, because he waved a hand dismissively. "I'll sort it, don't worry."

Marcus wasn't sure exactly what that meant, but he had a hunch he'd find out soon enough.

Warren Smith rolled in late that afternoon, the rumble of his battered International ute breaking the stillness of the station yard. Dust coated the bonnet in thick layers, and in the tray, a swag lay tossed among coils of rope and a battered water drum. He stepped out slow, unhurried, like a man who had nothing to prove but expected others to take note all the same.

He was tall and wiry, the kind of lean that came from years of hard labour, not lack of meals. His head was shaved clean, giving him a hawk-like sharpness, his eyes hooded, unreadable. There was something about him, an edge. Not hostile, not friendly. Just there. Like a man who had seen enough fights to know he could win most of them.

Bruce stepped forward, extending a hand. "Good to have you on board, Warren."

Warren met the handshake with a firm grip, nodding to the others before pulling his gear from the tray. "Shed's ready to go first thing tomorrow," Bruce added.

Warren slung his swag over one shoulder and gave a slow nod. "All good. Been a while since I shore a seven-stand, but I reckon I'll keep up."

The rest of the gang watched him as he moved toward the quarters, rolling out his swag in a dark corner without fuss or conversation. Marcus, eyeing the extra workload Warren's arrival would bring, rolled up his sleeves and muttered under his breath. If Bruce reckoned he'd "sort it," Marcus hoped that meant something more than words.

The tension surfaced before the first sheep even hit the board.

Bruce had Warren pegged for stand six, but Warren had his own ideas. As the gang filtered into the shed that morning, shaking off the last of their sleep, Warren strolled toward stand four like it was his by right.

Bruce, in good spirits, chuckled. "Jimmy's on four, Warren. Always has been. He's the ringer."

Warren barely looked at him. "Well, he won't be on four in this shed," he said, his voice calm but carrying weight. He glanced toward Jimmy with a smirk. "And I doubt he'll be ringing this shed."

Jimmy had just stepped onto the board, catching that last remark. He paused, eyes narrowing, reading Warren the way a man reads a horse before he decides whether to break it or shoot it.

"What's that?" Jimmy asked, his tone mild, but there was steel underneath.

Bruce, feeling the heat rising, cut in. "Warren wants stand four, Jimmy." He kept his voice even, throwing a quick look at Warren, trying to gauge how far this would go. The last thing they needed was a brawl before they'd even started.

Jimmy shrugged, surprising Bruce. "Fine by me. I don't really give a bugger where I shear."

That was that. No fireworks, no fists thrown. But the air crackled with unspoken challenges.

Then came the shearing itself. It was brutal, relentless, a test of endurance as much as skill. By day's end, Warren and Jimmy had both knocked over 187 sheep, neither man yielding an inch.

Warren, never one to let a moment go unclaimed, stretched his shoulders and muttered loud enough for all to hear, "Would've hit 200 easy if the shed hands weren't dragging their bloody feet."

The others exchanged glances, a few smothering chuckles. No one said a word, but the verdict was unanimous.

Dickhead.

Dinner was a feast. Marcus had outdone himself, roasting two legs of lamb to perfection, the meat tender and glistening under a thick, rich gravy. Golden potatoes, caramelised pumpkin, buttered peas, and sweet carrots filled the plates, and the men ate like wolves after a hard day's work. The mess hall buzzed with the usual low murmur of satisfied chewing, the occasional grunt of approval as someone reached for another helping.

Then Warren, because he never let a moment pass without souring it, leaned back in his chair and let his voice carry across the room.

"She's a bloody tough bit of mutton you've roasted there, young fella!" His tone was loud, edged with challenge, aimed squarely at Marcus.

Bruce barely paused, chewing deliberately before setting his fork down. His reply was calm, easy, but the steel underneath was unmistakable.

"Tastes fine to me. And no one else is complaining. Pretty good meal from a pretty good cook, if you ask me."

Warren smirked, shifting lazily in his seat. "Well, I wasn't asking you," he sneered. "And I wouldn't go calling him a cook either."

Then, without warning, he shoved his plate off the table. It hit the floor with a loud clatter, lamb and vegetables scattering across the boards, thick gravy pooling in a slow, ugly smear.

"I'm not eating this shit," Warren said flatly. "Do better, or I'm outta here."

Silence. The only sound was the slow creak of Bruce's chair as he pushed it back and got to his feet.

He moved across the room with the unhurried certainty of a man who had settled more disputes than he cared to count. He met Warren at the doorway, blocking his path.

"Pick up that plate and clean up the mess," Bruce said. His voice was calm, controlled, but there was an edge in it that made the other men glance at one another.

Warren let out a short snort, curling his lip. "Fuck off… old man."

Then he shoved past, shoulder first. It was a mistake.

Bruce moved in a flash, his left boot driving into Warren's backside with enough force to send him stumbling through the doorway. Warren caught himself before he hit the dirt, spun around, and glared back.

"You can wait, you arsehole!" he shouted, but he didn't stop walking.

The next morning, no one was surprised to see stand four empty. Sometime in the night, Warren had packed his swag and left Catalina without a word.

No one was particularly bothered. If anything, the mood at breakfast was lighter. The gang threw themselves into the work with fresh energy, pressing on through the relentless days. Even a man down, they ran hard, the rhythm of the shed tightening, the shears ringing against the wool.

By the end of it, eighteen thousand sheep lay shorn, the job done in just under eighteen days. And not a single man had missed Warren.

It was on Friday morning, the last day before the gang made their move to Stratheden, when Marcus made a discovery that soured the entire day. Both front tyres of his car were flat. A cursory inspection confirmed his worst fears, those tyres hadn't simply gone down; they'd been slashed.

The mood in the camp shifted immediately, like a storm front rolling in. A heavy silence settled over the crew as they processed the malicious act.

"Bloody hell," Dave muttered, crouching to examine the damage. His voice was tight with anger, his hands clenched into fists.

Bruce, standing a few paces away, let out a slow breath, his eyes narrowing as he surveyed the scene. "Doesn't take a genius to figure out who'd pull a stunt like this," he said, his voice low but firm.

No one needed to say the name aloud. It was as clear as the scorching sun overhead. Warren.

A few of the men exchanged dark looks, their faces tight with a mix of fury and disbelief. Slashing a bloke's tyres, there was no lower act, even for someone like Warren, who'd been an arrogant, sore loser from the start.

"Bastard must've done it during the night before he pissed off," Phil said through gritted teeth, his jaw hard enough to crack stone.

Marcus let out a sharp exhale, the frustration rising in his chest like a storm. There was no doubt in his mind that this was Warren's parting shot, a petty, spiteful act aimed at getting the last word.

By the time they hit Quilpie, the tension in the air had barely dissipated. The trip had been smooth enough, the crew making good time down the dusty, unforgiving roads of the outback. Quilpie itself was a welcome sight, a small town with wide streets and the familiar comfort of old weatherboard buildings. The Imperial Hotel stood on the corner like a sentry, its aged wooden façade a testament to countless years of travellers coming and going.

Marcus exhaled a sigh of relief as Bruce pulled the car to a halt outside. "First stop, the garage," Bruce said, eyes flicking to the tyres. "Let's see if we can get those wheels sorted before they shut up shop for the weekend."

The clink of coins and glasses greeted them as they entered the pub. Inside, the gang was already scattered around the bar, their laughter and casual conversation blending with the raucous noise of a few card games in progress.

Then, cutting through the noise, a voice rang out, sharp, mocking, and unmistakable.

"Well, well… was it a long walk for you, Cookie?"

Bruce and Marcus turned as one, instincts honed from months of working side by side in the harshest conditions of the outback. And there he stood, Warren, wearing his signature smirk like a badge of dishonour, his eyes glinting with malice.

Before either of them could respond, Warren locked eyes with Bruce. His grin twisted into something darker.

"Here's one I owe you!" he spat, the words barely out before his fist swung toward Bruce's head.

It was a split-second, but Bruce's training kicked in without hesitation. His body leaned back, narrowly avoiding the blow. But in doing so, he left Marcus directly in the line of fire.

With a movement born of instinct, Marcus dropped into a squat, low, fast, and fluid, his Silat training taking over in that instant. Warren, committed to his punch, sailed past Bruce, his body pitching forward with unstoppable momentum.

Marcus, poised like a coiled spring, didn't hesitate. He took the full weight of Warren's charge, rolling him straight over the top, his body using the momentum to drive Warren's head downward with brutal precision. The edge of the brass ashtray at the bar, polished to a gleaming shine, caught Warren just above the brow.

The sound of bone hitting metal was deafening. The sickening crack of it echoed through the stunned silence of the room.

Warren crumpled instantly, his body folding like a rag doll, his face smashing against the wooden floor. Blood began to pool around him, dark and spreading across the floorboards.

The bar was silent, utterly still. No one moved.

A few men rushed forward, checking for signs of life. But it was clear, Warren was out cold, his breath shallow, his body limp. Someone yelled for an ambulance, and the bartender hurried to make the call.

Minutes dragged on like hours. The wail of sirens finally split the quiet, and the paramedics moved in with cold professionalism. But there was no saving him.

Warren Smith, the troublemaker, the sore loser, the man who'd slashed Marcus's tyres and tried to pick a fight, was already gone. By the time they lifted him onto the stretcher, he had breathed his last. He was dead before the ambulance even reached the hospital.

Outside, Bruce's entire crew stood near the door, their faces a mixture of disbelief and resignation. The thick, dark stain of Warren's blood still pooled on the floor of the Imperial Hotel, a grim reminder of how quickly things could spiral in this unforgiving land.

The air was thick with the kind of tension that only came when a situation was about to reach boiling point. The sharp, rhythmic sound of boots on the dusty floor filled the bar as a uniformed officer approached, his heavy steps betraying the years of dealing with the outback's roughest. He was a man of solid build, his face carved from sun and hardship, the kind of man who had seen more brawls, drunken rages, and hard men than most would encounter in a lifetime.

He stopped just short of the group, his gaze sweeping over the scene, sharp and calculating. His hand instinctively rested on his belt, fingers brushing against the worn leather of his holster.

"All right, lads," he said, his voice a gravelly authority that carried weight. "Someone want to tell me what the bloody hell just happened?"

The crew went quiet, the atmosphere thickening further. Bruce, his jaw set and his eyes hard, took a slow breath and stepped forward, his boots clicking decisively against the wooden floor.

"I saw the bloke coming at me out of the corner of my eye," he began, his voice steady despite the tension in the air. "Didn't have much time to think, just leaned back, got out of the way."

The officer's eyes flicked to Marcus, who still stood with his beer in hand, the slight tremor in his fingers betraying his nerves. His heart hammered in his chest as he nodded.

"I saw Bruce move, and before I knew it, this bloke was coming right at me. Instinct took over, I ducked."

The officer regarded them both carefully, his eyes narrowing as if weighing their words. His gaze shifted over his shoulder, briefly resting on where the lifeless body of Warren, had sprawled across the floor, leaving the blood staining of the timber beneath him.

When he turned back, the skepticism was clear on his face, a silent challenge hanging in the air between them.

"Convenient," he muttered under his breath, his voice tinged with disbelief.

Before either Bruce or Marcus could respond, a voice broke through the quiet, sharp and laced with a knowing edge.

"Yeah, and he's the prick that slashed Marcus's tyres!"

The words came from Jerry, the roustabout, leaning casually against the bar, a knowing smirk curling on his lips.

The officer's head snapped around like a whip, his gaze now scanning the group. "That right?" His voice was dangerous now, an edge of authority creeping into every word. "Which one's Marcus?"

Marcus didn't hesitate. He raised his hand slightly, the sinking feeling in his stomach only growing as every eye in the room turned toward him.

"Déjà vu," he thought grimly, the words tasting bitter in his mouth.

The officer's stare lingered on him, unblinking and assessing, before he finally spoke, his voice a quiet command.

"Walk with me."

Marcus swallowed hard, the tension in his chest like a fist gripping his heart. The officer gave him a long, measured look before gesturing toward the door.

"Outside," he said, his tone leaving no room for argument.

With a resigned nod, Marcus set his beer down on the bar, the faint clink of glass echoing in the silence. He started toward the door, the weight of the moment bearing down on him, knowing that his fate, and maybe even the fate of the others, had just shifted.

The officer followed behind, his boots firm on the wooden floor, and as Marcus stepped outside into the blazing heat of the outback afternoon, the weight of what had happened, and what was yet to come, settled heavily on his shoulders.

Marcus had been in the small, oppressive interview room for what felt like an eternity. The air hung heavy, thick with the stale scent of old paper and sweat. The chair beneath him was a hard, unforgiving slab of wood that gnawed at his back with each passing minute. His stomach growled low, an angry protest against the long hours without food. Breakfast seemed like a lifetime ago, more than twelve hours, in fact, and he felt it now, the gnawing emptiness turning his insides into a twisted mess.

He glanced at the clock again. It was late, far later than he cared to admit. It seemed like no one was even aware he was still here. He was beginning to wonder if they'd forgotten about him entirely when, finally, the door creaked open.

A man entered, his presence immediately filling the room. He was in his late forties, with the easy swagger of someone who had walked the long roads of life and lived to tell the tale. Jeans, a button-up shirt with the top few buttons undone, and a look that told Marcus this man had seen it all, cattle rustlers, barroom brawls, and far more than his fair share of bloody confrontations. His posture, relaxed yet carrying authority, marked him as someone not easily ruffled by the chaos around him.

"Marcus, is it?" the man asked, his voice low but commanding as he pulled out a chair and slid into it.

Marcus nodded, feeling the weight of those two syllables pressing down on him.

"I'm Detective Senior Constable Russell Gilbert," the man continued, leaning forward just enough to make his presence known. "Can you walk me through what happened at the pub tonight?"

Marcus swallowed hard, preparing himself for what was to come. His mind flicked over the events, ready to recount the story. But as he opened his mouth to speak, his stomach betrayed him, growling loudly. The pang of hunger twisted deep in his gut, sharper than the tension in the air.

He paused, rubbing a hand over his face. The exhaustion in his limbs seemed to settle deeper, making it harder to focus. He'd been running on nothing but adrenaline all day, and now his body was demanding something to keep it moving.

"Look, mate," Marcus said, his voice rougher than he intended. "I'll tell you everything, exactly as it happened. But I haven't eaten since breakfast, and I'm starving. I could really use something to drink."

Detective Gilbert regarded him for a long moment, his eyes sharp as he assessed Marcus's words. Then, after a beat, he nodded, his demeanour unchanged.

"No worries, Marcus," he said in a tone that held no judgment, just a calm understanding. "I'll sort something out for you. Sit tight."

Gilbert stood, his boots scraping against the floor, and left the room, leaving Marcus alone with the echo of his own thoughts.

The wait stretched on, each minute dragging by like a weight tied to his chest. His eyes flicked repeatedly to the clock on the wall, but the second hand barely seemed to move. The stale air grew thicker, his senses dulled by hunger and the oppressive silence. Another twenty minutes, then thirty, then forty passed before the door creaked open again.

This time, Detective Gilbert returned, carrying a glass bottle of Coca-Cola in one hand and a small brown paper bag in the other. He set them down on the table with a casual air, as though he'd just come from a quick errand, rather than an hour spent scrounging together what little food was available at this hour.

"Here you go," Gilbert said, his voice quiet. "Best I could do at this hour."

Marcus didn't waste a heartbeat. His hands tore at the paper bag with the urgency of a starving man, the scent of rich, peppered meat and flaky pastry rising to meet him like a long-lost friend. Nestled inside were two square meat pies, their golden crusts cool to the touch but promising sustenance all the same. Freshness be damned, right now, they were a feast fit for a king.

He cracked open the Coke with a sharp hiss, the cold fizz biting against his parched throat as he took a long, greedy gulp. The bubbles stung, but it was a welcome burn, chasing away the dust that had settled in his mouth. Without ceremony, he sank his teeth into the first pie. The thick, savoury gravy and tender meat spilled onto his tongue, the taste both familiar and glorious. Hunger made everything taste better, and right now, this was ambrosia.

He chewed quickly, swallowing the first mouthful before diving in for another, hardly pausing for breath. The second pie was gone just as swiftly as the first, reduced to nothing but a few stray flakes of pastry clinging to his fingers. He licked them clean, chased the last of the meal with another swig of Coke, and leaned back with a satisfied sigh.

It wasn't fine dining. It wasn't even fresh. But to a man running on empty, it was salvation.

As he ate, the tension in his shoulders began to ease, and he started to talk. He told the detective about the confrontation at the pub, the fast, sharp movements that had sent him stumbling back, the shock of Warren's sudden attack, and the madness that had followed. Between bites, he recounted the earlier events at Catalina Station, the tension in the air, the slashed tyres, and Warren's hasty departure under cover of night.

Gilbert listened without interruption, his face unreadable, but his eyes never leaving Marcus's. Occasionally, he would jot down a few notes, but for the most part, he simply let Marcus speak.

When Marcus finally fell silent, his mouth dry from the pie and the late hour, Gilbert leaned back in his chair. The silence stretched, broken only by the sound of the Coke bottle tapping against the table.

"Well," Gilbert said, his voice thoughtful, "that's quite the story."

Marcus simply nodded, waiting for the detective's next words. He wasn't sure what would come, but at least, with the hunger finally abated, he felt steadier, more able to handle whatever came next.

"Can I go now?" Marcus asked, a flicker of hope in his voice. "I'm staying at the Imperial with the shearing gang," he added, then after a brief pause, added, "If you need me for anything else?"

Gilbert glanced down at his clipboard, finishing his notes, then looked up at Marcus. There was a moment of quiet deliberation before the detective spoke again, his voice casual but edged with a certain finality.

"Sounds good to me," he said. "I'll just have to check with the boss first. Sit tight."

With a nod, Gilbert stood and walked out of the room, leaving Marcus alone again.

The minutes stretched on like hours. Marcus leaned back in his chair, his arms crossed, staring at the blank wall ahead of him. Fatigue began to settle over him like a heavy blanket, the exhaustion from the long day catching up with him. His eyelids grew heavy, the adrenaline of the earlier events now a distant memory.

An hour passed. Then another.

The door opened again, and Gilbert stepped back inside, his expression unreadable. Marcus knew, before the detective spoke, what the answer would be. The long delay had told him everything.

"Boss wants you to stay put for now," Gilbert said, his voice flat. "They're still interviewing witnesses. Until that's done, you're not going anywhere."

Marcus let out a slow breath, the frustration rising inside him. He wasn't under arrest, but neither was he free. The uncertainty of it gnawed at him. He rubbed his face with a weary hand, the rough stubble on his chin a reminder of how long it had been since he'd had the chance to shave.

"How long are we talking?" he asked, his voice steady but tinged with exhaustion.

Gilbert shrugged. "Could be a few more hours. Could be overnight. Hard to say."

Marcus let out a short, sharp exhale, but didn't argue. There was no point. Instead, he leaned forward, resting his forearms on the table, and gave the detective a level look.

"Overnight?" he said, disbelief creeping into his voice. "It's nearly two in the morning now... Alright," he said, resigned. "Guess I'll get comfortable, then."

Just as the words left his mouth, Gilbert spoke again, his voice colder now, as if the weight of the situation had shifted.

"Err, no," Gilbert said, his tone sharp. "You'll be going to the cells shortly."

Before Marcus could process the sudden shift, the door swung open, and a uniformed constable stepped inside.

"Ready?" the constable asked, directing the question at Gilbert.

Gilbert nodded, then turned to Marcus, his next words hitting with the force of a hammer.

"Yeah… take him down and charge him with murder."

The words struck like a rifle shot, reverberating through the room, shattering the thin thread of reality Marcus had been clinging to. For a heartbeat, the world swayed beneath him, a slow, sickening lurch that sent his thoughts careening into chaos. Murder. The word crashed against the walls of his skull, a dull, ceaseless drumbeat that drowned out every other sound.

His throat tightened, breath coming in short, shallow bursts. He felt the blood pounding in his temples, but his body refused to move. He was frozen, caught between disbelief and the raw, creeping dread that coiled around his spine like a snake.

A shadow shifted in his periphery. The constable stepped forward, his face impassive, the weight of duty making him cold, mechanical. His hand reached out, firm and unyielding.

"Turn around and put your hands behind your back."

The words were flat, emotionless.

Marcus moved like a man wading through deep water, slow and disoriented, as if the moment wasn't quite real. His arms slid behind him, the cold kiss of steel biting into his wrists as the handcuffs snapped shut. The sound echoed too loudly in his ears, ringing with the finality of a judge's gavel.

This isn't happening. This can't be happening.

But it was.

A firm grip closed around his arm, guiding him forward. His legs carried him numbly, each step heavier than the last, as if lead had settled in his bones. He wasn't resisting, he couldn't. He was too caught in the maelstrom of his own thoughts, too busy grappling with the impossible.

They passed through the corridors like ghosts, the air thick with the weight of what had just transpired. The watch house loomed ahead, stark and merciless.

Marcus exhaled sharply, forcing down the rising tide of panic.

He was about to be charged with murder.

The harsh monotony of fluorescent lights buzzed above, casting their sterile glow over the bleak grey walls of the Quilpie Police lockup. Marcus sat on the edge of the cold, hard bench, feeling the weight of the weekend press down on him like a stone. The hours had crawled by, one indistinguishable from the next, each minute dragging him deeper into a pit of helpless confusion. In just a few short hours, he would stand before the magistrate, charged with a crime he hadn't committed, the word murder hanging over him like a noose. For now, though, he was left to stew in this barren holding cell, the unfeeling hum of the lights his only companion.

This was not the first time Marcus had found himself in this place, he had sat in this very lockup before, under circumstances that should never have happened. Twice now, he had come to Quilpie with nothing but good intentions, a simple visit to his aunt and uncle, a brief respite from the grinding monotony of the past. But each time, fate had dealt him a cruel hand. Twice he had been locked behind these same bars, charged with murder, accused of crimes he hadn't even been close to committing.

As he sat there, his back pressed against the cold concrete, a gnawing sense of déjà vu gripped him. It was as though the hands of fate had twisted his path, pushing him back into this very cell with all the inevitability of a river winding back into its course. His blood ran cold at the thought of the injustice he'd faced before. But this time felt different, sharper somehow. The dread in his chest tightened as he wondered if this time, the system might fail him, what if this was it? What if there was no way out of this nightmare?

Marcus shut his eyes, trying to block out the storm of thoughts threatening to overwhelm him. This wasn't how things were supposed to be. He was supposed to be on his uncle's farm, lending a hand with the cattle, enjoying the dusty air and the simple peace of family life. Instead, here he was, caught in a trap he couldn't escape, facing a charge that felt more like a sentence than a trial.

The minutes dragged on, each one heavier than the last. The stillness of the cell pressed in on him, the walls closing in as though the very air had conspired to make him feel smaller, weaker. The what ifs tormented him, what if the system was broken this time? What if the lies stacked against him were too powerful to overcome? He clenched his fists, fighting against the rising tide of panic that threatened to drown him.

The early morning light sliced through the small, barred window, a dull grey that reflected the cold hopelessness of his situation. The sound of footsteps echoed down the hall, the familiar rhythm of police boots heavy on the stone floors. Two constables entered the cell, their faces impassive as they approached him. One of them unlocked the door with the practiced ease of someone used to this routine, the cold clink of metal ringing in the silence.

"Stand up," one of the officers said, his tone as flat and emotionless as the walls around them.

Marcus complied, pushing himself to his feet. His wrists, still sore from the tightness of the cuffs the night before, flexed as he moved. For a moment, he could feel the crushing weight of his confinement pressing in on him, but he didn't flinch. He couldn't afford to. Not now. Not when his entire future hung in the balance.

The constables made no effort to ease his discomfort, their movements swift and impersonal as they guided him toward the door. As they led him down the corridor, Marcus felt the cold bite of reality. This was it. There would be no escape until the magistrate had his say. And when that moment came, who would believe his word against the weight of the evidence they had fabricated?

A feeling of finality settled over him like a thick fog. He had faced this before. And now, it seemed, he would face it again.

"Come on, mate," one of the constables muttered, his voice as flat and emotionless as the stone walls that surrounded them. "Time to face the magistrate."

Marcus's feet felt like lead as they shuffled along the sterile hallways of the police station. Each step was a struggle, his mind spiralling with a thousand questions, none of them with answers. The future loomed before him like a dark, impenetrable cloud. The trial, the whispers of guilt, the crushing weight of the charges, he couldn't escape them, no matter how hard he tried. What if he was wrongly convicted? What if the truth was never seen? The fear of an unjust sentence clawed at him, a gnawing certainty that threatened to swallow him whole. The air felt thick with it, suffocating with each step he took.

The clang of a door swinging open echoed in the silence as they reached the small courthouse. It was a place where hope seemed to come to die, where the air was thick with formalities, where justice often bent to the will of those with power. The room buzzed with the murmurs of legal staff, the weight of expectations thick in the air. People shuffled nervously in their seats, waiting for their turn before the gavel fell. Marcus was guided toward the dock, a small wooden box that separated him from the world outside. He might have been on trial, but he felt more like an animal in a cage, with eyes on him, judging, waiting for a mistake.

The magistrate sat at the head of the room, his face stern and unreadable, his wire-rimmed glasses perched low on his nose. His gaze flicked briefly to Marcus, as though the man before him were nothing more than a name on a piece of paper, a problem to be disposed of. The magistrate turned his eyes to the pile of papers in front of him, flicking through them with the casual efficiency of someone who had seen it all before.

"Marcus Diarmuid," the magistrate's voice rang out, cutting through the silence like a knife. His words landed heavily in the room, the chill in his tone spreading through the crowd. "You stand charged with the murder of Warren Smith."

The words hit Marcus like a blow to the gut. His chest tightened, a cold sweat beading on his skin. The sound of the charge echoed in his mind, a relentless drumbeat reminding him of the nightmare that had consumed his life. Murder. It was as though the very walls of the courtroom were closing in on him, the weight of the charge pressing down on him with suffocating force. The magistrate didn't look up, didn't seem to care. He merely glanced at his papers, his voice unfeeling as he continued.

"You are hereby remanded in custody until further notice," the magistrate announced, his words a cold decree. "Your trial date will be fixed in due course."

Marcus's heart pounded in his chest, but there was no time to react. The magistrate's voice droned on, indifferent to the life he was about to ruin.

"You will be transported to the Maryborough Correctional Centre in Queensland," the magistrate continued, his voice flat as he made his final ruling. "You will remain in custody until your trial is scheduled."

The sentence hung in the air like a noose, the words slowly sinking into Marcus's bones. Maryborough Correctional Centre. The name alone felt like a prison sentence, the grim certainty of it digging into his mind. He barely heard the rest of the proceedings. His mind was already miles away, trapped in a future he couldn't escape, each moment of his life slipping further into a nightmare from which he could not wake.

Maryborough. The name hung in Marcus's mind like a distant echo, cold and unyielding. It was a place he had heard of before, a sprawling remand centre far from home, a holding pen for the innocent and the guilty alike, where men waited for trials they could neither control nor predict. Now it was a place that loomed over him, its gates closing in on his future with a finality that sent a chill down his spine.

The magistrate's gavel had fallen, and as the officer beside him gave a sharp nod, Marcus was escorted out of the courtroom. The walk from the dock to the exit was a journey in itself, each step a reminder of how far he had fallen from the man he used to be. Once, he had known the certainty of his path, clear, untroubled by the fog of confusion and fear that now clouded his thoughts. But now? Now he was lost in the waiting, adrift in a storm of uncertainty that churned inside him like a tempest.

As they moved down the sterile hallways, the air thick with the weight of bureaucracy and indifference, Marcus's mind struggled to stay focused. He couldn't afford to lose himself in panic. He had to hold on. He had to survive. Whatever lay ahead, whatever horrors he might face, he had no choice but to endure them. He wasn't the first man to be swallowed by the system, and if he was strong enough, he wouldn't be the last.

The drive to Maryborough Correctional Centre was as silent and oppressive as the journey to the courtroom had been. The van rumbled over the uneven road, its tires bumping against the asphalt as though to remind him that there was no going back. Marcus could feel the handcuffs biting into his wrists, the air from the small vent above him doing little to cool the heat rising from his skin. His thoughts were a whirlwind, but they settled with grim clarity as the van slowed, drawing closer to the looming gates of the facility.

The correctional centre appeared out of the dust and haze like a monolith of concrete and steel, surrounded by high walls crowned with coils of razor wire. It was a place built to break men, to strip them of their dignity and turn them into nothing more than a number, a mark on a ledger. Marcus's pulse quickened as the van approached the entrance, the sound of the gates clanging open and closed ringing in his ears like the final toll of a bell.

Inside, the air smelled of antiseptic and sweat, of confinement and control. The guards moved with practiced efficiency, their eyes hard and their faces blank, as though they had long ago abandoned any pretence of compassion. The sound of Marcus's boots echoed against the concrete floors as he was led through the security doors, the weight of the place settling around him like a suffocating fog. This was it. This was the reality he now faced, and there was no escape.

They directed him to a small processing room, sterile, functional, cold. A low ceiling, fluorescent lights that buzzed overhead, and the bitter taste of disinfectant in the air. A small wooden desk sat at the centre, flanked by two rigid chairs. The officers stood on one side of the desk, their eyes unreadable. Marcus sat on the other, his back stiff, his hands resting on his lap as though he could somehow make himself smaller, as though it might help him fade into the shadows.

"Name?" The question was simple, but it landed like a hammer blow.

"Marcus Diarmuid," he replied, his voice a ghost of its former strength. Hearing his name out loud again felt foreign, like he was speaking of someone else entirely.

The officer jotted it down, moved on to the next question with mechanical indifference. "Date of birth?"

Amid everything going on inside his head Marcus had to think hard, he knew what it was, he just could not put it into words, "I said,…Date of Birth!.....and I need it now. The officer was becoming impatient. Suddenly Marcus could remember.

"The second of April, nineteen thirty three. Marcus had answered, his mind foggy but functional, the words leaving his mouth without the sense of ownership they once carried. He was no longer the man he had been; each passing moment in this place chipped away at him, hollowing him out. Each question, each form, was another step deeper into a maze with no exit.

Next came the search, the intrusive process of stripping away everything that remained of his humanity. He obeyed the command without a word, shedding his clothes and standing exposed in the harsh light of the room. The chill of the air cut through him, but it was nothing compared to the chill that had settled in his bones. His clothes, his last possession of any significance, were bagged and labelled, an impersonal ritual that underscored the reality of his situation.

The prison-issued jumpsuit was grey and utilitarian, the fabric rough against his skin, a far cry from the clothes he had worn just days before. His boots were replaced with sandals, the same kind worn by every other man in this place, each step reminding him that he was no longer an individual but a part of the machine.

The officers spoke little as they carried out the process, their movements efficient, their faces impassive. There was no compassion, no understanding, only the cold machinery of a system that saw him as nothing more than another body to be processed.

A photograph was taken, his face captured in stark, unflinching detail. He looked at the camera, and for a moment, he didn't recognise the man who stared back. His eyes were dull, lifeless, the fire that once burned within him now smothered by the weight of what was happening. The man in the photograph wasn't Marcus Diarmuid; he was a shadow, a fragment of someone who had existed before.

Finally, the officers took his fingerprints, pressing each of his fingers into the ink with a sound that seemed to echo through the room. Each mark on the page was another confirmation of his identity, another confirmation of his place in the system. His name, his fingerprint, his body, all reduced to nothing more than paperwork, a record in a ledger.

"Do you have any medical conditions?" the officer asked, his voice the same as it had been throughout, monotone, indifferent.

Marcus gave the briefest of answers, listing the injuries, the minor ailments that seemed insignificant now in the face of what was coming. He could feel the weight of his life, the years of memories, the faces of those he loved, slipping further away with every passing moment.

The officer made a few more notes, and then, with a final glance, he turned and left the room. Marcus was left alone in the sterile space, the hum of the lights overhead the only sound. He sat there, his heart heavy with the knowledge that this was his life now, locked away, stripped of everything he had been. A man caught in a trap of fate, waiting for the next move in a game he had no control over.

The moment the paperwork was completed, Marcus was led down a long, dimly lit corridor, his footsteps heavy, each one echoing off the cold concrete like a distant drumbeat. The walls seemed to close in around him, narrowing the passage ahead, each step taking him further into a world he knew he might never leave. At the end of the hall, a door clanged open to reveal a small, cramped cell, a hollow, soul-sucking space that could scarcely be called a room.

Inside, the place was as barren as the life he now faced. A thin mattress lay on a metal frame, its threadbare fabric mocking his situation. A stainless steel toilet, functional but uninviting, stood against the far wall, and a sink that seemed to serve only as a reminder of his helplessness completed the sparse furnishings. Overhead, the fluorescent light buzzed, its hum a constant companion, while the air was thick with the sour stench of stale disinfectant.

The heavy metal door slid shut behind him with a sound so final, it made his heart skip a beat. A deep, resonant click echoed through the space, sealing him in. The silence that followed was suffocating, pressing in from all sides. Beyond the thick concrete walls, the prison's rhythm continued, the distant clang of doors, the occasional shout of an inmate, but inside, in this tiny, isolated world, there was only Marcus and his thoughts. A storm that swirled and churned, a confusion of fear, frustration, and a bitter sense of injustice.

He sank onto the bed, his back pressed against the cold, unforgiving concrete wall. How long would he be here? Days, weeks, months? He had no way of knowing, but one truth was now undeniable: this was the beginning of a fight he had no choice but to endure. A fight against the system, against fate, against the chains of uncertainty. He closed his eyes, shutting out the suffocating confinement, the smell of antiseptic, and the weight of his circumstances.

Why me? Why again?

The question echoed relentlessly in his mind, a thought that refused to be silenced. His chest tightened, and he stood, pacing the narrow confines of his cell, his fists clenching and unclenching at his sides. The walls seemed to close in, each step making them feel even more oppressive. There was no escape.

He wouldn't do this again. He couldn't.

Eight years. Eight brutal years spent in the hellhole that was Boggo Road, a place that stripped men of everything, hope, dignity, and life itself, locked away for a crime he hadn't committed. He had barely tasted freedom, barely begun to rebuild the life that had been torn apart, and now, this.

His hand shot up to his hair, fingers trembling as the weight of his past, the cold memory of prison, threatened to crush him. The thought of returning to those hellish walls, where noise, violence, and brutality were the only constants, made his stomach twist with terror. The suffocating sense of being forgotten, of being nothing more than a faceless body lost in a sea of lost souls, it was a fate worse than death itself.

His breath came ragged, shallow, as the walls of his cell seemed to grow tighter around him. His throat tightened, and for the first time, he questioned his strength. Could he endure it again?

"No," he whispered, his voice hoarse, raw with desperation. "No, I have done nothing wrong!"

The words fell flat against the cold stone walls, swallowed whole by the indifferent silence of the prison. His pulse hammered in his ears as the weight of his fate pressed down harder than ever before.

Just as the suffocating silence seemed to consume him, a sharp voice shattered the stillness.

"Hands through the slot!"

Marcus blinked in confusion, the command momentarily lost on him. He stood frozen, unsure of what the guard meant, his mind still reeling from the weight of his own thoughts. The officer, a burly man with a no-nonsense air, sighed impatiently, as though Marcus were wasting his time.

"Put your hands through," the guard repeated, his voice rough and clipped.

Reluctantly, Marcus complied, his hands shaking slightly as he slipped his wrists through the rectangular opening in the door. Cold steel clamped down around him with the efficiency of a machine, the handcuffs biting into his skin as the officer secured them without a second thought.

"Where are we going?" Marcus asked, his voice strained with a mix of confusion and frustration as the door groaned open. The guard stepped forward, his hand gripping Marcus's arm firmly, steering him into the corridor.

"To see your lawyer," came the curt reply, as though the answer were as routine as anything else in this grim, unforgiving place.

Marcus's heart skipped a beat at the mention of a lawyer. His mind raced. Was this a fleeting chance to fight? To cling to the hope of freedom? Or was it just another cruel illusion in a place where hope had long since died?

As the guard marched him down the long, empty hall, Marcus couldn't help but feel the cold weight of his own doubts settle over him once more. Would his lawyer be able to save him from the nightmare? Or was this yet another step in the unrelenting march toward a future already written in stone?

The hallways of the correctional facility stretched out before Marcus, an unyielding expanse of cold, sterile concrete. Thick metal doors loomed at regular intervals, each one a silent sentinel, and overhead, surveillance cameras tracked his every movement with mechanical indifference. The air was thick with the murmur of distant voices, the occasional shout or curse, the echo of a world beyond the walls, a world he could only dream of returning to.

He kept his head down, eyes fixed on the dull floor as he was ushered through a series of heavy security doors, each one a fortress, a reminder of the cage he found himself in. The sound of the doors locking behind him sent a shiver down his spine, but he remained silent, his thoughts in turmoil. Finally, they arrived at a small, windowless room, a place as devoid of warmth as the cold concrete corridors they had traversed.

Inside, the room was bare, spare, functional. A single table sat at the centre, flanked by two chairs, both empty but for the lone figure seated at one side. The man was in his late fifties, sharply dressed in a navy suit that bore the marks of fine tailoring. His hair, neatly combed and streaked with grey, matched the air of quiet authority he carried. His expression was calm, unreadable, but his eyes, those eyes, were sharp, assessing, as though already sizing up Marcus, weighing him in a moment of silent judgment.

The prison guard gestured for Marcus to step forward, and with a click, the cuffs were unlocked, the cold metal sliding away from his wrists. Almost immediately, the man in the suit leaned forward, offering a practiced, easy smile.

"Relax, take it easy," he said smoothly, extending a firm hand across the table. "I'm Barry Dowling, your solicitor."

For a moment, Marcus hesitated, his mind spinning, but instinct drove him forward, and he took the man's hand. The grip was solid, reassuring, a touch of strength amidst the uncertainty.

"My brother, Bernard, will be acting as your barrister," Barry continued, his voice steady, never betraying any hint of doubt.

Marcus frowned, still struggling to piece together the fragments of his thoughts. He had never been one for lawyers, had never been thrust into such a world. But this? This was different. This was real.

"But... but who engaged you?" Marcus asked, his voice betraying the confusion still tangled in his mind.

Barry lifted a hand, palm outward, as if to calm the storm of questions swirling in the room. "Relax, please, Marcus. Let me explain."

He exhaled slowly, forcing his racing heart to steady itself. There was no choice but to listen now.

"My eldest brother, Bruce, you've been working with him in his shearing gang recently, "

At the mention of Bruce's name, Marcus sat up straighter. "Bruce... the shearing contractor?"

"The very one," Barry confirmed with a sharp nod, though a flicker of impatience crossed his face. He glanced at the clock on the wall, his patience thinning. Time was always a luxury in places like this.

"Bruce, along with your uncle, Miles Diarmuid, has retained our firm, Dowling, Dowling & Hearst, to act on your behalf. Now, you need to confirm this arrangement by signing the agreement."

From his briefcase, Barry pulled out a thick document, sliding it across the table. Brightly coloured stickers marked the places where Marcus's signature was needed, each one a small, silent demand for his acquiescence.

"We're filing for bail this afternoon," Barry continued, his voice crisp, businesslike. "And if everything goes to plan, you'll be out of here by this evening."

Marcus stared at the papers in front of him, disbelief still clouding his mind. It was as though a weight, heavy and suffocating, had been pressing on his chest for days, weeks, months, but now, just for a moment, it seemed to lift.

"All right," he murmured, reaching for the pen Barry handed him, his hand shaking slightly.

The solicitor rose smoothly from his chair, the action fluid and efficient, like a man accustomed to getting what he wanted. As the heavy metal door groaned open, signalling the return of the prison guard, Barry's expression remained unchanged, calm, controlled, yet there was an undeniable confidence in his voice.

"I should be back to collect you within a few hours, Marcus," he said, adjusting the cuff of his shirt beneath his crisp suit jacket. His gaze met Marcus's, firm, unwavering. "Stay strong. We'll get you out."

Marcus met his eyes, searching for any trace of doubt, any sign that this was just another false hope. But Barry's confidence was unshakable. For a brief moment, the possibility of freedom felt within reach, just a fleeting glimpse of light in the darkness.

The guard stepped forward, cuffs in hand. "Hands out," he instructed gruffly.

Without protest, Marcus extended his wrists. The cold steel clamped back into place, the familiar bite of the metal serving as a cruel reminder of the walls that still held him. The guard gripped his arm, leading him toward the door.

As Marcus was guided back down the cold corridor, he cast one last glance over his shoulder. Barry stood motionless in the room, watching him leave. His expression was unreadable, but the quiet confidence in his posture was unmistakable. The door swung shut behind Marcus with a hollow, final thud, and the sound seemed to echo long after.

The walk back to his cell was longer this time, each step heavy with the weight of what he had just learned. He didn't dare allow himself to believe it yet, to hope. But for the first time since his arrest, a flicker of hope dared to light in his chest.

Now, back in the dank, suffocating cell, he pressed his forehead against the cool steel of the door. What was happening?

He had to believe. He had to trust that Barry Dowling was telling the truth. That the bail would come through. That he wouldn't be trapped in this nightmare for a second time.

Because if it didn't,

He couldn't fathom how, or if, he'd survive.

The bail order had come through with the speed of a thunderclap, striking Marcus with a mixture of disbelief and profound relief. One moment, he had been trapped within the oppressive grey walls of his cell, consumed by the weight of uncertainty and dread; the next, he stood in the sterile, fluorescent-lit corridor of the correctional facility, signing the release papers, the distant clang of metal doors ringing in his ears like a prisoner's last call.

The outside air hit him like a wave of cool, cleansing freedom. It was raw and untamed, a stark contrast to the stale, suffocating atmosphere of his cell. He inhaled deeply, the fresh night air filling his lungs, as though trying to purge the foul taste of captivity from his soul.

Barry Dowling wasted no time, his voice low and efficient as he ushered Marcus into his car. The tires hummed steadily against the dark, deserted road, the occasional flicker of headlights from distant vehicles the only sign of life in the thick stillness of the night. The world outside seemed a different place now, one where, for the first time in what felt like eternity, Marcus could exhale without fear.

Nine miles later, as the night deepened, they pulled up outside the Old Sydney Hotel in Maryborough, a humble, yet solid, establishment nestled near the railway station. Its weathered facade, worn by the passing years, stood as a testament to the enduring spirit of the town. The place looked as though it had seen countless stories unfold within its walls, stories of triumph and failure, of heartache and redemption. Marcus stepped out of the car, feeling the weight of his own story settling heavily on his shoulders, but with a flicker of hope, a fragile promise of something different.

Inside, the warm light of the dining room offered a temporary reprieve from the cold edges of his thoughts. Barry led him to a table where the scent of food filled the air, a welcome distraction after days of emptiness and stale air. Marcus cut through the crisped golden crumb of the chicken parmigiana, the knife gliding effortlessly, as if even the food was willing to offer some small comfort. The taste of tomato and melted cheese burst in his mouth, the rich flavour soothing the hollow ache in his stomach. It had been days since he had eaten properly, and the food felt like a long-lost luxury.

He paused, taking a long pull from his schooner of beer. The cold liquid slid down his throat like a river after a drought, but the sensation was fleeting. He could almost hear the thrum of danger in the background, even in this quiet sanctuary. As he wiped his mouth with the back of his hand, the weight pressing on his chest seemed to linger, refusing to be fully eased by the meal. Tomorrow, the journey would continue, train rides, long stretches of open land, the ever-present thought of the trial waiting for him. Three months. Three months until the truth would either set him free or condemn him forever.

Barry had been clear, his instructions direct and unyielding. "In the interim, you keep your nose clean," he had said, his tone sharp, unyielding. "You stay put at Stratheden. No exceptions. No town, Marcus. Not even a step outside the bounds. Do you hear me?"

Marcus had nodded, the gravity of the words sinking in with each passing second, but now, as he sat alone in the dim light of the old pub, the reality of it all pressed down on him with the force of a storm. He had agreed, but the unease in his gut only grew stronger as the beer grew weaker. It wasn't just about lying low anymore. It wasn't even about surviving the trial. It was about surviving the silence that came with it, the isolation, the fear of a misstep, the pressure to remain unseen, unheard.

This wasn't just a fight for freedom. It was a battle to prove that he wasn't the man they accused him of being, a killer. For the second time in his life, he was forced into a corner, fighting against forces far bigger than himself. And this time, Marcus knew the stakes were higher than they had ever been before.

With a final swallow, he pushed the glass aside and sat back, letting the flickering shadows of the pub's dim light settle around him. Tomorrow would bring the train, then the long ride to Quilpie, and finally Stratheden Station. Three months of waiting. Three months of keeping his head down, his hands clean, and his secrets buried.

At last, he was heading to Stratheden. The name had lingered in his mind like a ghost, a place he had tried, and failed, to reach before. His first attempt had been eight years ago, when he was a raw-boned seventeen-year-old, stubborn and reckless, desperate to carve out a life of his own. He had been turning eighteen then, on the cusp of manhood, full of fire and ambition. That dream had slipped through his fingers like dry river sand.

Now, on this third attempt, he couldn't help but wonder, would he finally make it? Or would fate, ever cruel and unpredictable, snatch it away once more?

The journey from Maryborough had been a solitary one. The early morning chill clung to Marcus as he boarded the five o'clock rail service to Brisbane, the carriage half-empty, his only company the rhythmic clatter of the train against the tracks. By the time he reached the city at eleven-thirty, he would have just enough time to switch platforms and board the long, gruelling service to Quilpie.

Barry Dowling, on the other hand, had taken an entirely different route. A late-night phone call during dinner had upended his travel plans, forcing him to abandon the train in favour of a morning flight to Brisbane. Another case required his attention, and Barry, ever the meticulous lawyer, had adjusted course without complaint.

What had started as a single nightcap after their meal had stretched into three, the easy flow of whiskey loosening their conversation. Marcus had asked the question that had lingered at the back of his mind, how had two of the three Dowling brothers found their calling in the law, while the eldest had taken a shearing blade instead of a barrister's robe?

Barry chuckled, the corners of his mouth lifting as he swirled the amber liquid in his glass, watching the whiskey catch the dim light. "Bruce was, at one time, a brilliant barrister," he said, his voice tinged with something between admiration and regret. "It's in our blood, you see. We got it from our father, he was a magistrate back when we were coming up through high school. There was never any question about it; we were all vigorously encouraged to pursue law at Brisbane University."

He took a slow sip, then exhaled. "I remember Bruce objecting every step of the way. Swore blind that he'd fail just to spite Father. But, quite the contrary, he walked out with honours. Higher marks than Bernard and me put together."

Barry leaned forward, offering Marcus an Old Port cigar, the rich aroma filling the space between them as he struck a match and lit their smokes. Marcus took his first tentative draw, the tobacco burning smooth and deep in his lungs, a warmth spreading through him.

"Bruce was accepted to the bar, rose quickly, and became a QC," Barry continued, tapping ash into a tray. "Not long after, he took a position as a prosecutor with the Queensland Government, and a damn good one, at that. Then, just like that, when his two sons reached college age, Bruce walked out. Vanished."

Marcus paused mid-draw, frowning. "Walked out? Just like that?"

Barry nodded, watching the curling tendrils of smoke drift toward the ceiling. "That's exactly how it happened. We assumed everything was fine at home. He never let on otherwise. And then one day, bang. Gone."

Marcus leaned back, rolling the cigar between his fingers. He was intrigued, drawn in by the sheer abruptness of it. "So, he just went shearing?" he asked. "I don't quite follow."

Barry let out a short laugh, shaking his head. "Nor did we. For nearly ten years, we didn't see him, only heard from him in passing. He was drifting, first through New South Wales, then up through Queensland. We figured it was during those years he learned the shearing trade. By the time we laid eyes on him again, he was a different man. Hardened, tougher, like the land itself had claimed him."

Marcus took another slow draw from his cigar, considering the story. A man who had walked away from power, wealth, and reputation, into the dust and sweat of the shearing sheds. There had to be more to it. And somehow, Marcus suspected, he wasn't done learning about Bruce Dowling just yet.

As the evening wound down, Barry leaned back in his chair, swirling the last remnants of whiskey in his glass before setting it down with a decisive clink. His sharp eyes met Marcus's across the table, the flickering light casting deep shadows across his features.

"Bernard and I will be in Quilpie next week," he said, his tone firm, leaving no room for uncertainty. "We'll set the defence strategy in motion then. In the meantime, you keep your head down, stay out of trouble."

He pushed back his chair and stood, adjusting the cuffs of his crisp white shirt beneath his jacket. "Have a safe trip in the morning, Marcus. And a good night."

With that, he turned and strode toward the exit, his footsteps measured and steady. Marcus watched him go, the scent of whiskey and cigar smoke lingering in the air. A storm was coming, he could feel it, but for now, all he could do was follow Barry's advice. Stay quiet. Stay hidden. And pray that when the time came, the Dowling's would be ready for the fight ahead.

The train lurched to a halt at Quilpie station, the hiss of steam and the clang of shifting metal echoing in the quiet morning air. As Marcus stepped onto the platform, a flood of memories swept through him, ghosts of a past he wasn't sure he wanted to face. But before he could dwell on them, a familiar figure caught his eye.

Standing tall against the rising sun, arms crossed over his broad chest, was Bruce Dowling.

Marcus blinked, taken aback. He had expected Patrick, the mysterious station hand he had yet to meet, but not Bruce.

"Bruce!" he called out, genuine surprise lighting his voice. "How good is this to have you here?"

A slow grin spread across Bruce's weathered face as he stepped forward, extending a strong, calloused hand. His grip was firm, steady, the kind of handshake that spoke of confidence and years of hard-earned experience.

"Thought I'd come myself," Bruce said, his deep voice carrying that same quiet authority that Marcus had heard in Barry's tales. "Figured you'd need a proper welcome."

Marcus exhaled, some of the tension in his shoulders easing. If Bruce was here, then maybe, just maybe, things wouldn't be as bad as he had feared.

As Marcus strode away from the station platform, the gravel crunching beneath his boots, his eyes swept the quiet township of Quilpie. The air was thick with the scent of dust and cattle, the kind of dry heat that settled into a man's bones.

Bruce's '55 Chevy stood waiting in the car park, its polished chrome glinting beneath the early sun. But as Marcus made his way toward it, his instincts prickled.

At the station's entrance, a uniformed police officer stood with a small notebook in hand, his pen moving with slow, deliberate strokes. He didn't meet Marcus's gaze, but there was no need, his presence alone was enough to send a clear message. Observed. Noted. Logged.

Bruce must have caught it too. Without looking back, he flicked open the Chevy's door and nodded for Marcus to get in. "Ignore him," he muttered, sliding behind the wheel. "Just routine. You being here in

Quilpie is part of your bail conditions. He's just making sure you've turned up where you're supposed to."

The Chevy rumbled to life, the v8 engine settling into a low, steady growl. Bruce turned to Marcus, his expression unreadable in the shadowed interior. "I've rented a place just outside town. A small acreage, quiet, peaceful. You'll be staying with me."

Marcus stiffened. "But, " He stopped himself, his pulse kicking up a notch. "I thought I was going straight out to Stratheden?" There was a sharp edge to his voice, a flicker of unease curling through his gut.

Bruce's hands tightened on the wheel, knuckles whitening slightly. "Look, young fella," he said, his tone calm but firm. "We've got a lot to go through. Barry and Bernie will be here in a few days, and we need to plan your defence properly." His eyes flicked to Marcus, a warning glint in them. "Just hang tight until we get to the house, alright?"

Marcus exhaled, forcing himself to nod. But the unease didn't fade. If there was one thing he'd learned over the years, it was that when plans started changing without warning, trouble usually wasn't far behind.

Maxwell House made a decent instant coffee, nothing fancy, but quick and easy. Bruce scooped a spoonful into each cup, the steam curling as he poured in the hot water.

"Milk?" he asked, eyeing Marcus with a quizzical look.

"Thanks," Marcus said, reaching for the sugar.

Bruce stirred his coffee, then leaned back against the kitchen counter, his expression turning hard. "The fact is," he said bluntly, "they don't want a bar of you. And they sure as hell don't want you anywhere near Stratheden."

Marcus froze, the spoon halfway to his cup. Shock hit him like a cold slap. He opened his mouth to speak, but Bruce held up a hand.

"Look," Bruce continued, his voice edged with something between understanding and impatience, "they're old. And if there's one thing I know about old people, it's that they don't like trouble." He gave a dry, humourless grin, as if trying to soften the blow. But then, his expression darkened. "They see you as a murderer, Marcus. It's as simple as that."

Silence stretched between them. The words hung heavy in the air.

Bruce let it sink in before he spoke again, his voice lower now, measured. "And to be honest… so do a lot of other people." His eyes locked onto Marcus's, steady, unflinching. "But we won't go there just yet. For now, just try to understand how your uncle and aunt must feel."

Marcus swallowed, his throat dry. He understood, alright. But that didn't mean he had to accept it.

Marcus went with Bruce to collect his brothers from the Quilpie airport, which was more of a strip really. It was a small, remote airstrip serving the western Queensland outback. It featured a simple gravel or dirt runway, typical of rural bush airstrips at the time, catering mainly to light aircraft and regional services. Infrastructure was minimal, likely just a small terminal or waiting area, a windsock for wind direction, and a basic refuelling station.

The Gooney Bird came in low over the endless Queensland scrub, its twin engines droning like a tired old workhorse. The Douglas DC-3, stalwart of the outback skies, flared slightly before bouncing once, then again, before settling onto the dusty strip in a cloud of red earth.

Bruce and Marcus stood among a handful of others, stockmen, station wives, and a lone postal worker, watching as the aircraft taxied to a stop near the squat, weathered terminal. The building, little more than a glorified shed, remained shuttered and silent on most days, springing to life only when the tri-weekly flights arrived.

"Bloody reliable old thing," Bruce muttered, lighting a cigarette as he eyed the aircraft. "TAA's been running this route for years. Mail, supplies, the odd jackaroo coming or going, hell, half the time, it's the only real link these people have with the outside world. When the wet comes, this is all there is."

Marcus nodded, watching as the door swung open and the first passengers began to disembark. There was something about the DC-3, something timeless, enduring. Like the land itself, it was built tough. And out here, that was the only thing that mattered.

Marcus met Bernard, the third of the Dowling brothers, with a firm handshake and an appraising look. Bernard was the quiet one, with a lean build that hinted at the hard, unyielding nature of a man who'd spent decades working in their rewarding legal practice. His eyes, sharp and calculating, seemed to take in everything without saying much.

The three brothers, now together for the first time in years, began their tour of Quilpie, though it felt more like a necessary reconnaissance mission than a social outing. They drove through the town's dusty streets, past weather-beaten shops and low-slung buildings, the hot sun beating down from a sky as wide and unforgiving as the land itself.

Soon, their trip had led them to the Imperial Hotel, a weathered pub that had seen better days but still served its purpose as a local watering hole, and the scene of the incident. They were hungry, thirsty, and needed to clear their heads. The air inside was thick with the smell of beer and fried food, the dim light from the old ceiling lights casting shadows on the walls.

They settled into a corner booth where thy could observe the actual location and imagine the events for a brief moment. Then the conversation shifted away from the incident and turned to lighter matters, Bruce's latest health scare, his many misadventures, and tales from the long years spent roaming the country.

Bernard chuckled softly at Bruce's stories, though there was little warmth in his expression. It was clear the brothers had been through a lot together, and apart, but the bond between them, however strained, remained unbroken.

The counter lunch arrived, roast beef, vegetables, and thick gravy that clung to the plate like the dust of the outback. It was the kind of meal that could fill a man's belly and settle his mind, if only for a moment. But none of them were truly at peace. They sat in silence, each man lost in his own world, the weight of the coming days pressing heavily on their shoulders. The air was thick with unspoken thoughts, the same way the heat of the Australian plains clung to the earth, relentless and unforgiving.

After the meal, they gathered up a few takeaway drinks, enough to last the night, and made their way to Bruce's rented house. The house, perched just outside Quilpie, was a small, modest place, but it offered a quiet refuge for what lay ahead. The brothers would spend two nights there before returning to Brisbane, the airstrip their only connection to the outside world.

Once inside the dimly lit kitchen, they took their seats around the table, the evening stretched out before them like a long road with no clear end. Bernard, ever the blunt one, was the first to break the silence. His voice, though steady, carried the weight of truth.

"In a nutshell, Marcus," he said, not meeting his eyes, "you are fucked."

The words hung in the air like a dark cloud, and for a moment, Marcus couldn't find his voice.

Bernard didn't wait for a response. He continued, laying the facts out with the precision of a man who had spent his life dealing with hard truths. "The only person who really knows, other than you, whether you're guilty or not guilty of killing Warren Smith, is Bruce. Bruce tells us you're not guilty, and we believe him. But, there's a catch. Bruce, too, has a slight doubt. Things happened so quickly, so damn fast, he doesn't have all the answers."

Marcus's heart pounded in his chest as Bernard's words sank in. He tried to focus, to hold onto the thread of hope, but it was slipping through his fingers like sand.

Bernard went on, his voice low and steady as he recounted the details Bruce had shared with them. "Bruce remembers it all too clearly. Warren Smith came at him, fists clenched, that right hand swinging. Bruce says he leaned back, just in time, as Smith rushed past him. And then, as if everything happened in the blink of an eye, Smith was diving, or falling, over the top of you."

Marcus felt his breath catch in his throat, a cold shiver running down his spine. The image Bernard painted was vivid, too real, like a slow-motion replay of a nightmare.

"Bruce said you were in a squatted position, trying to avoid him, but then you rose up as Smith's legs came level with your shoulders. And just like that, Smith's head hit the corner of the ashtray. It was over. One moment, a man alive, and the next, he was gone."

There was a long silence after Bernard's recounting. The room felt smaller, the walls closing in, and Marcus could almost feel the weight of Warren Smith's death pressing down on him. It was the kind of moment where time itself seemed to hold its breath, waiting for something, anything, to happen.

Bruce, sitting quietly across from them, finally spoke. His voice was measured, almost weary. "It wasn't meant to happen like that. None of it was."

The words hung heavy between them. There were no answers, no guarantees, only the cold, hard truth that the road ahead was going to be far from simple.

Bernard leaned forward, his voice quiet but firm, the way a man speaks when delivering a truth too heavy to ignore. "Apparently, there are three witnesses who claim they saw you rise, fast, from a squat just as Warren Smith was falling over you. And that movement, they say, is what drove him headfirst into the brass ashtray at the base of the bar."

Marcus shook his head, his jaw tight. "That's not true," he snapped. "No way in hell that happened."

Bernard's gaze didn't waver. "Prove it."

Silence. The kind that settled thick and suffocating, stretching long enough to remind them all just how deep in the mire Marcus truly was. His hands clenched into fists, then released. His mind worked furiously, grasping for something, anything, to counter the accusation. But the answer never came.

"I can't," he admitted finally, his voice barely above a whisper.

Barry exhaled through his nose, slow and deliberate. "And it doesn't end there," he said grimly. He tipped his glass, swirling the amber liquid inside before taking a measured sip. "There's the motive, Marcus. Revenge for the slashed tyres on your car." He shook his head, the movement slow, deliberate, as though he were unwillingly spelling out the inevitable. "And then, there's the precedent."

Marcus lifted his gaze sharply.

Barry met his eyes, his expression unreadable. "The death of Palmerston at the Terrace Hotel."

The room seemed to contract, the air thick with unspoken weight. Outside, the night stretched endless and silent, but inside, the past had just crashed headlong into the present, and neither was willing to let Marcus go.

Now it was Bruce's turn, and he leaned forward, his voice taking on the weight of someone who'd seen the inside of too many courtrooms. "Mate, I was once a prosecutor. A case like yours, I could let the clerk handle. The jury wouldn't even have the door to the courtroom closed before it'd swing back open with a 'guilty' verdict." He paused, his eyes dark with a sorrow that reached beyond the present moment, a weariness that spoke of battles lost long before. "This bloke here," he nodded towards his brothers, "he's like a challenge to me, but this... this is too far. Too far from any kind of challenge worth fighting."

He looked Marcus in the eye, the weight of the truth crushing, and the air grew thick between them. "When it comes to defending you, mate, there's nothing they can do. To take this case to court... it's a one-way ticket. 'Prison time', and no matter what we do, there's no escaping that."

The words landed with the finality of a hammer strike, and Marcus felt the weight of them slam into his chest, cold and brutal. It hit him unexpectedly, like a brick shattering his last hope. These men, his brothers-in-arms, the ones he'd trusted with his life... they couldn't help him. They wouldn't help him. The fight was over before it had even begun.

But then Bernard spoke, his voice steady, slicing through the silence like a lifeline thrown into a storm.

"But... we do have a plan."

The Plan

Marcus turned the plan over in his mind, again and again, each loop tightening around his thoughts like a noose. But for every way he twisted it, another hard truth came back to bite him.

Convict him? For Christ's sake, he was innocent!

He had done nothing wrong, nothing except running from that hotel room in Brisbane. That had been a mistake. Taking the man's wallet? Also a mistake. Not going to the police? Yes, another. But he had paid the price for those missteps. He had served his time, taken his punishment. That part of his life was settled.

And now, for standing in a hotel bar, enjoying a drink, and watching, just watching, as a man accidentally, by sheer misadventure, fell hard onto the sharp corner of a brass ashtray... that was supposed to be his crime? That was what they were going to hang him for?

He had asked the lawyers, pressed them, demanded answers. How could they blame him for this? How could this possibly be his fault?

And each time, all three had given him the same answer. The evidence pointed to his guilt.

Three witnesses. Three different angles. And every single one of them had sworn that it looked deliberate. Some kind of calculated move.

Each had said they saw Marcus dip low, a quick, precise motion, just as Warren Smith lunged at him. They said it looked like a practiced technique, a trick designed to send Smith stumbling forward. And then, as Smith tumbled over him, Marcus had snapped upright, driving him, headfirst, into the brass ashtray that lined the length of the bar and curved sharply at the corner.

And just like that, Warren Smith was dead.

It didn't matter what Marcus knew to be true. What mattered was what the jury would believe. And right now, they had all the proof they needed to see him swing.

Bernard fixed Marcus with a hard, unwavering stare. His voice was steady, the weight of experience pressing down on every word.

"Between the three of us, we have seventy years in Australian criminal law," he said. "And let me tell you something, Marcus, it doesn't matter one damn bit if we believe you're innocent. And we do believe it. But belief doesn't win cases. Proof does. And we don't have any."

He let that sink in before continuing. "The only reason we're convinced of your innocence is because of Bruce. He was there. He saw Warren Smith, full of rage, charging straight at him. Bruce ducked back, he didn't see what happened after that. And that's the problem. The rest of the room saw something else. And what they saw was enough to damn you."

Barry, ever the pragmatist, exhaled slowly and leaned forward. "The way I see it, our only move, the only move, is to plead self-defence. A manslaughter plea could get the charge knocked down. Maybe fifteen years. Maybe twenty. It's not good, mate, but it's better than life."

The room fell silent.

The truth of it settled over Marcus like the scorching weight of the outback sun. It didn't matter what was real. It only mattered what could be proven. And right now, proof was the one thing he didn't have.

Marcus leaned forward, his jaw tight, his voice edged with steel.

"And what is Plan B?"

Bruce didn't hesitate. "You go back to England," he said flatly, reaching for the fridge door. "When you get there, change your name. Keep your head down. The Brits won't waste much effort looking for you, and there's no way in hell an Aussie cop is flying halfway across the world to drag you back for this."

The fridge door swung shut with a dull thunk as Bruce pulled out a couple of cold beers. He cracked one open, the hiss of escaping gas filling the silence. Then he tossed the other to Marcus.

"That's it, mate," Bruce said simply. "That's your way out."

Marcus took a slow swig from his stubbie, the cold beer doing little to cool the firestorm raging in his mind. He lowered the bottle, fixing Bruce with a hard, searching look.

"And just how the hell do you expect me to get out of the country?" he asked, his voice edged with doubt. "They'll have me flagged at every bloody port."

Bruce smirked, leaning back in his chair, utterly unbothered. "That's just it, mate. They probably won't." He took a sip of his own beer before continuing. "Far as the cops are concerned, your passport expired while you were rotting in Boggo Road. They don't have a damn clue that you renewed it to sort out your bank account."

Bernard nodded. "That's right. The British Consulate isn't obliged to inform Australian Immigration about renewals, and even if the police went sniffing around, they'd hit a brick wall. It's not their jurisdiction."

Bruce grinned, tapping his stubby against the edge of the table for emphasis. "So, in theory, you could just stroll onto a Qantas Constellation flight to London and disappear into the crowd."

Silence settled between them, thick with the weight of what was being proposed.

Marcus let out a slow breath, staring at the label on his stubbie as if it held the answer to his troubles. His voice was flat, resigned. "So much for my new life in Australia. Two train rides from Brisbane to Quilpie, eight bloody years locked up in Boggo Road, and cooking for shearers at two different sheds. And now, after all that, I just turn tail and run back to where I came from, spend the rest of my life in hiding?" He scoffed bitterly. "Maybe it'd be easier to disappear here. I could work the shearing circuits, keep moving, stay ahead of trouble."

Bruce gave a short, humourless laugh. "Yeah? And how far do you think that'll get you?" He leaned forward, fixing Marcus with a knowing look. "You never even got to see your uncle and aunt. Australia's a vast place, but it's a damn hard place to hide. A foreign accent sticks out like a sore thumb. Plenty of cops in the cities, and plenty of law-abiding citizens who get a real kick out of recognising faces from wanted posters. And small towns?" He shook his head. "They're full of friendly people, but they've got long memories and sharp eyes. You'll last a few months, maybe a year if you're lucky, but sooner or later, someone will put two and two together."

Bruce took a sip of beer and set the bottle down with a deliberate clink. "No, mate. If you want to disappear, Britain's your best bet. In London, you'll walk into a pub and see a dozen different nationalities drinking side by side. No one will blink at a bloke with an accent. You change your name, keep your head down, and you'll be just another face in the crowd."

Marcus said nothing. He just stared at his beer, rolling the idea over in his mind.

After a long day of drinking and strategising with the three lawyers, good blokes, Marcus thought, and damn sharp, too, he finally accepted Plan B as the only way forward. There was no choice, not if he wanted to stay out of prison. The brothers, each with decades of courtroom battles behind them, agreed unanimously.

Before they caught their flight back to Brisbane, they hammered out the finer details. Getting to Brisbane itself would be the first challenge. The train was out. So was the plane. The local coppers would be watching every departure, making sure Marcus remained in Quilpie, just as his bail conditions demanded. Driving out, in the early hours of the morning, was the best option. Slip away unnoticed. No tickets. No records. No questions.

Once in Brisbane, he'd have to lay low for at least a month. The withdrawals from his bank account had to be gradual, draining it too quickly would raise flags. And under no circumstances could he access any bank once he was back in the UK.

"Don't grow a beard," Bernard had warned. "Don't dye your hair. Don't change a damn thing about your passport photo. You don't want some nosy customs officer jotting down notes when you check in."

Marcus had time, just under three months before he was due in court. The trick was patience. Most bail-jumpers made their move early, right after being charged, when the police were expecting it and watching closely. But as the court date drew nearer, the watchful eyes would grow dull, the urgency would fade. That was when Marcus would vanish.

Marcus had said his farewells to Barry and Bernard at the airport, shaking their hands with the quiet understanding that this might be the last time they ever saw each other. He'd also clocked the local coppers loitering near the terminal, their eyes sweeping the comings and goings with casual interest, too casual. They were watching. Not him specifically, not yet, but they were waiting for any excuse to tighten the noose.

Back at the house, he gave his FC Holden a thorough once-over, checking the oil, the tyres, the fuel. It had to be ready. There would be no second chances. Satisfied, he settled into the rental, knowing it would be his hideout for the next month or so. A waiting game.

Bruce was leaving the following morning, heading back to his shearing gang, back to normal life. For Marcus, normal life was already a distant memory. That night, over a quiet farewell dinner, they didn't speak much of the plan. There was nothing left to say. Bruce had done all he could. Now, it was up to Marcus.

Finding Joseph Rascher's number in the Brisbane telephone directory had been easy. Now, standing in a cramped, graffiti-scrawled phone booth near Joseph's shop, Marcus fed coins into the slot and dialled. He hadn't been able to call from Quilpie, too risky. If the police were listening in, it could have ended everything before it had even begun.

The phone rang twice before a familiar voice answered. It was Hilda, Joseph's wife. The warmth in her tone was instant, unmistakable. He was welcome. More than welcome. When he hesitantly suggested staying for three days, her excitement only grew. And when Joseph came on the line, his old friend's pleasure at hearing from him was just as genuine.

That night, over steaming mugs of coffee at the Rascher's modest home, Marcus laid it all out. The Imperial Hotel, the fight, the fall, the accusation. He watched as their faces shifted from shock to disbelief, then finally to sadness. They understood. Of course, they did. And when he told them he was leaving, going back to England, perhaps forever, Joseph sighed, shaking his head.

"We had high hopes for you here, Marcus," he said.

Marcus nodded, swallowing hard. "So did I."

The three days spent with Joseph and Hilda had been a whirlwind of quiet but urgent preparation. Every morning, he set out early, moving between different bank branches across Brisbane, withdrawing precisely three thousand pounds at a time. By the end of it, he had secured the bulk of his funds, leaving just under seven hundred pounds in the account, enough to avoid raising any unwanted curiosity.

The Qantas ticket had been another stroke of foresight from the Dowling brothers. A return fare, London and back, for the princely sum of £585. On paper, it made perfect sense. If, by some ill twist of fate, he was recognised, there would be no immediate cause for alarm. He was, after all, just another traveler set to return to Australia.

Marcus had to admit, it was a clever touch. A lifeline hidden in plain sight.

The moment had arrived with a quiet, almost inevitable finality. Marcus stood at the gate, his flight to London just moments away. Joseph and Hilda had driven him to Brisbane Airport in the FC Holden, a car he had passed on to them despite their insistence on refusing it. They had, however, accepted it with the understanding that should he ever return, it would be waiting for him. A small piece of home, should he need it again.

As Marcus boarded the flight, the second person to board, everything seemed to fall into place. He found his seat, number eighteen, of thirty, and the plane was nearly full. Settling into the cramped space, he ordered a scotch and soda, savouring the fleeting comfort before the long journey ahead. The flight to London would stretch on for 63 hours and 45 minutes, a span of time and distance that felt surreal.

The woman seated next to him eyed him curiously. "Is this your first time going to Britain?" she asked, her voice casual but probing.

Marcus, his mind momentarily distracted by the long haul ahead, replied smoothly, "No, I'm returning after spending eight years in Queensland."

The woman arched a perfectly sculpted brow, amusement flickering in her eyes as a knowing smirk curled the corner of her lips. "Going backwards, then," she said, her voice laced with dry humour.

Marcus offered a polite smile but said nothing. His silence, however, did not mean indifference. The words echoed in his mind, bouncing off the walls of his thoughts like a bullet refusing to rest. Going backwards. The more he turned them over, the more they took root, growing like a tangled vine around his resolve.

Because she was right. Damnably right. He was going backwards. Back to England. Back to the grey, soulless cold. Back to a life he had spent years trying to escape. He had no one there. No future, no warmth, no fire. What kind of man chooses exile over the freedom of a land like this? Even gaol time in this country seemed preferable to the drudgery that awaited him across the sea.

A decision formed, swift and absolute. He turned to the woman, meeting her gaze with sudden clarity.

"Excuse me, please," he said.

Before she could react, he was already moving. He stepped past her, out into the aisle, striding toward the front of the aircraft. And then, without hesitation, Marcus walked off the plane, leaving England, and the past, behind him. Again.

The Revision

The calls of the hostess and the ground staff rang out behind him, urgent and insistent, but they might as well have been the cries of gulls lost in the wind. He heard them, but he did not listen. His mind had already severed the tether to that world, to that fate.

Somehow, without fully recalling the steps that had brought him there, he found himself outside the terminal, the heavy tropical air wrapping around him like a cloak. A taxi idled at the curb, the driver watching him with the practiced indifference of a man who had seen it all before.

Marcus didn't hesitate. His hand found the door handle, his body moved on instinct, as if following a path carved by destiny itself. He slid into the back seat, the worn leather creaking beneath him.

"Joseph's shop," Marcus said, his voice firm, the decision settled in his bones.

The taxi driver turned in his seat, his expression flat but laced with curiosity. "I give up, mate. Who the bloody hell is Joseph?"

For a brief moment, Marcus blinked, thrown off by the question. Then it hit him. The street name. That was what mattered.

"Ballow Street," he said, his mind snapping into focus. "Ballow Street, Fortitude Valley."

The driver gave a short nod, as if this made far more sense, and with a flick of his wrist, he threw the car into gear. The taxi lurched forward, rolling away from the terminal and merging into the pulsing veins of the city beyond.

Marcus let out a slow breath, his body sinking into the seat as the airport, and all it stood for, slipped away behind him. The past, the cold, the emptiness of England, all of it receding into nothingness. He had broken away.

His bag? He had not given it a thought. It was still on the aircraft, forgotten in the overhead compartment. But now, as his mind circled back to it, he realised it didn't matter. He would need nothing where he was going. Gaol awaited him, and in gaol, a man had no use for baggage.

Hilda answered the insistent knocking at the back door of the workshop, expecting a delivery or a late customer. But as she swung it open, her breath caught in her throat. Standing before her, flesh and blood, was Marcus.

For a long moment, she simply stared. Only minutes ago, she had heard the distant roar of an aircraft overhead and imagined Marcus aboard it, flying away, lost to them forever. And yet, here he was.

Joseph emerged from the workshop, wiping his hands on an old rag, and when his gaze landed on Marcus, the colour drained from his face. He had long since resigned himself to never seeing his old friend again. Yet Marcus stood there, as solid as the ground beneath their feet, as if he had stepped out of a forgotten past.

They moved to the kitchen, where the heavy silence between them was filled with the clink of coffee cups, the slow pour of schnapps, and the weight of unspoken questions.

Finally, Marcus exhaled, his voice calm, resigned. "So simple," he murmured, rolling the glass between his fingers. "I'm going to face the music. Serve whatever sentence they impose. Death or life imprisonment, it makes no difference." He looked up, meeting Joseph's gaze, his expression devoid of fear. "I've thought it through. This is the right way. The only way."

A heavy stillness settled over the table. The weight of his words pressed into the room like a gathering storm.

"Your room is still made up, just as you left it this morning," Hilda said with a smile, though there was something unreadable in her eyes. "Good to have you back." She let out a soft laugh, but Marcus could hear the tension beneath it.

He only nodded, offering nothing in return. The decision had been made. There was nothing left to discuss.

Tomorrow at ten, he would stand before the court. Face the judge. Face his fate.

Joseph pulled the FC to a stop at the front steps of the courthouse. The engine idled, a low, steady growl beneath the tension that hung between them. He turned to Marcus, his brow furrowed with concern.

"Are you sure you don't want me to come in with you?" he asked, his voice gruff.

Marcus had one hand on the door handle, the other resting on his knee. He shook his head, a slow, deliberate motion. "No!" he said firmly, then, with a sudden grin, added, "But I'll call you if they let me off!"

His laugh was sharp, cutting through the thick morning air. The door swung shut with a solid thud.

Joseph watched as Marcus strode toward the courthouse steps, his posture straight, his pace steady. He didn't look back.

The court receptionist barely glanced up as Marcus approached, busy assisting someone else. When it was his turn, the man gave him a perfunctory nod.

"How can I help you, sir?"

Marcus met his gaze evenly. "I'm due to appear in court this morning at ten o'clock, but I don't really know where to go."

The attendant flipped open a ledger and skimmed through the pages. "What are you appearing for, sir? Traffic offence?" he asked without much interest.

"Murder," Marcus said, his tone as casual as if he were ordering a cup of coffee.

The receptionist's hand froze mid-turn. His eyes flicked up, locking onto Marcus, searching his face as if waiting for a punchline. When none came, he hesitated, then cleared his throat.

"Name?"

Marcus gave it, and as soon as the man found it in the records, his entire demeanour changed. His back stiffened. His fingers gripped the ledger a little tighter.

"Where's your solicitor? Your barrister?" His voice had lost its detached professionalism, replaced by something closer to disbelief. "You should already be in the courtroom with them."

Marcus only shrugged. He had made his decision. There was no need for lawyers now.

The receptionist was already on the telephone, speaking in hushed but urgent tones, while Marcus stood waiting with quiet patience. It was an odd feeling, being here like this, under no guard, no escort. He had walked in of his own free will.

Of course, he realised now, the Dowling legal team would never have turned up today. They had known he was absconding his bail, had likely written him off the moment they discovered he had vanished. Well, he thought grimly, that's not true anymore.

A tall, thin man in court robes strode into the reception area. The clerk of the court. He barely glanced at Marcus before gesturing for him to follow.

"This way," he said briskly, leading him down the dimly lit corridor to the courtroom. The chamber was not yet in session, the judge's chair still empty, the rows of seating devoid of the usual audience.

The clerk pulled back a heavy wooden chair and motioned for Marcus to sit. The accused's seat. A place he had once vowed never to occupy.

"Where is your counsel, sir?" the clerk asked, his voice edged with professional curiosity.

Marcus met his gaze without hesitation. "I have none," he said simply. "The lawyers responsible for my bail are no longer retained by me."

The clerk hesitated, his expression betraying the first flicker of uncertainty. He glanced toward the heavy doors that led to the judge's chambers, then back at Marcus.

"I see," he said at last. He straightened his robes, clearing his throat. "I will advise His Honour."

The courtroom was heavy with expectation as Marcus Diarmuid took his seat in the dock, his posture straight, his expression unreadable. He had entered this chamber alone, unrepresented, defiant in his decision to face the charges without the shield of legal counsel. The murmurs of the gathered spectators, journalists, legal observers, and the curious public, were hushed as the judge entered, his black robes flowing behind him as he took his place at the bench.

"Mr. Diarmuid," the judge began, peering down at him over the rim of his spectacles, "you stand before this court charged with the murder of Warren Smith. How do you plead?"

Marcus stood, his voice steady. "Not guilty, Your Honour."

A ripple of surprise swept through the courtroom, though it quickly stilled beneath the judge's stern gaze. He exhaled slowly, regarding Marcus with the kind of patience reserved for men he deemed foolish.

"I must strongly advise against this course of action," the judge said, his voice measured. "You are facing a charge that carries the gravest consequences. The complexities of a murder trial require skilled legal expertise. I will not have this court descend into chaos due to your lack of representation."

"I understand the risks," Marcus replied evenly. "But I will defend myself."

The judge's expression darkened. He turned his gaze to the prosecution table, where the Crown's barrister sat, his case meticulously prepared, his witnesses ready to be called. A man who would wield the full force of the law against Marcus without hesitation.

The judge sighed, then struck his gavel against the bench. "This is highly irregular and, in my view, entirely inadvisable. I will not allow a man to stand trial for his life without competent legal representation. Therefore, I am ordering a two-day adjournment so that counsel may be appointed for you, Mr. Diarmuid. You may refuse their services at a later date if you so choose, but I will not allow these proceedings to continue without ensuring you have been given every opportunity for a proper defence."

Marcus clenched his jaw. He had anticipated resistance, but he knew arguing would be futile, for now.

"Very well," he said.

The judge nodded, his decision final. "Court is adjourned. We reconvene in forty-eight hours."

The gavel struck once more, echoing through the silent chamber. Marcus was led from the dock by two guards, his fate still hanging in the balance.

Marcus spent the rest of the day in the Brisbane watch house, the walls pressing in on him as he waited. Hours passed with nothing but the dull murmur of voices from the other cells and the occasional clatter of boots on the concrete floor. The cold steel bench beneath him was unforgiving, but Marcus had long since learned to ignore discomfort.

A meal was slid through the slot that evening, something vaguely resembling stew and a chunk of dry bread. He ate mechanically, neither enjoying nor detesting it. Morning came, bringing another meal of the same uninspired fare. Still, no lawyer had appeared.

It wasn't until nine-thirty that a barrister finally arrived. A tall, thin man with neatly combed silver hair and a well-tailored suit stepped into the holding area. He carried himself with the confidence of someone accustomed to command, though there was a hint of reluctance in his eyes, as if he would have preferred another case, any other case, besides this one.

"I'm Nigel Sutcliffe," the barrister announced, glancing at Marcus with the critical gaze of a man sizing up a thoroughbred at auction. "I've been appointed by the court to represent you."

Marcus said nothing.

Sutcliffe took this as his cue to continue. "Now, you do have the right to object and request another barrister, should you feel I am unsuitable. The court may assign someone else, though, let me be frank, I doubt you'll get a better option on such short notice."

His tone was clipped, businesslike. A man doing his duty but not wasting unnecessary energy on pleasantries.

Marcus leaned back against the cold wall, arms crossed. "And what if I say I don't want any barrister at all?"

Sutcliffe exhaled sharply, as if he'd been expecting the question. "Then you'll be making a damn foolish mistake. But, as I understand it, you've already made a few of those." He folded his arms and raised an eyebrow. "So, what's it to be?"

Marcus studied Nigel Sutcliffe carefully, his eyes cold and unwavering. He had no intention of letting the barrister see any weakness, but he couldn't help but feel a pang of frustration at the man's blunt approach.

"I just don't want to waste your time," Marcus said slowly, his voice low, each word measured.

Sutcliffe regarded him with a faint smirk, as if he'd expected that answer. "Allow me to be the judge of that, Marcus," he replied sharply, his tone one of quiet authority. "Now, let's get down to business, shall we? You've stated your plea as 'Not Guilty,' but let me tell you, considering the evidence, that might not be the wisest course of action. I read the brief yesterday." He flipped open a leather-bound folder and tossed it lightly onto the table between them, his fingers tracing the edges of the documents within.

"Three witnesses," he continued, not giving Marcus a chance to respond. "Not one, not two, but three witnesses who have solemnly sworn they saw you physically pushing the deceased into that brass ashtray. You understand the implications of that, don't you? The details of their statements are damning, to say the least." Sutcliffe's gaze hardened, the full weight of his words sinking in like a stone.

He leaned forward, his fingers steepled together in front of him, eyes narrowing. "Now, what do you say, Marcus? Shall we change your plea before we find ourselves drowning in this mess?"

Marcus leaned forward, his eyes locked on Nigel Sutcliffe's, a quiet resolve in his voice as he spoke.

"I'm telling you straight, Sutcliffe," he began, the rough edges of his accent thickening, "I'm not guilty. Not now, not ever. And nothing you or anyone else says will change that plea." His gaze sharpened, a flicker of something fierce burning beneath his calm exterior. "But I'll tell you this, I've got a statement to make. Not for you, not for anyone else, but for the court and the jury. Just for the record, you understand?"

He paused, allowing the weight of his words to settle between them. The room, the air, everything seemed to still in that moment, the tension taut as a drawn bowstring.

"I'm not backing down," he continued, his tone steady, unwavering. "I'll face whatever they throw at me. I'll submit to whatever ruling they hand down. But I'll stand tall, and I'll have my say. That's all."

Nigel Sutcliffe looked at Marcus, his eyes narrowing as he weighed the man's words. There was no mistaking the sincerity in Marcus's voice. This was a man who had made up his mind, who would not be swayed by anything or anyone. And if nothing else, Nigel could respect that.

"Well then," he said after a beat, his voice cool but acknowledging, "we'll get your statement ready. But you're going to have to trust me, Marcus. This isn't going to be easy. But you've made your decision, and we'll see it through."

Marcus nodded once, his jaw set, eyes never leaving Sutcliffe's. This was his fight now, and he would fight it with everything he had. No matter the outcome.

Supreme Court

The heavy wooden doors of the courtroom groaned open as Marcus Diarmuid entered, flanked by his barrister, Nigel Sutcliffe. The scent of polished wood and the hum of anxious voices filled the air, but Marcus held his ground, his back straight, his steps measured. He had been here once before, but now, the weight of the day felt heavier, the outcome uncertain. The audience, the jury, and the judge all awaited his next move, and Marcus was ready to make his stand.

Nigel Sutcliffe, his briefcase in hand, walked beside him, offering only a brief nod of encouragement. As they took their seats, the judge, a stern figure whose gaze had already swept across the courtroom, called the court to order with a sharp rap of the gavel.

"Mr. Diarmuid," the judge intoned, his voice deep, commanding, "you are charged with the murder of Warren Smith. How do you plead?"

Marcus met the judge's gaze without flinching. His voice, when it came, was steady, unwavering.

"Not guilty, Your Honour," he stated, the words resounding through the room.

The judge nodded, motioning for the proceedings to continue, and it was at that moment that Marcus, with a quiet determination, stood up. The murmurs in the courtroom slowly died down as all eyes shifted to him. Even Sutcliffe, who had been watching the proceedings with his usual detached professionalism, now focused his attention on Marcus.

"Your Honour. The court, members of the jury," Marcus began, his voice calm but strong. He paused for a moment, gathering his thoughts as the weight of the moment pressed upon him. "I wish to, attempt, to explain the unusual circumstances that bring me here today."

He scanned the faces of the jury, noting the mix of skepticism and curiosity in their eyes. He could not afford to back down now. This was his only chance.

"The events that led me to stand before you today began long before any of you knew of me, long before my name became a whispered thing in this courtroom. It began in London, on the day I boarded the ship that would carry me to distant shores," he continued, his voice growing in strength with every word. "I had come to a decision, one that I believed was right for me, and so I left everything behind, my life, my ties, everything I thought I knew."

Marcus paused, his mind retracing the path that had led him to this very place. He took a deep breath, his eyes never leaving the jury as he continued, "I arrived in Brisbane, a man set on his course, eager to leave the past behind. I was a stranger in this land, unfamiliar with its people, its ways. But even so, I was drawn to it, as though the very air of this place called to me. But then, as fate would have it, I was thrust into a situation I had never expected. And in that moment, I made a choice. A choice that would, as you can see, bring me here."

The courtroom was silent, the air thick with tension. Marcus's words seemed to hang in the air like smoke, swirling and shifting with every passing moment.

"I did not intend for things to go as they did. I did not intend for anyone to be harmed, especially not Warren Smith. The evidence you have heard, the witness statements, are not the whole truth. They do not account for the truth of that night, the confusion, the chaos. The circumstances surrounding that event are far more complicated than they appear. I stand here today, not because of the man I am accused of killing, but because of the misunderstanding that led to his death. And for that, I am truly sorry."

Marcus's words echoed through the courtroom. He stood tall, his gaze unwavering, as he addressed the jury. He could see the flickers of doubt, the flickers of humanity in their eyes as they began to process his statement.

After a long moment of silence, the judge spoke, his voice grave.

"Mr. Diarmuid, the court acknowledges your statement. We will now proceed to the jury deliberations."

The jury was called to retire, and as they exited the courtroom, the tension in the air thickened, like a storm brewing on the horizon. Marcus remained seated, his hands clasped before him, his heart pounding in his chest. There was nothing more to be done now, nothing more to say. His fate lay in their hands.

Minutes stretched into hours as the jury deliberated, but finally, the doors opened, and they returned. The foreman, a stout man with a weathered face, stood up, his voice steady but firm.

"Your Honour, we have reached a verdict."

The courtroom fell silent once more.

"Not guilty," the foreman declared.

A wave of disbelief and relief washed over Marcus, and he felt his chest tighten as the weight of the verdict sank in. Not guilty. The words were like a lifeline, pulling him from the abyss.

The judge nodded, acknowledging the jury's decision, and the gavel struck down with a finality that echoed through the room.

"Case dismissed," he said, and just like that, the ordeal was over.

As Marcus stood and walked out of the courtroom, his heart still racing, he felt a sense of freedom, a freedom he had not known in months. The journey had been long, and the road had been filled with uncertainty. But in that moment, he knew he had won.

Nigel Sutcliffe clasped Marcus's hand firmly, his grip sincere, his expression one of admiration and respect. "Marcus," he said, his voice carrying the weight of genuine pride, "today you have won a case beyond all odds. Against the counsel of the most seasoned minds within the Queensland law faculty, you stood your ground. You have proven yourself to be a man of rare conviction and wisdom. I sincerely congratulate you."

He paused for a moment, his eyes narrowing slightly as he spoke again, this time with a slight smile, as though considering the future. "And I would add, Marcus, that should you wish to pursue a career within law, our chambers are open to you. You have the mind for it, and more importantly, the courage to walk a difficult path. A quality few possess."

Marcus took a moment before replying, his expression unchanged, though there was a quiet gratitude in his gaze. "Thank you, Nigel, for your kind words," he said, his voice calm, yet laced with a depth that reflected his understanding of the journey. "But, let me make one thing clear. The words I spoke in that courtroom, to the judge, the jury, and the court... they were not a performance. They were from my heart, unembellished, without shade or adjustment. The truth, as I saw it, and as it has always been."

Nigel regarded Marcus thoughtfully, a flicker of understanding passing between them. The barrister, a man well-versed in the art of persuasion, had seen many cases, many victories, but this one, Marcus's unyielding pursuit of truth, had resonated in a way few could truly comprehend.

"Well said," Nigel responded, his voice low and filled with respect. "The law is an instrument of truth, but truth, my friend, is often the hardest thing to uphold. You've done what many could not. I'm honoured to have represented you, though I suspect your destiny lies in different hands."

Marcus offered a brief nod, the fire of conviction still burning within him. "Perhaps," he said simply, before turning toward the doors, his mind already drifting to what lay ahead, and to the uncertain horizon before him. Marcus leaned forward, his eyes locked onto Nigel with quiet intensity. "Just one thing, Nigel. Why didn't the Dowling Brothers take the same approach I did? They could have easily done what you've done, pushing for a fugitive statement to be heard. Why didn't they?"

Nigel exhaled, running a hand over his jaw. He was calm, measured, as though explaining the laws of nature rather than the cutthroat realities of the courtroom. "It's called 'reputation,' Marcus," he said, his voice smooth, unwavering. "The beak could have just as easily rejected my motion as he accepted it. And then what? Those boys sit very high on the legal ladder, and they weren't about to risk a blemish on their standing for something that could go either way."

He leaned back slightly, studying Marcus with a look that suggested he was measuring his words carefully. "In my personal opinion, I don't believe Barry or Bernard were ever truly interested in taking your case. If you ask me, and I'm just speculating here, it was Bruce who pushed them into it."

Marcus frowned. "Bruce?"

Nigel nodded, his gaze unwavering. "Yes. I think Bruce is a real mate, the kind of man who was willing to put himself on the line for you, even when his own brothers wouldn't. And, if I may say so, I don't think you've fully grasped just how much he's done for you."

And with that, he walked away from the courtroom, leaving behind a case, a victory, and a future that no one, not even the most seasoned barrister, could predict.

As Marcus walked from the courthouse, his boots striking the pavement with a steady rhythm, his mind was a maelstrom of thoughts. The weight of what had just transpired, the verdict, the relief, the untold story of his life in those harrowing months, pressed down on him like the hot winds of the Kalahari. He could scarcely believe that the decision to stand and fight, to face the music head-on, had come to him in the quiet solitude of the aircraft bound for London.

The image of himself, a fugitive, haunted him like a shadow on the edge of his vision. Had he stepped off that plane in London, a hunted man, would he have survived? The thought of becoming a hunted animal, chased by the relentless forces of the law, gnawed at him. In London, there would be no refuge. There would be no escape from the reputation of a murderer, branded in the eyes of all who crossed his path. What would he have done? Where would he have gone? His world, already shattered, would have cracked further beneath the weight of his choices.

And yet, here he was, alive, free, and not shackled by the lies or the chains of his own making. He had chosen this path. Chosen to fight for his innocence. It had been a gamble, a desperate move, but one that had paid off. Now, with the court's ruling behind him, Marcus could not help but feel a faint glimmer of hope stir deep within him, like the first light of dawn creeping over the horizon of a long, unforgiving night.

The streets of Brisbane stretched before him, unfamiliar yet full of possibility. He had been given a second chance, an opportunity to rebuild, to reclaim what was once lost. The question now was where to go, what to do with the life that still lay ahead of him.

But for the first time in what felt like an eternity, Marcus allowed himself a breath, slow and deep, as the sound of his footsteps echoed through the empty streets. He would walk this path, no longer bound by the mistakes of the past, but by the hope that perhaps, just perhaps, there was a future still waiting for him.

Marcus stepped onto the sunlit street, the heat shimmering off the pavement, and only then did the truth strike him like a hammer blow, he had nothing. No money, no watch, no means to even buy himself a meal. Three days ago, the police had stripped him of everything when they took him into custody, and now, though free, he was as good as a beggar on the streets.

He turned back, pushing through the heavy courthouse doors into the foyer, his keen eyes sweeping the grand space. It was near empty now, the energy of the trial already dissipating like dust in the wind. Nigel was gone. The judge, the jury, the clerks, even the spectators who had sat in silent judgment of him, vanished.

For a long moment, he stood there, his hands resting lightly on his hips, considering his next move. He had fought for his life in that courtroom, against odds that would have broken lesser men, but now, standing here with nothing but the clothes on his back, he felt the weight of the world settle upon him once more.

He exhaled sharply. No time for self-pity. He needed to retrieve his belongings. And there was only one place to do that, the police station.

Having no idea in which direction the police station was as he had been transferred from the station to the courts through a tunnel, thinking that there may be a shortcut that he could take he approached the same person at the reception that he had spoken to when he had first arrived at the court on the first day.

"Excuse me, could you tell me where the police station might be?" he asked the man politely.

"Directly behind the court house sir." The man said without interest.

"I thought that I might be able to access it through the court house?" Marcus added. But the man just shook his head rather than answer.

Marcus stepped back from the reception desk, pressing his lips together in frustration. The man's indifference was palpable, his disinterest almost offensive. It was the same clerk who had eyed him with suspicion on his first day here, as if already convinced of his guilt.

Now, Marcus was a free man, yet the man's demeanour had not changed.

He exhaled, pushing down the irritation that threatened to rise. No use in wasting time on bureaucratic arrogance. He turned on his heel and strode towards the courthouse entrance, stepping out into the glare of the midday sun.

The police station was behind the courthouse. That much he knew now. What he did not know was how to reach it. The tunnel through which he had been transferred from the station to the court had given him no sense of direction, just the cold, damp passage of the underground, the weight of shackles on his wrists, and the silence of men who had already judged him before the verdict had been read.

Now he was on his own, and he had no choice but to find his own way. Squinting against the sunlight, he took a deep breath and set off, determined to reclaim what was his.

The young constable at the reception desk carried himself with the crisp discipline of his uniform, yet there was an easy politeness in his manner. Marcus met his gaze squarely as he explained his situation, his voice measured but firm.

"I was remanded here while on trial," he said. "The court has discharged me. I've come to reclaim my personal effects, taken by the police when I was first brought in."

The constable nodded, his expression unreadable as he reached for the necessary records.

The young constable barely glanced up from his ledger as Marcus stepped forward. His voice was flat, uninterested.

"Your name?"

There was no courtesy, no "sir," just the blunt mechanics of officialdom. Marcus noted it but let it slide. There were more important battles to fight.

"Marcus Diarmuid," he answered evenly.

The constable dragged a finger down the list of names on the logbook, then tapped the page with finality. "And a description of the items?"

Marcus spoke with the clarity of a man who had counted his belongings a hundred times in his head. "A Tissot watch, a wallet with twenty-seven pounds, a Bank of New South Wales passbook, my driver's license, and a money belt containing nine thousand." He paused briefly before adding, "Oh, and a boarding pass for a Qantas flight."

The constable's pen hovered for a second before scratching across the paper. He did not look up, nor did he question the sum of money, though Marcus saw the slight twitch of his jaw. Without another word, he muttered, "Just a moment," and disappeared through an interconnecting door.

Marcus stood alone at the counter, the silence stretching out before him. A clock on the far wall ticked methodically, a measured reminder of time lost. Then, the door swung open again, and the constable reappeared, not alone.

A stocky sergeant entered, his polished boots clicking against the floor. He held Marcus's belongings in one hand, the weight of authority in the other. But something was missing. The money belt.

Marcus's eyes flickered over the items before looking up. The sergeant met his gaze, expression unreadable. The moment stretched between them, taut as a drawn bowstring.

The sergeant's gaze was steady, probing, as he gestured toward the door behind the counter. His tone was firm but not unkind.

"Just a few questions for you. Please come through and take a seat."

Marcus followed him into a small office adjoining the reception area. The room was spartan, functional, grey walls, a metal filing cabinet, and a desk that had seen years of use. A single wooden chair stood opposite the sergeant's own. Marcus lowered himself into it as the officer took his seat, fingers laced together on the desk before him.

"I'm Sergeant Neilson. Geoff Neilson," he said, his voice even. "Now, tell me, why were you carrying so much money?"

Marcus met the man's gaze without hesitation. "I was leaving the country, but I changed my mind."

Neilson considered that for a moment, his expression unreadable. Then, leaning back slightly, he asked the next question, his tone sharpening.

"Did you declare the money you were carrying?"

Marcus's instinct was to answer with a simple no, but then his mind flicked to the boarding pass, still stapled to his ticket. His ticket was for a return flight. He straightened slightly in his chair.

"No, because I was returning on another flight."

That gave the sergeant pause. Marcus watched as the man's brow furrowed slightly, the flicker of doubt creeping in.

Neilson wasn't done yet. His fingers drummed lightly on the desk before he continued. "Where did you get the money? Where did it come from?"

Marcus did not flinch. "From the Bank of New South Wales. The withdrawals are all recorded as transactions in my passbook."

For the first time, the sergeant's features relaxed, just slightly. He exhaled through his nose, perhaps annoyed that the interrogation had yielded nothing questionable. Without another word, he reached for the money belt, along with the rest of Marcus's belongings, and slid them across the desk.

"Have a good day," Neilson said at last, a faint trace of reluctance in his voice.

Marcus took the money belt and fastened it securely beneath his shirt, then picked up his wallet and watch. Rising from his seat, he gave the sergeant a brief nod before stepping out of the office and into the fresh air beyond.

He was a free man. And enjoying a feeling that he hadn't for quite a while. No more, surely no more, he thought as he hailed a cab for Ballow Street, Fortitude Valley.

Neither Hilda nor Joseph had any inclination to go out and revel in Marcus's so-called victory. It was a victory, yes, but one that should never have required a fight in the first place. It had been an injustice, in its purest form,

Instead, Hilda had a different idea. "We'll celebrate at home," she had declared, her tone leaving no room for debate. "It'll be safer, more comfortable, and I'll cook a proper feast on the barbecue." There was a warmth in her voice, the kind that made it clear she wanted to mark the occasion with something real, something more than the hollow clinking of glasses in a crowded bar.

Joseph, always the willing accomplice, nodded in agreement. "I'll get the drinks from the hotel drive-through," he said. "We'll make a night of it."

And so, the plan was set. An evening of fire-kissed meat, good liquor, and the quiet satisfaction of survival. But Hilda, ever the orchestrator, had one more surprise up her sleeve.

"There's someone special coming to dinner," she said, her eyes gleaming with something unreadable. "I think you'll be pleased."

Marcus had only just opened his first bottle of beer, Hilda was cooking on the BBQ and nobody with any brains at all would go anywhere near her, when the was a knock on the door.

Marcus's face just dropped when Joseph had opened the door to let in the special guest that Hilda had organised. Bruce was carrying two magnums of champagne as he walked into the room.

"I reckon that this is the least that I owe you, and congratulations Marcus" he said as he placed the bottles onto the table.

"I reckon, it is I that owe you Bruce" Marcus approached Bruce and shook his hand, "Thanks!..Mate!"

During around of toasting drinks, Marcus, for the millionth time, thanked everyone, but this time added "I really do owe the freedom that I have today to a woman, a woman I do not know, nor do I know her name. She was the woman that sat next to me on the Qantas plane. The woman who told me that I was

'Going Backwards'.

Three Strikes and Out?

Marcus stood in the small, glass-panelled phone booth at Charleville, the receiver cool in his hand. His fingers gripped it tightly, his nerves pulsing with a tension that matched the silence of the empty streets outside. The faint hum of the telephone line buzzed in his ear, mingling with the soft murmur of his own thoughts.

"Number please?" The voice on the other end was neutral, neither welcoming nor dismissive, just a voice doing its job.

"Quilpie 382, thank you." Marcus's words were steady, but beneath them, a storm of emotions churned. He wasn't sure what kind of reception he would receive, if any. The Dowling's had told him his family wanted nothing to do with him, and he'd carried that bitter truth with him ever since. But now, standing in the shadow of his own freedom, he needed to hear something different. He needed to know whether his uncle, his last remaining family, had any shred of forgiveness left.

The phone rang once. Twice. Then the line clicked, and a familiar voice echoed through the receiver.

"Hello, Stratheden, Miles speaking?"

Marcus's heart skipped a beat, and he steadied himself, trying to keep the tremor out of his voice. "Uncle Miles!… This is Marcus."

There was a brief pause on the other end, and Marcus could almost hear the surprise and hesitation in his uncle's voice. He didn't blame him. It had been years since Marcus had last made contact. But he'd always hoped that his family would understand, would one day realise that he was not the man they'd thought him to be.

"Hello, Marcus… We heard all about the case. Congratulations, Marcus. We're so happy to hear that you've been cleared of all charges."

Relief surged through Marcus like a wave. The knot in his chest loosened, but he didn't allow himself to fully relax. There was still so much left to say, and so much left unsaid.

"I was just wondering, Uncle," Marcus continued, his voice calm but edged with tension, "if I might call around and collect my bags. I presume you still have them?"

He waited, the words feeling heavier now, as though they carried more than just a request for belongings. This was his past, his life, still in the hands of those who had once cared for him. He had no idea how his family would react to his return, but he needed closure. He needed to know where he stood.

"Yes, of course, my boy," his uncle replied, and Marcus could hear the warmth in his voice. "They're here, safe and sound, in your room waiting for you. You're welcome to come by anytime."

A wave of emotion hit Marcus like a sudden gust of wind. The tears, long held back, threatened to spill, but he steadied himself, his throat tight with a mix of gratitude and sorrow. It had been so long since he'd felt anything resembling belonging, and yet, here was his uncle offering him the one thing Marcus had desperately needed: acceptance.

"I'll be there later this afternoon," Marcus said, his voice barely a whisper now. "Thank you, Uncle. I'll see you soon."

As the line went dead and the receiver clicked back into place, Marcus stood still for a moment, his heart racing in his chest. He had expected nothing from his family, but in that simple conversation, he had found something, something he hadn't dared hope for in a long time.

And with that, Marcus turned away from the telephone box, his steps carrying him toward Stratheden, where a piece of his past, and, perhaps, his future, awaited him.

End..........

Did you enjoy this book?...

If so please tell your friends and I would appreciate it greatly if you could rate it.

Thanks! ... Max

Other Books By Max Barrington

Woolgar River Park

Task

Dying To Find Gold

Harry Croft

The New March

Bad Company

The First Ten Years in Australia

Fifty Five More Years

You Couldn't Make This Stuff Up

The Writer & The Written

What's Mine is Yours

The Darkie's Gold

The Intrusion

The Premonition

Revelation at Narern

King to Spare

The Telephone